REAL MAGIC

BY STUART JAFFE
AND CAMERON FRANCIS

Real Magic is a work of fiction. Names, characters, places, and incidents either are the product of the author's imagination or are used fictitiously, and any resemblance to any persons, living or dead, business establishments, events, or locales is entirely coincidental.

REAL MAGIC

All rights reserved.

Copyright © 2013 by Stuart Jaffe and Cameron Francis
Cover art by Littera Designs

ISBN 13: 978-1490353982
ISBN 10: 1490353984

First Edition: June, 2013

For

Dad and Lori

Beth and Gianna

ALSO BY STUART JAFFE

Max Porter Paranormal Mysteries
    Southern Bound
    Southern Charm
    Southern Belle

The Malja Chronicles
    The Way of the Black Beast
    The Way of the Sword and Gun
    The Way of the Brother Gods

Gillian Boone
    A Glimpse of Her Soul

The Bluesman
    The Bluesman #1: Killer of Monsters
    The Bluesman #2: Tattoo Magic Showdown
    The Bluesman #3: Death House Jam Session
    The Bluesman #4: Hospital Blood Night
    The Bluesman #5: Sacrifice

Stand Alone Novels
    After The Crash

Short Story Collection
    10 Bits of My Brain

Non-Fiction
    How to Write Magical Words: A Writer's Companion

For more information visit www.stuartjaffe.com

ACKNOWLEDGEMENTS

From Stuart:
    First off, thanks to Cameron for saying *Yes*. If he hadn't been interested and willing to work on this project, this book simply would not have happened. Thanks also goes out to Julie Henderson of Design Archives for some great help with 1930s clothing and style; Rachel of Littera Design for a wonderful cover; Ed Schubert for sanity support; and always, Glory and Gabe, my closest and dearest. Most importantly, I want to thank you, the reader. Without you, none of this matters.

From Cameron:
    There are so many people to thank for their direct and indirect help with this book that it's hard to know where to begin.
    First, special thanks to Peter Duffie and Jack Carpenter for their help with some of the magic and gambling research. They are two giants in the world of card magic and I feel fortunate to call them my friends.
    Also special thanks to magic's past masters who were huge inspirations on the material included in this book: Dai Vernon, Al Baker, Jean Hugard, John Scarne and too many others to name.
    And finally, a big thank you to Stuart Jaffe for calling me up and asking if I would be interested in collaborating on this novel. Stuart and I went to college together and hadn't spoken in close to twenty years, so the call itself was most welcome. And collaborating on a book ... well, the prospect was both exciting and terrifying at the same time. The result was thrilling. I will always be extremely grateful to Stuart for inviting me to share this incredible creative journey with him.
    Finally, a big thank you to my wife, Beth, and daughter, Gianna, for all of their love and support.

REAL MAGIC

PART I
2013

Remove any five cards from a deck.

Keeping them face down, shuffle the five cards.

Turn over the top card, remember it, and then turn it down again.

CHAPTER 1

WHEN IT CAME TO THE RISKY ENDEAVOR of cheating at cards, Duncan Rose had been taught well. Choose your marks with care — people with money to spare and little brains to keep it in their wallets. Choose your location well — a place with a lot of distractions and an easy escape route should the situation turn ugly. Choose your time wisely — play an honest game for the most part, setting up patterns of behavior that will look innocent later, and actually cheat for the big pot. Duncan Rose knew all of this, but he still screwed up.

He had ignored the fourth crucial choice — choose your partner like your life depended on it. Duncan's partner, Pancake, was a friend with an apartment. Agreeing to help Pancake with a cheat in exchange for a month on the couch had seemed smart at the time. Cheat a few of Pancake's friends, get a free month with a roof over his head, and probably mooch some food into the deal too. Besides, he had known Pancake for years, and though the bone-thin guy brought along trouble like flies to a carcass, Duncan tried to help him out whenever he could. That's how they met.

Near the end of his senior year at Reedsburg High, Duncan happened upon three guys beating up a scrawny kid. Though Reedsburg, Pennsylvania had barely enough population to show up on a map, he didn't know the kid or the guys. He had no stake in it whatsoever. But he heard the whimpers and the laughter, the cries and the taunting, and he knew that if he walked away, he'd continue to hear that awful combination of sounds every night for the rest of his life.

"Hey, fellas, I wonder if you could help me out," Duncan said, standing behind the guy he thought to be the ringleader — the biggest of the three.

The big guy turned around with a confused look that, under other circumstances, would have sent Duncan rolling in a fit of laughter. "Get out of here."

"I want to show you something." Duncan pulled out a deck of cards.

"You want to do a card trick?"

"I want to make a bet. You ain't afraid of a bet, are you?"

The big guy glanced at his buddies. "I ain't afraid of nothing."

"Okay, then. I'll do a trick, simple one, and if you can't figure it out, you let that kid go free. If you do figure it out, I'll give you a hundred bucks."

That got the guy's full attention. "You got a deal."

"Cool." Duncan pulled out a second deck of cards. "Here. Shuffle these while I shuffle mine." One deck had blue backs and the other red. "All shuffled? Now, we trade decks, and I want you to do everything I do with your deck."

Duncan placed the red deck on the ground, and the big guy placed the blue deck on the ground. "Now cut the deck wherever you want, take the next card and remember that card." Duncan cut the deck and placed the top portion to his right. The big guy did the same with his deck. Then Duncan picked up the top card of the left hand portion and looked at the card. "Memorize that card now, and then place it on top of the half of the deck you cut off, then place the rest on top." Duncan picked up the left packet and placed it on top of the rest. The big guy did so, too.

"Go ahead and cut the deck as much as you want. Good. Now, we switch decks again, and I want you to go through the red deck and pick out the card you saw in the blue deck. I'll do the same with the blue deck. Place the card face down." Duncan and the big guy found their cards. "Okay. Just so we're clear: we shuffled, switched decks, found a random card from a random cut of the deck, cut the decks more, switched decks again, and have picked out our cards. Right? Now, turn yours over."

The big guy turned over the Queen of Spades.

Duncan smiled. "What do you know?" He turned over his card — also the Queen of Spades.

The big guy's friends laughed in amazement while the big guy stared at the cards with a stunned look.

"Any idea?" Duncan asked, but the big guy didn't answer. "No?" He walked over to the kid they were pummeling and said, "Come on, let's go."

As they walked away, he could still hear the bullies talking out the trick. Duncan knew they'd never figure it out even though it was extremely simple. All he had done was look at the bottom card of his original deck before the first switch. This time it turned out to be the Six of Diamonds. When the big guy cut the deck and placed the Queen on top of the cut, he then placed the other half on top of the deck, positioning the Six just behind the Queen. The rest of the trick was nothing more than putting on a show because when they switched decks again, Duncan simply looked for the Six of Diamonds and selected whatever card was in front of it — this time, the Queen of Spades. Simple, easy, and it saved Pancake from a brutal beating.

Pancake never forgot what had been done for him that day. Even when he screwed up the most, he always knew he could count on Duncan. At least, that's how Duncan saw it. Pancake always looking up to him, always wanting to show off.

So he should have seen this coming, should have known that any cheat set up by Pancake would end in disaster. But Duncan had been blinded by the free room. More than that, though, he had to admit that sometimes he wanted to show off for Pancake, be the hero Pancake saw in him. The moment he stepped into the tiny, smoke-filled room, however, he knew they were in trouble.

Three men crowded a round table, smoking cigars and drinking beer. Each one had a shoulder-holster and each holster had a handgun. One of these guys had more muscles than Duncan knew existed on the human body, his blue t-shirt stretched taut to reveal every one of them. The other two were thin and harsh, looked like they killed people every day and boy, was work a grind.

Behind them, shoved into the corner, a hairy man hunched over two laptops. One showed surveillance footage from the outside alley. The other displayed a game of mahjong. Two women were in the room as well. Both were nude, pretty once, but acted like drugged-out slaves — giving Muscles a back rub, serving beer, or sitting on a bed and smoking pot. All these people and tobacco and pot and alcohol blended into a nose-turning stench.

"Hey fellas," Pancake said, his voice always high and congested. "Ready to play?"

The three glanced at him, and Duncan wanted to bolt. These were not the kind of guys he could afford to be caught cheating, and this was not the place to do it either. Cramped, only one exit, guns and muscle. Bad, bad, bad.

But Pancake had their bankroll and plunked it on the table before Duncan could fumble a lame excuse to leave. "I'm feeling lucky tonight," Pancake said, sitting down and winking at one of the girls. Duncan stayed at the door. He could still turn away, maybe even get Pancake to follow him. But he knew better. Pancake would forge ahead without him, if for no other reason than to show Duncan that he could do it all on his own. In the end, Duncan would be identifying Pancake's body, pulled from the stinking river, and he'd never sleep well again.

"You coming in or what?" Muscles asked in a thick Slavic accent.

Forcing a smile, Duncan scooted into the room. He sat at the table, took his chips, and tried to hide his shaking. Muscles snapped his fingers at one of the girls. With dead eyes, she pulled bottles from a cooler and passed them around. Duncan drank a little of the nasty, cheap beer — enough to appear sociable but not enough to get drunk.

One of the killers dealt a hand of poker. "I'm Peyter. I don't like stupid games. Just five- and seven- card stud or draw. That's it. No pussy crap with wild cards or anything like that. This is a real man's game. You understand?"

"Of course." Pancake slapped Duncan on the shoulder. "That's why we're here, right? A real man's poker game."

Since Peyter dealt the first hand, Duncan could relax a tiny bit. It would be a fair hand, and he could play it out as anybody would. Dmitri, the other killer, won with two pair — aces and threes. The deal rotated to Muscles and another fair hand hit the table.

When it reached Duncan, he made sure to reach for all the cards rather than let anybody pass them in. This was the first step to establishing a pattern. He dealt a regular hand, which Dmitri won again, and the deal moved on to Pancake.

Pancake didn't have much skill as a card cheat but he could perform a few blind overhand shuffles well enough to fool anybody not paying attention. For this false shuffle, he held the deck in his left hand, grabbed a chunk of cards, lifted them up and over to the back, then brought another chunk to the front. This gave the impression of the cards being shuffled overhand when, in fact, Pancake maintained an ace or two on the bottom for use whenever he needed them. Duncan cringed as Pancake launched into cheating on his first deal. Not surprisingly, Pancake won his hand with three aces. These thugs might not be paying attention yet, but a few more deals like that and they'd notice.

The evening progressed like a well-timed machine. The three gun-toting men each dealt a fair hand of poker. On his deal, Duncan made sure to pull in the cards himself and then deal a fair hand. Pancake cheated, trying to give the winning aces to either himself or Duncan. Each time Pancake's deal came along, Duncan flirted with one of the nude girls or asked Peyter a question or told a joke or bumped his hand on the table or anything else he could think to do to distract the men from watching the deal.

After three hours, Duncan had noticed Peyter paying closer attention to Pancake. Not good. Even Duncan's attempts at misdirection lost their effectiveness. Whether he wanted it or not, he knew the time to finish this game had come.

When his turn to deal came around, he collected the cards as he had every time that night — reaching out and pulling them in on his own. This time, however, he pulled them in, sliding the cards he wanted on top of the rest, so that they stacked up in a specific order. He made sure that he had three queens in a row and a full house at the top. Then as he shuffled he shifted the full house to the bottom of the deck and let the queens stay on top. He went a step further, making it look as if he riffle shuffled the whole deck several times, creating that classic snapping shuffle sound as the two halves laced together into one deck, but in fact only used the top half. The result was that the queens were now spaced apart every four cards and the full house remained intact on the bottom.

When the deal came, Duncan would deal seconds — dealing out the second card from the top until he reached Muscles who would get the top card, the queen. The next card on top would be the next queen which would sit there until Duncan reached Muscles again. For himself, Duncan would deal from the bottom of the deck. In this way, Muscles would end up with three queens, a strong hand that he'd be willing to bet big on and Duncan would beat him with a full house.

Stacking the deck and going through the false shuffles went smoothly. Nobody, not even Peyter, appeared to notice. Just to be safe, as Duncan launched into the riffle shuffles, he asked one of the girls for a beer. Peyter and the others all wanted beers, too, and they all turned their attention to the nude girl for a second.

Duncan readied his hands to start the complex deal when the hairy guy playing mahjong in the corner chirped up. "Boss is here."

All three thugs straightened in their chairs. The stifling room grew hotter and even the stoned women found the energy to show fear. Duncan's throat tightened.

"Wait for the Boss," Peyter said. "He'll want to play a hand."

Duncan nodded and shuffled legitimately several times, destroying the stacked deck he had carefully put together. No way would he try to cheat a guy who bossed around these men. Even if he didn't fear for his life, he followed certain codes of conduct when it came to cheating. He didn't cheat good people out of hard-earned money. He only cheated dumb thugs and criminals — people too stupid to notice and too brutish to deserve better. A thug's boss, however, would be calculating and vicious. That's how guys like that became bosses in the first place.

After shuffling the deck clean, Duncan let out a sigh and placed it on the table between him and Pancake. He had been thinking how they had dodged a bullet — had the Boss come in after the hand had been dealt, who knew what would have happened? Except from the corner of his eye, he spied Pancake pick up the cards and begin shuffling. He hoped Pancake understood what he had done — that he had scuttled the stacked deck, that he wanted to play a straight hand and get out of here, that the time for cheating had ended. But as the door opened, Duncan caught sight of Pancake re-stacking the deck.

The Boss filled up most of the doorway. More brute than brains, his thick, tattooed arms made Muscles look puny. He had a shaved head that only added to his monstrous appearance. But when he spoke, Duncan saw the smooth, intelligence come through. "Mind if I sit in for a hand?" he asked as he placed a chair next to Peyter.

One of the women handed him a beer while the other leaned against him so he could rest a hand on her rear. The Boss looked at the chip stacks and gestured to Pancake. "Looks like you've done well tonight."

"I've had some luck."

"You're Pancake, right?"

Pancake nodded, looking as nervous as the rest of them.

"That's right."

"Congratulations, Pancake. Not many people can beat these guys at cards. It takes some serious brains and huge balls to do that. You got huge balls, Pancake?"

Duncan looked to the door, not sure how they could possibly get there and then out of the building before bullets pierced their backs. Sweat trickled down his side. Even if they could manage all that, the Boss knew Pancake by name. What else did he know?

"Five card draw okay with you?" Pancake asked.

The Boss flashed his teeth in an expression that mixed a surprised grin with a snarl. "If that's what you men are playing."

Pancake dealt out the cards but nobody made a move to pick them up. They all watched the Boss as he took a long pull on his beer. With a satisfied belch, he said, "You gotta love this country. A bunch of guys sitting around a poker table, a couple beautiful women on their arms, and a cold beer. Where we grew up, this was just a fantasy. Right, Peyter?"

"Yeah, Boss."

"But in America, you have so much at your fingertips that a night like this could be any night of the year. Nothing special to it at all. That's amazing. I mean what other country but America could a couple of guys like you two join a bunch of immigrants like us and all happily play a friendly game of cards? And you, Pancake, you're even winning. Any other place and there'd be bodies thrown out the windows by this time in the night." The Boss chuckled and his men laughed along with him. They laughed too hard. "Let's play," he said and picked up his cards.

Duncan picked up his hand and knew right away that Pancake had lost his mind. He had dealt Duncan a ten, a five, and three aces. Undoubtedly, Pancake held two pairs and the Boss would be given three jacks. The three of them would get in a bidding war that resulted in a heavy pot which only Duncan could win.

The initial round of betting started and when it came to

Duncan, he hesitated. He wanted to throw his cards in but that wouldn't solve anything. Another hand would be dealt. And another. And Pancake would keep trying to cheat. With Peyter already suspicious and the Boss watching, too, Pancake would eventually get caught. And that would be the start of a long, painful night which might be their last.

But if Duncan bet, if he played along, Pancake would bet as well. Pancake would bet big to force the Boss to bet big. And if Pancake lost everything to the Boss, then there wouldn't be another hand to play. No cheating would be suspected. No pain would be inflicted. While losing all their money didn't sit well with Duncan, losing his life sat worse.

The Boss leaned forward. "Having trouble? Relax. We're all friends here. I mean, my boys wouldn't have invited you in to play unless they knew it was all good. It's not as if Dmitri took a look at that walking stick called Pancake and thought he'd be an easy target. Right, Dmitri?" Dmitri suddenly found something interesting to look at out the window. "So, there's no pressure. Just a friendly game. Bet, don't bet. It doesn't matter. It's all for fun."

Duncan bet. More than he should have, but he knew he could back off later. A sliver inside him considered taking the Boss for all the money just to show up the bully, but as Pancake raised the bet, Duncan's sensibilities returned. Getting one up on a guy in organized crime was a fast way to die. If he played this right, he'd save Pancake's butt once again. Then when they got back to the apartment, he'd kick it all over the place.

Muscles and Dmitri folded but Peyter called. The Boss raised again and so did Pancake, but it finally worked around with everyone calling. They drew one round of cards, and when Duncan's turn came, he asked for three cards.

Though Pancake had missed or ignored Duncan's other signals, he couldn't mistake this one. Duncan had broken up his three-of-a-kind and Pancake should know that he had canceled the cheat. But when Duncan turned up his new cards, he found the fourth ace to be among them.

The betting started with Peyter. He folded fast. The Boss tossed in a hundred dollars and Duncan had to call it. If he folded too early, Pancake would also fold since he knew he couldn't beat the Boss's three jacks. Duncan had to keep Pancake in for the whole bankroll. At least he had greed on his side. It had blinded Pancake into this situation, and if Duncan's plan worked, it would blind Pancake right out of it.

The Boss raised, Duncan called, Pancake raised. They locked into this pattern and the pot grew richer with every pass.

The Boss chuckled. "I like this guy," he said, pointing to Pancake. "He's crazy. Keeps raising and raising. I mean, look there, he's barely got anything left. That's America right there. All out. No holding back. Things look tough, what do you do? You double down. Am I right?" Dmitri and Muscles nodded. "I like you, Pancake. But I ain't going to go soft on you either. That would be an insult to you and to this incredible country." The Boss put in a final raise of one hundred dollars — large enough to commit the rest of Pancake's money.

Duncan had about twenty dollars left. Though he put on a show of looking disappointed, he happily folded. He slid his cards in amongst the other folded cards, hopefully mixing them enough to hide his three aces.

"What are you doing? You're folding?" Pancake asked. "After all this?"

"I don't have enough to bet," Duncan said.

"You should've asked me. I could've loaned you the money."

The Boss sneered at Pancake. "Hey, stop worrying about your lover and get on with this. There's a lot of money on this table."

For a second, Duncan feared Pancake would fold. The way the Boss eyed him, such an action would have screamed out that he had been cheating and something went wrong. After all the betting and raising, Pancake had no choice but to play on. Tight-faced and tight-lipped, he tossed the rest of his money in, his eyes locked on Duncan.

As the hands were revealed, the Boss and his men laughed

up the win. Duncan smiled and stood. "Well, it's been fun. Wish I had more to show for it, though."

Peyter said, "You had a good run for a while, but nobody can beat the Boss. He's too good."

"Maybe next time," Duncan said, inching towards the door.

"Don't leave. We got beer, we got girls, maybe a little pot, a little coke. How about it? Besides, the Boss won. Let's have a party."

Pancake perked up and leered at the girls. Duncan grabbed his arm and yanked him towards the door. "Thanks for the offer, but we've got an early day of work tomorrow."

"See that, boys," the Boss said while stacking his chips. "That's what's wrong with this country. No sense of perspective. Worrying about work when they should be enjoying our hospitality."

"Yeah," Pancake said, "we should stay. We don't want to be rude."

Duncan froze. He didn't want to know what kind of *hospitality* the Boss had planned. "S-Sorry. We really do have to go. Maybe we can play again sometime."

"Maybe we'll get all our money back someday, too," Pancake said.

The Boss turned an eye on him, his face cold like the guns each man wore. "Nobody beats my boys. They're too damn good." Then his mouth opened into a wide grin. "You guys crack me up. Get the fuck out of here. You come back when you got more money to lose."

Duncan didn't take the chance that things might change again. He pulled on Pancake's arm and got out of there as fast as they could move without looking too anxious. The alley reeked of trash and urine, but anything was more pleasant than another hour of that stifling, stinking room. Once they hit the street and headed towards Pancake's apartment, Duncan steadied himself for what he expected would come.

Despite his lanky size, Pancake found enough strength to send Duncan to the ground with one punch. "What the fuck was that? You blew all our money!"

Rubbing his chin, Duncan had to admit, he was impressed. Perhaps Pancake had outgrown his puppy dog admiration. Still, that didn't excuse any of what had happened. "First off, it was my money. And second, you nearly got us killed."

"Oh, for crying out loud, is that what got you all pussying out on me? You were afraid of those guys? They're just small time scum and you know it. No different than any of the other jerks you cheat."

"This was different." Duncan got back on his feet. "Very different. Everything was wrong about this set up and you were so careless, we're lucky we didn't get made."

"I was smooth. They didn't see a thing."

"Oh, now you're an expert?"

"You're the one who taught me that cheats take skill and risk. I took the risk. Where were you with the skill?"

"Look, sometimes you've got to trust your instincts. When the Boss came in, you should've known it was time to lose and leave. I mean, come on, that guy's probably killed more people than I've ever known."

Pancake shook his head. "You're full of it, you know that? You act like you know it all but when your time came to prove it, you turned chickenshit."

"Can we just forget it? I'll get you some money and we can—"

"You got twenty bucks there, don't you?"

Duncan pulled out the twenty in his pocket. "You want my last twenty?"

Pancake swiped the bill and walked away. "Don't ever talk to me again, you lying sack of crap. And go find some other place to stay. You ain't welcome anymore."

Standing alone on the street of a crime-ridden neighborhood was never a smart thing to do, but Duncan had nowhere to go. A surge of pride filled him — he had saved his friend's life, even if his friend didn't know it. But he had no money and no place to stay.

That's not true. There's one door that's always open.

He hated to call upon his great-grandfather, the man had

been so good to him over the years, but he couldn't think of another option. Pappy would let him crash on the sofa for the night, offer up some breakfast, and even give a small bankroll to get Duncan started again. After all, Pappy was the one who taught him how to cheat in the first place.

Chapter 2

"No."

Duncan stared at Pappy, waiting for the old man to crack a smile, but after a long moment of silence, nothing changed. Pappy had been losing it a bit lately, but this showed no signs of dementia. He simply had refused to help.

"Listen," Pappy said and sat in a hardback chair. Despite his frail body losing weight every day and his skin loosening to the point of slipping off his face, he looked pretty good for a man over one hundred years old. He had a strong voice and a spark of life in his eye. But he carried an odor of impending death that seeped into the walls and carpet of his cramped apartment. "I've given you everything I've got. All the tools I know. And you're welcome to spend the night here, but I don't have the money to bankroll. I doubt your father would want me to do it anyway."

"Since when has *his* opinion mattered?"

Pappy gave a sly wink. "I'm not sure I approve, either. I taught you these skills so you could follow your dream of becoming a magician. Not so you could cheat at cards."

"You're not really going to pull that argument on me?"

"All I mean is that there's more to it all than simply taking people's money."

"I'm doing what I have to do. Some people can work a nine-to-five they hate to make ends meet. I'm not one of those people. I've got that artistic temperament. Heck, you're the one who taught me all this — that a magician is an artist and all artists suffer under the strict limits of a regular life. Now that I'm living the irregular life, everyone wants to tell me how wrong I am?"

Pressing out his hands in a placating manner, Pappy said, "Okay, calm down." He struggled to his feet and shuffled toward the kitchen. "You want something to eat? Something to drink?"

Pappy's apartment should have felt like a mansion. It wasn't overly large but it had high-ceilings and beautiful floors. He rarely let anything go. He hoarded to the point of covering all the walls with stacks of books, magazines, and trinkets. If he weren't so old, Duncan would consider getting him on a reality show, but at his age, what was the point? He had earned the right to live however he saw fit.

"Here," Pappy said. Duncan looked up expecting a glass of iced tea or water. Instead, Pappy tossed over a new deck of cards — he had hundreds of them. "Let me see your shuffles."

Duncan sighed. They had been through this routine countless times, but he knew better than to argue. He revealed the Ace of Spades on the top of the deck and shuffled. After a few overhands and a riffle of the deck, he revealed the top card — still the Ace of Spades. He turned the card back over and shuffled downward, keeping the cards on the table like a Vegas dealer. Then he turned the top card over — still the Ace of Spades.

"Not bad," Pappy said. "Now deal."

Duncan dealt out four hands of five cards each. When he finished, he turned over the top card of the deck — Ace of Spades.

Pappy grimaced. "You're still not buckling the bottom card early enough. You need to press the corner, popping the card away from the deck a little to make it easier to position, so you can then pull it out when you're ready. But if you wait to buckle it, you can't get it out in time. That's why you're pausing too long before you deal the bottom. Breaks up the flow of the deal and looks suspicious. You need to rock your left hand more, too. That back-and-forth motion is natural when you hold the deck in that hand and it helps hide that you dealt the first three rounds as seconds and the last two as bottoms. Now, show me your Classic Pass."

The Classic Pass was always Pappy's final test. Not surprisingly, it was one of the most difficult maneuvers in sleight-of-hand. Duncan had to hold the deck in his left hand, break the cards and use his pinky to maintain the break while making it look like the deck was held solid, then while appearing to shore up the deck, he slipped the top half over and brought the bottom half up. Now the bottom half had become the top half.

"Sloppy," Pappy said. "Might work in a card game if the players are drunk or not paying attention, but if someone's burning you, really studying your moves, they'll catch you no problem at all. For one thing, you keep flashing the break just before you do it."

"Maybe a little, but it doesn't matter. That's what misdirection is for."

"You'll never fool a real magician with that pass. Especially when they burn you."

"I don't care about fooling magicians. I'm not going to be a magician. I don't even care about the Classic Pass. You rarely use that when playing cards."

"You mean *cheating* at cards. Let me tell you something — just because modern sleight-of-hand grew out of card cheating doesn't mean we have to make our living that way. You've got real talent with this, and you've worked so hard for so long at it. Why bother with cheating when you could be a real magician? Now, what you need to do—"

"I need money," Duncan snapped. "I don't mean to be rude but I need a little bankroll, anything to get going again."

Pappy studied Duncan. Then he tapped his temple. "I might have something for you."

He left the room, muttering to himself. Duncan sat alone and waited. Off to his right, behind a chair cover with a stack of books was a door — *the* door. The one he never opened.

No. He shoved those thoughts away and kept his eyes focused straight ahead. He looked at the photos on the wall, the details well-worn into his memory. Fishing with Pappy ("All boys should learn to fish"), hunting with Pappy ("Learning to properly handle a gun is crucial information"), and performing magic with Pappy ("The greatest art in the world"). All the pictures were of the two of them. Somewhere in the place, he must have kept photos of his late wife, but Duncan had never seen them. Nor did Pappy bother with pictures of his own son or grandson. The only person he ever showed interest in was Duncan.

Maybe that's why the rest of the family resents me, Duncan thought, but before he could let his mind wander down those depressing avenues, Pappy returned wearing a bathrobe.

Pappy smiled as he sat down. "Good to see you. When did you get into town? Oh, wait, before we get to any pleasantries, let's first check out your card handling. Now, now, don't argue with me. You've got to learn to handle the cards before you can do anything good with them."

Duncan could only think that the old man had really lost it for good. An idea sparked in Duncan's head, an idea he felt both curious about and slimy for thinking. A lump formed in his throat that he couldn't swallow away. He walked to the chair with the stack of books and slid it all to the side. He stared at *the* door.

It was made of a light wood and had a simple knob. Nothing ornate on the door at all except for a series of long slash marks connected to geometric shapes that had been burned into it like some bizarre artwork — part Jackson Pollock, part Pablo Picasso. The strong lines stretched the entire height of the door. Duncan had never opened it — never dared. Pappy would have killed him.

Growing up, he would catch Pappy staring at the door in wonder, but whenever he inquired about it, Pappy would snap at him. "You must never go through that door," he would say. "It's real magic, and you should never mess with real magic."

"Pappy," Duncan said, staring at the door as if it were an exotic dancer. He knew he was taking advantage of Pappy's lost faculties, but when else would he ever get a chance to open the door? "You ever notice this door before?"

Pappy turned to Duncan, and the terror on his face prickled Duncan's skin. "You stay away from that door." His voice rose as he struggled to his feet. "You stay away, you hear me. I don't care if I'm lying dead in my chair, you must never never never go through that door. Not for anything. You got me?"

Backing away, Duncan said, "Okay, no problem. Calm down, please. I was just asking."

"I know exactly what you were doing, and you should be ashamed of yourself."

Duncan had the decency to look down. It had been a stupid thing to do. But Pappy didn't understand what he had done to Duncan over the years with that door. The more he said to never open the door, the more Duncan wondered about it. What was behind it? If it was so terrible, why have the door in the first place? Why not board the thing over? And what were those markings all about?

As a kid, Duncan spent equal amounts of time thinking up one horrible scenario after another — bodies in the walls, a secret torture chamber, a door in the mouth of a slime-covered monster. He even tried to open the door once, got as far as putting his hand on the knob, but Pappy caught him. It was the only time Pappy ever seriously punished him. Took out a belt and made it so Duncan couldn't sit for the rest of the night.

But now, as an adult, the door's allure grew even stronger. He still imagined what would be on the other side, only he now approached it with more experience. Sadly, the scenarios he arrived at were every bit as horrendous as those from his youth — sex slaves held in a secret room, some bizarre sacrificial altar, and bodies in the walls, always bodies in the walls.

Duncan's cell phone chirped, startling him. He glanced at the ID — Pancake. "I'll be right back," he said to Pappy who fussed with covering the door back up.

Once he reached the guest room, he said in as light a tone as he could manage, "Hey, Pancake, you talking to me already?"

Before Pancake spoke, Duncan heard the panic in his breathing. Not just panic, crying and maddening fear. "T-They figured it out."

"Figured what out? Who?"

"Peyter and Dmitri! They know we were cheating."

"Don't be paranoid."

"They cut off my fucking hand," he screamed. Then his tears came back and through heaving sobs, he said, "My hand. It's gone."

"Oh shit. Where are you?" Adrenaline jolted through Duncan's system. "Have you gone to a hospital?"

"Are you fucking crazy? They're going to kill us. I ain't worried about a damn hospital. I'm worried about my life."

"You'll probably die if you don't worry about a hospital."

"They'll come after you next, you know."

"Okay, just calm down. Tell me where you are. I'll come get you."

"You better come. You better. Or we're dead."

Chapter 3

Before Pancake gave his location, Duncan knew the answer. Pancake had never been too inventive, so when it came to hiding — especially when frightened — there were only a few options available. First among them was the haunted house.

Deep in the woods on the edge of town, the foundation of an old relic of a house still stood. Like a grave marker in an open field, you couldn't miss it, and lots of teenagers knew about it. On weekends, they slipped out there to drink beer, smoke pot, and screw around. As a kid, Duncan would sneak around the perimeter to watch and learn the secret ways of teens. As a teen, he and Pancake would hang out there getting drunk. But that was weekends from long ago. Nobody bothered with the place anymore.

Duncan approached the ruined house as quietly as he could manage. He had taken a circuitous route in case the Boss's men had followed him, but he couldn't be sure Pancake had been so smart. He spied Pancake pacing near a jagged, knee-high wall, whining like an injured dog. He held a stump wrapped in a blood-stained shirt close to his chest. Soaked in sweat and ghostly pale, his steps looked wobbly, like he might pass out at any moment. Nobody else appeared to be around.

"Psst," Duncan said. "Pancake."

"Duncan?" Pancake asked full-throated, alerting every living thing to his presence. "What the hell are we going to do?"

Duncan approached, cautious but less worried since nothing bad had happened to them yet. "First thing, we need to get your hand taken care of."

"Gee, you think? Or maybe we should stand around here and wait to get our asses shot off. You think that's a good idea? Huh?"

"You're the one who was acting so brazen. If I had let you go through with your big cheat, we'd both be dead right now."

"Oh, I see. I should be thanking you."

"You can't go cheating on every round you get. That's why they figured it out."

"Now it's my fault?"

"How else do you think they noticed? We didn't win any money." Duncan looked at Pancake like a lost child — he just didn't understand. But no way would Duncan take the blame for this.

With his good hand, Pancake wiped back the tears in his eyes. "It doesn't really matter now, anyway. They found out and they're going to do a lot worse to us if we don't pay them."

"Pay them what? We let them win."

"You did. And we pay them to say we're sorry for trying to cheat them. We pay them so they won't kill us."

Duncan frowned and turned away. He worried about Pancake's hand, but since Pancake didn't seem concerned enough about it, he stopped trying to help — horse to water and all that. This other thing, though, this was a way he could help, and if Pancake was to be believed, he had to help. Get the money or die. The choice couldn't be clearer.

"How much?" Duncan asked.

Pancake let out a breath that said it all. The hand, the fear, the panic — all had been used to get that question out of Duncan. "Twenty Gs by tomorrow morning."

"Twenty thousand dollars? How am I supposed to get that?"

"You're the great card cheat. Go cheat." Pancake's face paled. "Or rob your Pappy. I don't know. And maybe get me to a hospital."

Duncan caught Pancake before he hit the ground. He was light enough to carry, so Duncan took him to the road. A cell phone call got a cab to take them to the hospital. Duncan slid Pancake's watch off his wrist and handed it to the cabbie as payment. Once the cabbie stopped cursing and sped off, Duncan left his friend by the ER entrance. He didn't dare stick around. There would be too many questions he couldn't answer.

As he strolled away, his hands in his pockets, his head low, he heard a nurse find Pancake and call out for help. He felt the urge to throw up but he had to keep his cool. He had to keep thinking — where could he come up with the money? Not all of it. No way could he do that in one night. But enough to assuage the Boss.

A sharp blade of guilt cut into his gut at the thought of robbing Pappy. He wouldn't, he couldn't, do it. And since Pappy refused to bankroll him, he couldn't cheat a game even if he had one set up — which he didn't. There had to be a way, any way he could avoid the one person he knew had the money. But that meant he'd be forced to do something even worse than robbing Pappy or cheating idiots, something he hadn't done in years — he'd have to call his father.

CHAPTER 4

DUNCAN TRIED THREE TIMES TO REACH HIS FATHER, and each time he canceled the call before it could ring twice. After the third attempt, he put his cell phone in his pocket and pulled out his car keys. It would be too easy for his father to say *No* over the phone. But in person, Duncan thought he'd have a better chance of leaving with some help.

After a two hour ride, he pulled into the driveway of his father's lovely home. Two stories on a half-acre of land with a manicured lawn and a heated pool in the back. Not bad for ignoring your kids your whole life.

Duncan sat in his car with the engine idling. He couldn't call his father, so what made him think he'd find the strength to ring the doorbell? He glanced down at his hand and pictured a bloody pulp. He had to give it to the Boss — losing a hand or dying were strong motivators.

Before he could step out of the car, the garage door slid open. His father, Sean, stood with hands on hips and scowl on face. A beer belly had begun to form, enough to hang over his belt, and he had lost a lot of hair since the last time they had seen each other — over two years ago. His legs poked out from his khaki shorts like stilts on a balloon. Even from the street, Duncan could smell Sean's heavy cologne. That man never did understand the word moderation.

Duncan got out and walked toward his father. The scent of the recently mown lawn and the click of his shoes against the driveway — concrete with brink inlays — turned his stomach. It was all a plastic show. He didn't bother with a fake smile or a friendly greeting. Might as well be something honest in this place.

"What the hell do you want?" Sean said.

Duncan didn't know what to expect — one never did when it came to Sean — but years of growing up under the man's rule had left him with one approach. There would be no appeal to a familial connection or even pointing out that death hung over him. The only way through was straight.

"I'm in trouble," Duncan said.

Sean barked out a laugh. "Of course you are. No other reason you'd be here. How much do you need?"

"Don't you want to know what's going on?"

"Same thing that's always happened to you. You try to take the easy way out of things, it backfires, and you lose your money. I'm guessing whoever you screwed over is serious about getting his money back because you wouldn't be here otherwise. So, I'm curious, how much?"

"Twenty thousand," Duncan said, feeling his body shrink into a twelve-year-old with every passing second.

Sean laughed full-voiced this time. "I'll say this for you — when you screw up, you don't screw up small."

"Anything that can get me close to it will buy me a few more days," Duncan said, but his father continued to laugh. "Please. They'll kill me."

"Yeah, for that amount, I suspect they will."

An awful silence settled between them. A silence poisoned by years of mutual distrust and disappointment.

"So that's it?" Duncan said. "You'll just let me die?"

Sean leaned against the back of his Cadillac. "I tried with you every way I could. Get you into football or baseball. Heck, I'd have been happy if you were into comic books or video games. But it was always Pappy. That's all you ever wanted to do. Learn his little card tricks."

"What did you think would happen when you dumped me on his porch every chance you could get? Mom died and you didn't waste a minute trying to hook up with someone new."

Sean folded his arms. They had been through this fight so many times the accusations no longer held the same venom. However, instead of coming back with another assault on Duncan's lifestyle, his father said, "I never understood Pappy and neither did your grandfather. He tried to raise me right but Pappy spent all that time driving us around the country, and well, you don't know Pappy nearly as well as you think you do."

"I see. Now, Pappy's the villain."

"No. But he's no hero, either." Sean scrunched his face at a memory and looked as if he might walk away. But he scratched his arms and said, "One time — I must've been about fourteen since your grandfather was still alive — Pappy came to the little apartment we were living in. He was all smiles and excitement. He'd hit it big, he said. Really worked his magic and got us lots of money. But we had to move fast, get out of town, or there'd be trouble. I say this like it's something new, but it happened all the time with him. But this time, my father shook his head. He said there was no way he would keep going on like this. He stood up for me. And you know what your tough ol' Pappy did? He stood down. He had to leave, of course, but he promised to return when things cooled down, and he did. About two years later he bought a place and got all crazy with that stupid door of his. Point is — I thought he had changed. Why else would he come back if he hadn't figured out what family was for? That's why I looked to him to help raise you. But I was wrong to do that. It was my big mistake. I admit it. And I lost you to him."

Duncan kicked at the driveway. This was just his luck. All he wanted was some cash, but his father decides tonight's the night to offer an olive branch. Except the man hadn't even done that. He wallowed in his regret, sure, but nothing else. Heck, they still stood in the driveway.

"I guess I should go," Duncan said with a flicker of hope

that his father would hand him a little money before he left. Sean said nothing. He watched Duncan drive off and never even moved from the garage.

Duncan drove for five miles before he pulled to the side of the road. He stared down the long road and smacked the steering wheel. Breathing like a bull facing a matador, readying to strike, he smacked the steering wheel again. He lowered his head and rubbed the back of his neck.

Family issues don't matter tonight. I don't get that money, family won't ever matter again.

He had one last option. He could call his sisters. He didn't expect much from them, they had sided with Sean long ago, but perhaps they would care more about his impending death than his father.

He called Samantha first. She didn't hate him, though she didn't go out of her way to have any contact with him. Her husband, Chuck, despised him, though, so Duncan felt a twinge of hope when it was Samantha who answered the phone.

"I'm sorry, Dunc," she said. "Really, I am. But I don't think feeding your problems is any way to help you. Why don't you leave town and come visit us? We can look into some programs for you. I'm sure Chuck could arrange a job. Come on. Stop this crazy lifestyle of yours before you get yourself killed."

That's all Duncan needed — spend his days pushing paper for a manager like Chuck. Duncan didn't even know what kind of papers Chuck pushed, but he would never work for a cocky fool like that. No way.

That left Mary — the longest of long shots. She never got over that he won three thousand dollars off of her stupid friends during her wedding reception. "They were drunk and celebrating and you cheated them of serious cash," she screamed at him when she learned what had happened. He shrugged it off. "That's cards," he said, knowing he had done wrong but figuring the whole thing would blow over in a few months. Mary never let it go.

No surprise, then, that she didn't pick up the phone. He tried her cell, too, but she ignored him.

Duncan put the phone away and glanced in the rearview mirror before pulling back on the road. A beat-up car idled under a streetlamp a little way back. The headlights were off. He made out the silhouette of a big man with a thick head.

Waiting to see what happened seemed like a horrible idea, so Duncan slammed on the gas, screeching his tires as he tore off down the road. He couldn't be sure but he swore the car followed him, keeping its lights off. Duncan hit the brakes, turning hard left, hit the gas to straighten out, and shot through a side street.

When he reached another major road, he slowed the car, turned into traffic, and casually drove on. His heart hammered blood throughout his body. He could smell the sweat that stuck to his arms.

Two more ideas came to him. He could rob a few convenience stores. Except he knew he couldn't. The thought of stealing from somebody who worked hard all day left Duncan with a sour taste. Cheating crooks had a Robin Hood feel to it. That was different. No, he couldn't rob anybody.

Which left him with only one alternative. He'd have to pawn something belonging to Pappy. The man had so much stuff in his apartment, there had to be enough of value to pool the money he needed. He could pawn it, and then get back to work at cards. When he raised back the money, he'd return the pawned items to Pappy's house. Most likely, the old man would never even notice.

Duncan didn't like it, but he didn't like any of this. At least, pawning a few items kept him from having to commit a serious crime that endangered people. The more he thought of it, the more Duncan settled in to his plan. His shaking hands eased a bit.

"Sorry, Pappy," he whispered to the empty car. "I hope you understand."

CHAPTER 5

THOUGH DUNCAN HAD WALKED DOWN the apartment building's hall so many times he knew where to avoid tripping on the threadbare carpet, though he had opened Pappy's door with his personal key so often that he knew to pull up on the knob before turning or else the door would stick, though he had entered the cluttered apartment so much that it had become like entering his own home after a long day at work, this time felt new, different, and terrible. This time he walked down that hall and the hall lengthened to the horizon. Each step weighed upon him heavily enough that by the time he reached the door, he barely had the will to pull up on the knob. Even then, he did it wrong and had to try again before he could push the stubborn door open. And when he finally entered the apartment, he did not experience the warm embrace of a home. Instead, he felt exactly like what he was — an intruder.

"Pappy?" When no answer came, Duncan flicked on the living room light, and a new fear took him over. The room had been cleaned out.

All the books, all the papers, all the magazines. The jewelry, the glasses, the little porcelain figurines. Every bit of hoarded junk had been removed. The blankets had been taken off the furniture and someone had dusted everything well. The carpeting bore track lines of a vacuum, and the sharp fumes of lemon-pine cleaner drifted in from the kitchen. Even the marked door had been spruced up so that it didn't look so oddly out of place. The entire room looked like something one found in a model display home.

He knew, Duncan thought. Pappy knew, must have known the moment Duncan left, that he'd be back. Duncan pictured how hard Pappy would have worked to clean out this place. Maybe he called Mary — she'd love to screw Duncan over and would've helped eagerly. They would have had to work fast, sweating and grunting, never taking a break. When Duncan called Mary's cell phone, it would've been a final alarm bell that they only had a short time left. All that work to keep him from having anything to pawn.

He dropped onto the couch and buried his head in his hands. Of all the times for these people to start caring. All their caring was going to get him killed.

Tears welled and he had a hard time breathing. It wasn't just threatening words in his head anymore. He had no other option he could think of. This was real. The Boss and his men — they were going to kill him. His life would end. And though it had never amounted to anything important, it was still his life. Heck, even Pancake clung to the hope of living.

From the couch, Duncan could see a sliver of the kitchen. He considered stomping over there, grabbing a sharp knife, and ending his own life. At least it would be on his terms, then — and probably less painful than whatever psychotic torture scenario the Boss would think up.

But he stayed on the couch. The thought soured his stomach. Suicide in Pappy's kitchen — no way.

He glanced to his right, and his wet eyes rested upon the door. All those crazy markings called out to him. Something important lay on the other side. Something so valuable that Pappy had protected it all these years. Possibly dangerous, too, but at this point, what did he have to lose? If he survived whatever the danger was, then he'd be able to get a hold of the valuable thing — whatever it was. Something that special wouldn't be able to be pawned with ease. But playing cards with criminals had introduced him to several fences. And if he couldn't get them to help him out, he could hand the object directly to the Boss. Probably call it even and walk away. He'd have a terrible time explaining it to Pappy, might even lose the last family member on his side, but he'd be alive. Live Duncan trumped a dead Duncan any day.

On weak legs, Duncan stood and approached the door. He thought he felt waves of energy pulsing off the door, pounding into his chest, but then realized it was his own heart beating. He licked his lips. Took a deep breath. His hand hovered over the doorknob, his fingers tapping out a fast rhythm. Heat rose from the knob, warming the palm of his hand.

He glanced back to the clean room feeling smaller and smaller. Any remaining swagger left him. He turned away from the door and stepped toward the exit. He could leave now, forget he ever considered this, and find some other way to solve his problem.

Not one that could happen fast enough to save his life, though.

"Damn," he said, turning back to the strange door. This time, he didn't allow himself the luxury of thinking. He hurried to the door, grabbed the knob, and pulled it open.

He couldn't see anything inside. It was pitch black as if all the light from the living room stopped at the door frame and refused to go any further. He could hear something, though. A whisper of laughter? Not an eerie, creepy laughter, but a sound of joy.

One more deep breath, and Duncan stepped through the door.

PART II
1934

Starting on your left,
deal the cards into two alternating piles.

Pick up the left packet of cards, drop it on the right, and
then pick up the combined packet.

Chapter 6

Duncan stood on the wooden porch of a narrow house. A black metal railing followed the edge of the porch, stopping before a small yard. The chipped white paint on the house matched the chipped white paint on the picket fence marking the property. On either side of the house stretched more, similar homes. American flags hung from balconies. American red, white, and blue flag bunting decorated the fences. Dusk covered the land in a soft orange hue, but the day had been a hot one and the air felt thick with humidity. Duncan didn't dare move. He could barely breathe.

People strolled along the brick sidewalk. The men wore gray suits and hats. Every man wore a hat. The women wore slim dresses, kept their hair short and wavy, and many of them wore wide-brimmed hats or smaller types that tilted at an angle. A few children jogged by waving tiny American flags in their hands.

The thought hit Duncan that he had stepped into an old movie — the way people moved arm in arm, laughing and chatting, as if an early-evening stroll could be the height of a day. But he could taste the air in this movie — rich and clean. And he could smell this movie — an odd combination of gasoline and horse manure. He saw it transpire a short distance away as if projected on the greatest, most encompassing screen ever developed, yet what he saw clung to reality the way a movie never could.

He might have stayed that way, frozen to the wooden porch, but a car drove by and honked its horn. Duncan watched this relic slip down the street — a boxy, classic automobile with a long nose and runnerboards, cloth top and flat front, just like an old movie gangster's car. The quacking horn melded with the fresh air and the gentle chatter and the cool metal railing on his hand — this was really happening.

He glanced down to find his own clothes had changed, too. Like the other men, Duncan now wore a modest, gray suit with a black tie. The motion of his head brought his attention to the hat he wore — a classic fedora. Except, if this was all real, then it wasn't a classic any more than the cars driving by were antiques.

Duncan's face brightened. This had to be the greatest illusion he'd ever seen. That's why Pappy had forbidden him to use the door before. Pappy must have been working on this illusion for most of his life. But why had he kept it secret for so long? If he had shared this, Duncan would have helped him develop it. They could have been partners. And the money they could make would do more than pay off the Boss. The money from an illusion like this would make them famous. David Copperfield, Penn & Teller, Criss Angel — amateurs compared to what the name Duncan Rose would be with a trick like this.

He watched life pass by for a few minutes, basking in how real the whole world felt. There was an extra layer of calm in the environment that Duncan had never experienced before. No cell phones, no computers, no busy push push push. Just a quiet evening within a quiet town. Part of him wanted to stay forever.

Questions filled his head — How did this work? Mechanical? Computers? Some mix of stock footage and modern 3D technology? And what still needs to be done? As far as he could tell, the illusion neared perfection. Only one man would have the answers. "Okay, Pappy," he muttered, "time for you to come clean."

Duncan turned around, gripped the cold doorknob, and turned it. But the door was locked. He tried again. Nothing. Pressing his shoulder into the door, he attempted to open it with brute force. Still, the door did not budge.

Pounding on the door, he called out, "Pappy! Open this thing up." A few passersby glanced in his direction but most paid him little attention. Duncan jostled the doorknob again, his pulse increasing with each passing second.

The door whipped open so fast, he nearly fell into the young lady behind it. She had a round face and her eyes widened as she stepped back. "What do you want?" she snapped.

Dumbfounded, Duncan stared beyond the lady. He saw the home inside — a narrow, wooden staircase on the right, a brown-wallpapered living room sparse of furniture, and a fireplace sooty from constant use. On the wall next to the stairs hung a mirror, and even at a sharp angle, Duncan could see the backside of the door. The blank, normal door. A door without a single marking or ancient symbol upon it.

The lady crossed her arms and jutted out her chin. "You gonna just stand there gawkin'? I'll call somebody. You get outta here. You hear?"

"S-Sorry," he said as he backed off the porch.

"Watch it," an older man said as Duncan backed into the flow of pedestrians.

Duncan walked away from the house and its door. He itched to turn back, and when he glanced over his shoulder, each step away felt as if he drifted further from a lifeboat. Except that wasn't his door. Where was *his* door?

Another car passed by and a young boy leaned far out of the window. He waved a flat, straw hat in one hand and a tiny American flag in the other. "Happy Fourth of July! Woo! Happy Fourth of July!" he shouted while someone else in the car tossed out bits of paper. All the men and women walking waved their hands. Some even shouted back.

"Spare a penny?" asked an unshaven man sitting against a brick wall. He had brown pants, a threadbare shirt, and a dirty bowler. Add a little mustache and the man would have been a perfect Charlie Chaplin.

Duncan shook his head and kept walking.

The man stood and shattered a glass bottle on the ground. "You'll wish you helped out when it's your turn, bub. Everybody's gonna get a chance at having nothing!"

With each passing second, this illusion felt more real. An amazing visual was one thing, but Duncan didn't see how Pappy could create an entire town. How could such a thing fit in the apartment? He tried to convince himself he was still at Pappy's home. Perhaps he fell and bumped his head. This could all be a dream.

But it isn't, he thought.

A wooden newsstand, dark green and leaning to one side, marked the beginning of the downtown area. Newsstands — another relic from the world Duncan only knew in the movies. As he walked by a cigar-chomping man wearing a dark green visor and an apron, he glanced down at the local newspaper — *The Reedsburg Gazette July 4, 1934.*

That did it for him. Seeing that date in print made it real. Pappy had not devised some grand illusion. Nor had Duncan banged his head sending him into a hallucination of epic proportion. What had happened was simple — incredible, unfathomable, miraculous, but simple none-the-less. Duncan had walked through a door and back in time.

Stating this helped solidify it in his brain, and he walked on with a more confident stride. He refused to become a character in *The Twilight Zone,* spending the entire show denying what had happened to him or wondering the why of it all. In his opinion, the *why?* was easy enough — because he walked through a door he had been warned never to go through.

Only one question really had any importance to him now — *how do I get back?* This answer seemed to be both easy and complicated at the same time. The easy part — he had to find the door again. The hard part — he had to find the door again.

Duncan leaned against a closed bakery, the sign in the window reading *Fresh Baked Loaves 5¢!* Thrusting his hands into his pockets, he felt the distinctive textures of paper money and heard the clink of a few coins. He glanced back the way he had come. He could have given that guy some cash. Too late, though. Besides, looking along the street showed him that there were plenty of others in the same boat. Lots of people meandered about, dejected and destitute. And thin. Duncan was a healthy 147 lbs. but he felt chubby compared to these people. About a block up, he saw a line of people working its way around the corner. Some held bowls, some held Army mess kits, some only held a spoon. 1934 — The Great Depression was in full swing.

He pulled out the money in his pocket. Four dollars and twelve cents. Not much. Then again, it was 1934. If a loaf of bread cost only five cents, then his money would probably go pretty far.

Duncan crossed his arms and considered what he knew beyond The Great Depression. Life was hard for most people. If this little town was the same Reedsburg, Pennsylvania he knew, then not much important would be going on here for a long time. Thankfully, World War II hadn't yet begun for America. He was fairly certain Roosevelt was President. And, he thought with a grin, Prohibition had officially ended.

To his right and across the street, he saw what had to be a 1934 bar. Should he call it a saloon? Regardless of the name, that would be a place to start. Especially because even though his 1934 dollars would go far compared to 2013, they wouldn't go far enough. But they would be a good bankroll to start.

All he had to do was get a drink, observe the crowd, and he would find the makings of a poker game in no time. And while things went bad with Pancake, this time Duncan would run the show. Besides, these people are from the 1930s. They won't know any of his techniques — some of which had yet to be invented. He'd clean them out of their money with ease. Then he'd have the funds to mount a search for the door.

Armed with a plan of action, Duncan adjusted the brim of his hat and headed towards the bar. As he crossed the street, making way for a backfiring car spewing out black smoke, he saw a little girl and her mother coming the other way. The mother held her head up, stern expression firmly on her gaunt face, while the daughter wrapped her hands around a tiny cup.

"I hope it's chicken noodle," she said. "Do you think it'll be chicken noodle, Mama?"

The mother's cheek twitched, but she didn't say a word. Duncan turned right around and walked up behind them.

"Excuse me," he said with a smile. The mother grabbed her daughter and pulled her close. Duncan raised his hands. "No, no. I'm not going to hurt you. I just ... I heard your daughter and well, I've got a little change to spare. Twelve cents. May I give it to you?"

The woman glanced around warily. "That's quite a bit."

"Please."

"I'm not that kind of lady."

"And I'm not that kind of man." He put out his hand, the coins sitting in his palm. "Get that girl a full meal."

He could tell the mother liked the idea of taking charity even less than the idea of being propositioned, but twelve cents would make a difference and she had a child to take care of. With a resigned sigh, she snatched the coins. "Thank you," she said. The daughter rushed over and hugged his legs. Duncan laughed and the mother allowed a smile to crack her lips. "Thank you," she said again.

Duncan turned back towards the bar. He could feel the faces of those in the soup line watching his back, wondering why he hadn't helped them, too. He could have bought loaves of bread to feed them all, feed their families, give them something to be happy about for once. But then it would end. They'd be just as broke and back in the line the next day, only he'd be there with them. Stuck in 1934.

Sorry, folks, but I got to get home.

He walked into the bar, Joey's Corner, and a distinct smile crossed his face. No matter the decade, a bar was a bar — some things never changed. This one had the bar on the left side and it ran the entire length of the room. Large mirror behind with rows of empty glasses and filled bottles. The right side had a few stools lined down the way and the rest of the space had been left empty for the crowds to stand in. Not many people, though. Duncan guessed most were either at home having dinner before going out for a drink or already out celebrating July Fourth. In a few hours, Duncan expected this place to be hopping — Great Depression or not, people always found a way to afford a drink.

Two men dressed in white coats buttoned to the neck stood behind the bar. One cleaned glasses while the other wiped down the bar top. "Evening," the one cleaning glasses said. He had his hair slicked down and the streaks of gray looked like racing stripes. "What'll it be?"

Duncan nodded. He had to force himself not to laugh — the man had spoken in earnest but the old-timey sound of *What'll it be* tickled Duncan. He felt like he had stepped into an old Bogart film. "Manhattan," he said, figuring that would be a safe bet to have existed in 1934.

Listening to the clink of glass and the glug of pouring liquids settled over him — warm and friendly in its familiar song; dark and dangerous in its origin. The dark drink slid before him in no time. Duncan gulped down a bit and coughed hard, nearly spitting the drink back up. These folks didn't joke around with their alcohol — this was the strongest Manhattan he had ever tasted. He guessed that after so many years of Prohibition, they were happy to let the stuff flow. That wouldn't last long.

The bathroom door in the back creaked open, and a young man strode out. Like everyone else, this man wore a suit, but it fit him better. He had his blond hair slicked back, and it gave him an older, cooler vibe. He sauntered over to Duncan — straight-backed but not stiff — and he smiled in a way that set the world at ease.

"Joey, I'll have another scotch," the man said, emphasizing the owner's name.

Duncan knew this type well — confident, smart, smooth, but likes to be noticed.

The man put out his hand. "Hi there, fella. Haven't seen you around here ever."

"I just got in." Duncan shook the hand.

"Name's Vincent. Vincent Day. I gotta tell you. I like you. I can tell about a man when I shake hands with him and you're the kind of guy I like. Joey, get this man another Manhattan. What's your name?"

Vincent spoke fast. In 2013, the trait would have turned Duncan away. He never liked that old time, used car salesman speech. But sitting in a dark bar in 1934 gave the words a unique and free-flowing feel.

"I'm Duncan Rose."

Snapping his fingers at Joey, Vincent pointed to Duncan's empty glass. Joey raised an eyebrow. "Who's gonna pay for that?"

"That's no way to talk to one of your best regulars. Why I have a mind to—"

"When you settle your tab, then you can order drinks for your friends."

Duncan waved a hand between the two men. "It's okay. I've got it."

Vincent took his scotch with a scowl. To Duncan, he smiled and tipped his glass. "To you, sir. Already a true friend."

As he sipped his second Manhattan, careful not to make the same drinking mistake twice, Duncan wondered how old Vincent might be. He found it difficult to judge with everyone wearing suits. A young man looked much older when not dressed like a college bum. Vincent was young, that much was certain, but how young — how naïve — was the real question? After all, no matter how Duncan thought of Vincent, he had one objective. A guy like Vincent might make a good contributor to the Get Duncan Home fund.

Leaning into the bar, Duncan gestured for Joey to come close. In a low voice, he asked, "You wouldn't happen to know where a man might find a good card game, would you?" Duncan figured that bartenders were bartenders in any age. They knew all the local secrets.

Joey shook his head. "Sorry, pal. We only run a legitimate business here." He never looked at Duncan while he spoke. He kept eying Vincent.

When Duncan turned to his new friend, Vincent wore a big smile. "Cards, is it? Why I might know a few things or two about cards."

"I don't have much, but I'm hoping for a little fun and little luck."

Vincent slid one barstool closer. "Well, pal, you've got the luck part down. You met me. As for the fun — stick with me and I'll show you a great time. What kind of cards you like to play?"

"Anything, I suppose. Poker is always a good one, right?"

Vincent's shark smile nearly chomped a bite. "Then poker it is. Come with me. I'll get you in a game. You got five bucks?"

"Not quite."

Vincent dismissed the whole thing with a wave of his hand. "Don't worry about it. You pay in what you can and you owe the rest."

"You'll let me do that?"

"Heck, half the guys I know can't pay the buy in. Who's got five bucks to burn, right? So, you buy-in on credit. As long as you got something to put up for collateral, you'll be fine."

Duncan felt around his pockets. Other than the little cash he had, he couldn't find anything. He checked his wrists — no watch.

Vincent laughed. "You sure you want to play poker? You don't seem too bright."

"I'm sure I've got something we can use."

"I'm sure, too," Vincent said, and placed his hand firmly on top of Duncan's head — Duncan's covered head.

"This'll be enough?" Duncan asked, taking off his fedora.

"Of course. Every man wants a new hat. Nobody'll mind taking it from you if you lose. So, whadya say?"

Duncan shrugged weakly and hid his own shark smile deep inside. "I say that it's time to play a little poker."

CHAPTER 7

Everything changes.

Nothing changes.

When he stepped into the small, smoke-filled room, Duncan couldn't decide which was true. Perhaps both at the same time.

Two men, cigarettes dangling from their mouths, crowded a round table with a green felt cloth. They kept their hats on but had them tilted back. Their coats hung over the backs of their chairs. One of the men had a pencil-thin mustache and pock-marked cheeks. The other guy was a square-jawed package of muscle with a boxer's nose. A pretty girl dressed sharp and with a fur shawl also sat at the table.

Might as well be Peyter and the boys.

Vincent had led the way here (two blocks up and one block over) as if he had been this way a thousand times. That could be good or bad for Duncan. A regular game might mean less money, especially during The Great Depression, but three "pals" would have their guards down.

Nothing to do but make the best of it.

The girl saw them first. "I'll leave you boys to your games," she said and kissed the big guy. Squeezing by Duncan, she gave him a wink.

"Don't get any ideas," the big guy said. "She's mine."

"She's anybody's for a price," the thin guy said with a chuckle.

The big guy shrugged. "Well, I'm paying, so she's mine tonight."

The thin guy laughed until he started coughing. Vincent laughed as well, so Duncan joined in as they sat at the table.

Vincent pointed to the big guy. "This is Freddie. And that's Sammy. Gentleman, this here is Duncan Rose. Duncan and I are a bit short on the entry fee."

"How short?" Sammy snapped.

Duncan put out all his cash. "I got four dollars."

Before he had finished speaking, the money vanished and a stack of chips made its way in front of him. Sammy opened a deck of cards and started shuffling. He nodded at Vincent. "What about you?"

"Aw, you know me. I'm good for it."

"You owe me five from last week's game."

Freddie leaned on the table. "And five from the week before when Sammy was sick."

Vincent opened up a friendly smile. "Can I help it if you guys keep cleaning me out?"

"You ain't provided us nothing to clean out."

"Okay, okay," Vincent said with placating hands. "I just thought my pal Duncan here would enjoy the game. He's not played much poker before, and you guys are usually so sporting. But I understand. Come on, Duncan. Cash in and we'll go find another game."

"Now hold on," Sammy said. "There's no reason to get all huffy. We're all friends here." Before Duncan had a chance to react, before he could even decide whether it would be advantageous to go along with or correct Vincent's assessment of his abilities, Sammy had a stack of chips out in front of Vincent.

And with that, they dealt the first hand.

Duncan played honest hands for the first few rounds, keeping his attention on all the information he could glean about his three opponents. Sammy was the easiest to read —

full of tells and nervous energy. Freddie played a harder game. His stoic face and steady body posture gave away little. Vincent was impossible. He acted inconsistently — full of exuberance one moment, quiet and serious the next. He distracted easily and spoke non-stop the whole time. And when the cards laid down, his hands never correlated with his behavior in any repetitive pattern.

Nobody appeared to be dangerous, though, and that was the real reason for watching them. Tells are nice to know but unnecessary when one planned to cheat. Duncan's only real concern was Freddie. Sammy and Vincent didn't look like fighters, but Freddie could hold his own, no doubt.

Since Vincent had done a fine job of setting up Duncan as a novice, Duncan decided to play a game of beginner's luck. He'd cheat more often than usual and feign ignorance as to how he even won a few of the hands. Most people would chalk up the extra winnings to beginner's luck and none would be suspicious.

He kept the cheats rather simple. Holding an ace on the bottom of the deck for use whenever he wanted it. Stacking the deck to favor his hand but not worrying about what the other's received. Nothing too flashy. Nothing too big.

An hour into the game, Freddie stretched his arms. "I'm tired of beer. How about a shot of whiskey?"

Duncan wanted to decline — getting drunk would impair his abilities — but nobody took the time to even answer the question. Sammy simply produced four shot glasses and poured the drinks. "Your health," he said and tipped back his drink. Vincent and Freddie followed.

"Bottoms up," Duncan muttered to himself and drank. The whiskey hit hard and warm. The other men barely seemed to register that they had any alcohol in their system. Duncan shook his head. The tolerance of the 1930s man was astounding.

Another hour of play passed and Duncan had raked in fifteen dollars. He still had no firm grasp of what to expect when it came to prices, but he suspected fifteen dollars would be considered a good haul for a night. Not enough to live off of for long, but a good start.

A harsh bell rang from behind Freddie. The big guy reached back and brought around a phone. The old kind. The ancient kind. A black contraption that looked like a tube with a flared mouthpiece on top. A separate ear piece attached to the base with a cord. Freddie put the ear piece to his ear and brought the rest of the phone close to his mouth.

"Hello?" Freddie said in a louder than normal voice. "Yeah, Boss. Just playing poker."

Sammy turned to Vincent and tipped his head to the door.

"Come on," Vincent said to Duncan. "Break time."

They walked down a narrow hall and into an alley. The cool night air felt refreshing after all the smoke. Duncan took a deep breath and had no trouble ignoring the sour odors of trash.

Vincent lit up a cigarette and kicked away a rock. "You know, you're gonna get caught."

"What?" Duncan asked, his nerves igniting.

"Don't get me wrong. You've got excellent card control. Even if they were wise to you, they wouldn't see a thing. But I caught it. You're a bit slow dealing seconds, and how many more times are you gonna hold a bottom ace tonight? Now, don't worry. They don't suspect a thing. But they ain't stupid either. You keep being as greedy as you're doing, and they'll spend the night thinking over the whole game, trying to figure out how they lost so much money in one night."

Duncan hated to do it, but he had to bargain his way out of this. If they had been playing a cash game, he could have run, but all he had in his pocket was fifteen dollars in chips. Of course, bargain was the polite way to say what really was happening — he was being shaken down.

"How much?" Duncan asked.

"Excuse me?"

"You stay quiet, and I'll cut you in on some of my winnings. How much you want?"

Vincent lifted his hat and patted back his hair. "You don't get it." He pulled a deck of cards from his coat pocket. He proceeded to false shuffle, stack and re-stack, control aces, and display all manner of card control. With a sly smile, he said, "I've been working these guys for a long time. Losing on purpose week after week. Tonight is when I planned to strike."

"And you wanted to use me as cover."

"Exactly. If I won big tonight with a novice playing, they'd figure I got lucky or that you screwed up the flow of cards or some other malarkey like that." Vincent glanced up and down the alley, then moved in close to Duncan. "It ain't too late. You've had a good run with your beginner's luck, but any more and we're done. You give me a little trust, and we both can clean up tonight. I mean really clean up, not the little bit you've got now. So, the big question is: will you trust me?" Vincent put out his hand and waited.

"I have to admit," Duncan said as he shook Vincent's hand, "you're really surprising me. That doesn't happen often."

"I could say the same about you. In fact, I think I just did." Vincent checked his watch, then opened the door. "When we go back in, you watch carefully and be ready. And don't do anything until you understand what's going on. Okay?"

"Tell me the play now."

"No time. We don't get back there, they'll get suspicious."

Duncan went back in, his head spinning at the change in Vincent. He wanted to pause the world and find out all he could about this man who had caught his cheats. But he had a big job to do now. Playing the straight man in a two-person cheat can be difficult, especially after all the hours already played. He had to pretend nothing had changed, that his relationship with Vincent had not changed, that though everything had changed, nothing had changed.

At the same time, he had to watch Vincent carefully without being obvious. And as the hands were dealt, Duncan couldn't believe what he saw. Every time Vincent pulled in the cards to deal, he dropped a card to his lap. An Ace, a King, a Ten. It was so smooth, Duncan failed to catch it at first. And he knew deep in his heart that he would never have caught it had he not been told to look for it. In fact, he felt pretty sure that Vincent had slowed slightly to aid Duncan in catching the move.

Two rounds of cards didn't reveal what he was looking for, but after another five rounds had passed, Vincent had dropped a Heart straight flush into his lap one card at a time. Freddie and Sammy never suspected that they were playing rounds missing cards, especially because they kept winning. Whenever Duncan or Vincent had a winning hand, they folded. Whenever Duncan had a Heart to help, he made sure to get it close to Vincent.

When the deal fell to Duncan, he glanced at Vincent and received a slight nod. This was it. He dealt out the cards.

Vincent put in a minimum. The others followed but Duncan raised. The bet got called and they did a round of card exchanges. So far, all played honestly. But now came the crucial moment, and Duncan knew he had to be the misdirection.

He turned his body to face Sammy. "I really like your hat."

Sammy raised an eyebrow, took off his hat, and inspected it. "This thing?"

Freddie pointed to a tear in the back. "That's a piece of crap." He then took of his hat and tossed it to Duncan. "Try that one."

Duncan made a production of trying on the hat. "It is nice."

"I know."

Vincent chimed in, "Freddie's always got the best hat."

That was Duncan's cue. Vincent had successfully switched the winning hand in his lap with whatever Duncan had dealt. As long as Vincent remembered to pocket the extra cards, all would be good.

Vincent opened with another minimum bid. Freddie called. And, thank goodness, Sammy raised. Duncan raised, too, and they were off. Freddie stayed in another two rounds before bowing out but Vincent, Duncan, and Sammy kept raising each other until Duncan had all fifteen dollars in the pot. Vincent and Sammy went on further, forming a side pot just between them. By the end, the side pot reached fifty-two dollars. Add to that the original pot of forty-eight, and they would win a round one hundred dollars.

And they did.

Freddie laughed as Vincent laid down his straight-flush. Duncan frowned and crossed his arms while Sammy's pissed scowl said everything.

"I think that's a good place to stop for the night," Vincent said.

"Oh no," Sammy said. "You stay right here until I say you can go."

Freddie slapped Sammy's shoulder. "Quit your whining. You lost. So did Duncan. So what? Vincent never wins. Let him have his victory. Besides, you'll get it all back next week."

"Yeah, well, I better." Sammy put his hand out to Vincent. "You still owe me fifteen bucks for the past week's entries."

"And a dollar for mine, too," Duncan added.

Sammy liked that. "That's right. You pay for this kid's fee, too."

Vincent made a show of wanting to argue but knowing better. "Okay, fine." He peeled off three five dollar bills and tossed them on the table along with a one dollar bill and a smile. "Goodnight boys."

As he walked out, Duncan remained seated. This was the real moment of truth — the real test of trust. He had another drink with Freddie and Sammy before he made his own exit, and he hoped Vincent would be back at the bar where they met. If not, he had wasted his evening and lost all of his money.

CHAPTER 8

DUNCAN WANTED TO RUN straight to Joey's Corner, but he knew he had to play his role. He sauntered off in the opposite direction and around the block, making sure to hang his head low. If Freddie or Sammy bothered to watch, they would see a guy dejected at his loss, ready to join the masses suffering through the hard times, maybe even contemplating a visit to the soup kitchen.

Once he turned the corner, however, Duncan tossed away that cloak of sorrow, put a little bounce in his step, and headed to the bar. Though he walked at a brisk clip, he kept at a walk. Running would only draw attention, and that was something a card cheat never wanted.

As Duncan neared the bar, Vincent stepped out and waved. "Joey's is too crowded," he said. "I'll take you somewhere else."

"Sounds good." Duncan put a firm hand on his partner's shoulder. "First, let's settle up."

Vincent's eyes darted all around them and his hands pulled his coat tightly together. "Are you crazy? Keep your voice down and stop with the loony business. We don't do it out here." Shaking off Duncan's hand, Vincent went on, "Just follow me and you'll get your money."

He led the way around the block until they came to Sal's — a small Italian joint with only a few people inside. Like Joey's Corner, Sal's had a bar but alcohol wasn't the main attraction. Several wooden booths with high backs lined the wall, and at the occupied booths, every customer wolfed down a plate of pasta. Garlic and parmesan perfumed the air, and loud voices rattled off Italian from the kitchen.

"Two spaghettis and some beers," Vincent said as they made their way to the back corner booth.

Once they sat, secluded from the world, Duncan felt a hand on his knee. He reached under the table and received a wad of paper bills. He glanced down to count it.

"You can trust me," Vincent said. "Heck, I didn't run off, did I?"

Duncan counted it anyway — fifty dollars. He put the money away, looking around for prying eyes and pleased to see nobody paid him any attention. The waiter arrived with two heaping plates of pasta and two beers.

Vincent swirled up a forkful of spaghetti. "You've got some nice card skills. Nice skills, indeed. Who taught you?"

"My great-grandfather." The pasta tasted fantastic and the beer washed it down well.

"I picked it up from a few traveling magicians and that book, *Expert at the Card Table*. You ever read that? It's quite good. Really opened my eyes back when I was a kid. Even thought about making a go of being a professional magician."

"What stopped you?"

Vincent gestured into the air. "Life. People have no money, no jobs. I take care of my sister and that costs, too. We get by, but a professional's life requires constant travel which is expensive. What are you gonna do? That's just life. What about you? You could be a professional."

Duncan chuckled. "Not for me. Pappy always wanted me to do that, but that's a life that never would have worked for me. For one thing, you've got to deal with all the venue owners and their rules and audience expectations and all of that."

"Ain't that the truth. And worse, you work all those years to perfect a handful of effects, and then you're stuck doing them over and over and over. Nobody wants to see anything new from you. It's like that guy, Goldin. He's out in New York. Coney Island, I think. He does this trick where he saws a lady in half. You ever see that?"

"Of course, that's a classic—" Duncan stopped with a fork of pasta waiting to go into his gaping mouth. He stared at Vincent in disbelief. It wasn't a classic trick — not in 1934.

In fact, the trick started out in England, developed by P.T. Selbit in the '20s, and became hugely popular worldwide. Horace Goldin worked out his own method for the illusion and licensed it to other magicians — fifty bucks a week plus a percentage of the house. It was a gold mine for him, and he went after anybody who dared to perform the trick without a license. He even prevented Selbit from performing his own trick during an American tour.

It was one of the great stories behind magic, and Pappy loved to tell it. But that was all less than a decade ago here. And that reminded Duncan of his situation.

He had money now which meant focusing on finding that door. Chatting up with a guy and making friends was not a smart move. Especially considering that he had traveled back in time. Duncan had never gotten into time travel stories much, but he understood the concepts and dangers involved. He had to be careful of what he said to Vincent. Everything he had done already, everything he would do, everything he would say, all of it could have an enormous impact upon the future. Couldn't it? He wasn't sure but he thought that's what most time travel stories were about — screwing up the future and then trying to fix it. Had he already messed things up? Cheating those guys at cards — had that somehow screwed up the universe?

"Hey pal," Vincent said, "you okay?"

"I don't know," Duncan said for fear of saying anything else.

"Don't look so glum. We cleaned up tonight. We got some cash to spend. Heck, there'll always be plenty of days to look glum. So, let's have a few more beers and relax." Vincent snapped for the waiter's attention and pointed to the beers. After finishing the last of his old beer, Vincent reached into his pocket and brought out his deck of cards. He tossed them on the table near Duncan. "Let me see your pass."

Duncan stared at the cards. Vincent sounded just like Pappy, and for a horrifying moment, he wondered if Vincent was Pappy. His stomach swirled at the idea. But then he remembered that Vincent had mentioned a sister and Pappy had no siblings. With a relieved sigh, Duncan picked up the cards.

Vincent pointed at him. "I see it in you. The second you put those cards in your hands, you were feeling better."

"In a way," Duncan said, shuffling the cards and enjoying the feel on his fingertips. "It was hitting me just now how little control I have in my life, but these cards — I can control these." And with that, he decided he couldn't worry about the future. If he fretted over his every word or action, he'd be paralyzed. He'd never be able to find the door and get home. He had to focus on what he could control and let the universe handle the rest.

Vincent watched closely as Duncan performed the pass. He kept a steady poker face and said, "One more time, please." Duncan obliged. "Okay," Vincent said. "Drink up. Time to go."

"I haven't finished eating."

"Hurry up then."

"Why? Where are we going?"

Vincent smiled. "We're going to steal a car."

DUNCAN HADN'T ACTED THIS RECKLESSLY since his high school days. At first, he had agreed because he needed an ally and Vincent seemed like a good one to have. But he liked Vincent, too. He liked how Vincent fit so perfectly in this time period, and how that perfect fit helped him fit in, too. He liked Vincent's carefree bravado. And he liked that as they careened down the old back roads, kicking dirt and stones behind them, he wanted to smile.

Here he was, lost in 1934, yet he smiled.

And sang.

He stood on the runner, held onto the car door with one hand, and sang out to the sleeping world with a flask in his other hand. When he belted out the first lines of the chorus to Tom Petty's "Free Fallin'", Vincent gave him the oddest look. Duncan laughed and quickly mumbled his way into the only thing he could think of that definitely existed at the time — "The Star Spangled Banner." With all the July Fourth celebrations, the choice made plenty of sense.

Vincent swerved off the road, back on, off the other side, and back on again. Though the Ford they had lifted couldn't have been going more than forty-five miles-per-hour, it felt like ninety while hanging from the runner. When a squirrel darted into the road and Vincent over-reacted, the car moved fast enough to slam into a tree and send Duncan hurtling through the air.

He tumbled in the dirt and tall grass, coming to rest under a pine tree. The fragrant pine needles were soft to lie on as long as they didn't poke him in the side, and Duncan considered closing his eyes for a while. He burped and tasted alcohol, and his eyelids lowered. But then he remembered they had just crashed and Vincent might be hurt.

Wobbling his drunken way toward the car, he saw smoke drifting from the long, narrow hood. Vincent sat in the driver's seat, his head against the steering wheel, blood trickling down the side of his face. He looked up, dazed and smiling.

"I think I had an oopsy," he said.

Duncan fell backwards laughing.

Vincent stumbled out of the car. "It's not my fault somebody put a tree in the way." He glanced around until he found the road. "Come on. We gotta walk back."

"Okay, okay," Duncan said, snorting out another laugh.

As they headed back, Duncan noticed a faint light poking out from the dark trees. "What's that?"

Vincent belched. "Some nutcase still lives out there. Won't come join the rest of society. He'll probably die out there, too. His house is all wood except for the foundation and he smokes like locomotive."

"You know him?"

"Never met him. Just telling you what I heard."

"Wait a second." Duncan stopped and looked around. He tried to picture where they stood in relation to the town. "Oh, wow." That hermit's house had to be the burned out ruins he and Pancake would hang around while they got drunk as teens.

"What's up?" Vincent asked.

Duncan laughed. "Nothing. Just got a weird feeling is all."

"That, my friend, is because you're drunk."

They walked on, and an hour later they had sobered enough to stay mostly on the road while walking, no longer dropping into fits of laughter for no reason at all. At one point, Duncan put his arm around Vincent. "We did good tonight. I bet the two of us could clean up a lot more money working together from the start."

"We could at that. But we can't do anything for a while. We've got to lay low on the poker cheats because of that big guy, Freddie."

"I ain't afraid of him."

"It's his boss you should be afraid of — Nelson Walter. Owns The Walter Hotel in town. He used to go by the name 'Thumbs' on account of the fact that he liked to break them off his victims. Especially magicians. Liked to ruin their careers."

Duncan's face screwed up in confusion. "Why the heck would he care about magicians?"

"We're really good at cheating at cards, for one thing. For another, he's not."

"So he's jealous?"

"Who knows? He's a Jew and they're a strange lot."

Duncan bristled but kept his mouth shut. This was 1934. Anti-Semitism, like all forms of racism, wasn't necessarily frowned upon. Or even questioned, for that matter.

Wait a few years, Duncan thought. *World War II might change a few minds.*

Vincent shuffled his feet to a halt. He pointed into the sky as if he expected a UFO to appear suddenly. "Look there."

Squinting, Duncan said, "I don't see anything."

"Wait. It'll come."

A few seconds later, the sky lit up with Fourth of July fireworks. Reds and blues streamed across the sky while explosions popped everywhere. In between shots, Duncan could hear the dim noise of a crowd applauding.

"How close to town are we?"

"Not far," Vincent said. Minutes later, they passed under a lone streetlamp. "You'll be able to find your way back from here, no trouble." He started to walk away, then spun with a snap of his fingers. It all looked rather choreographed to Duncan. Especially when Vincent said, "You know what you should do? You should try to join my magic club. It's an amateur group, mostly, but we get together at the Magic Emporium and trade secrets, work on effects, and have fun. It's a blast. It's also a good place to lay low without seeming suspicious."

Duncan didn't quite catch why being in a club would make him any less suspicious, and he figured Vincent's drunkenness was doing the talking here. But joining the club might help him learn the area a little faster, would certainly provide a few new contacts, and might be the right kind of people to learn about a magic door. At the least, it would be a place from which to conduct his search for the door. "Okay, I'll join your club."

"Hold on, there. Not so fast." Vincent pulled out a fresh deck of cards with a red patterned back. "I know you can handle cards well, but everybody in the club has had to pass this test. I can't go making exceptions just because I nearly killed you in a car. That wouldn't be right." He opened the deck and began to shuffle. "I'm going to show you a trick. All you have to do is figure it out. You do that, you can join the club."

"Are you serious?"

"I'm not so drunk that I can't pull off a card trick. And, yes, I'm serious. The club members are serious, too. They care about magic. I figured you were serious, too. Anybody willing to put in all the hours it takes to handle cards like you do has to be serious. Or crazy."

Duncan smirked. "I might be both."

"I suspect you are." Vincent sat on the side of the road. "You ready for this?"

Duncan sat next to him. "Okay. Let me see."

Vincent gave the deck to Duncan. "Go ahead and shuffle the cards."

As Duncan shuffled, he watched Vincent closely. When magicians performed tricks for each other, the tension always raised since they always knew they were being burned. In this case, though, Vincent invited, really demanded, that Duncan burn him — watch close enough to figure out the trick.

After the shuffle, Vincent took the cards and held them face down in his left hand. "Now, I'm going to deal cards until you tell me to stop, okay? Stop me whenever you want." Vincent started placing cards into a small pile on the road.

Duncan studied Vincent's hands, looking for a bottom deal or some other manipulation. After about eight cards, he said, "Stop." He hadn't seen anything wrong.

"Okay," Vincent said, a devious smile on his lips. He turned over the next card — the Seven of Hearts. "This is going to be our Magic Card." He then placed the rest of the deck on top of the card, so that the Seven was face up in the deck. He handed the deck to Duncan. "You go ahead and deal out as many cards as you want. Stop when you're ready and flip over the next card. That's your card. Remember it and place it face down on the pile you dealt."

Duncan took the deck and held it in a dealer's grip — the natural way a person holds a deck with the index finger at the upper side, the other three fingers on the right side, and the thumb resting on the left side. If Vincent had palmed a card or two, Duncan couldn't tell. *Not that I could tell,* he thought. Five or six cards missing, Duncan would feel the difference. But only one or two — *Pappy could do it, but I've never been that good.*

"Just to be completely amazing, I'll turn my back for this,"

Vincent said and turned around.

Duncan dealt out a bunch of cards, then made a bunch of dealing noises by re-dealing the same card back into place — just in case Vincent was trying to count the number of dealt cards. After a little of this, Duncan stopped and flipped over the Five of Spades. As instructed, he placed this card face down on the pile.

"All done," he said.

Vincent turned back. "Great. Now put the rest of the deck on top of the dealt pile. Good. Now you can give the deck as many cuts as you want. Nothing fancy, just normal cuts."

Duncan cut the deck a few times but figured if he was being allowed to do this, it couldn't really matter that much to the trick. When he finished, Vincent picked up the full deck, shored up the cards, and began dealing two alternating piles.

"You can watch my hands as close as you want, but trust me here, I'm just dealing out the deck. Nothing very exciting."

Duncan watched carefully. At one point, he saw the face-up Seven of Hearts go by, but otherwise noticed nothing unusual.

"Okay," Vincent said when he dealt the last card. He picked up the left deck. "So far, we found a Magic Card, and you dealt out your own card. You then cut the deck as much as you wanted, and I've dealt out the entire deck. Your card could be anywhere. In fact, let's see what we have on top." He lifted off a few cards — King of Clubs, Nine of Diamonds, Three of Diamonds. "Those your card?"

"No."

He lifted off another card — Four of Clubs. "How about that one?"

"No."

Vincent put those four cards on the bottom of the packet he held. He placed this on the road next to the other packet of cards. "That's okay. Watch this." He then lifted one card from each pile and placed it face down in front of the pile. He kept doing this over and over — his left hand lifting from the left pile, his right hand from the right pile. Duncan had to admit that Vincent's hands moved with grace and presence like the best magicians. "We'll keep doing this until we reach the Magic Card," he said, and a few cards later, that face-up Seven of Hearts sat on the left pile. "Moment of truth time. Tell me, Duncan my new friend, what was your card."

"Five of Spades."

Vincent lifted the card on the right pile and turned it over. It was the Five of Spades. "There you are. All you have to do is figure it out, come by the Magic Emporium and show us. Do that, and you're in. Do that, and we can share all the card cheats and effects and illusions that we know."

Duncan played out the trick in his head a few times, going over all the basic maneuvers Pappy had taught him. He had never seen this one before and it had a lot of steps to it, any one of which could be the key to the whole thing. Or it could be the type of trick in which none of the steps matter, all of it is nothing more than misdirection, because the trick is essentially set up from the very start.

Vincent patted Duncan's shoulder and headed down the road. "You think on that, pal. And I'll tell you what — you come on by the Emporium tomorrow, even if you haven't got the answer yet. I want to introduce you to the gang."

"Wait," Duncan said. "Where are you going?"

"Home. Gotta sleep a little. Goodnight." Vincent hummed a roaming melody as he walked off, leaving Duncan standing on the road next to two piles of cards.

Duncan considered chasing after Vincent, but he needed to run through the card trick before he forgot the details. He plunked down on the road, scooped up the cards, and tried to recall the performance. He couldn't get the actual trick to work, but he could recall the steps presented and that was important if he wanted to deconstruct the whole thing.

After about fifteen minutes, he felt satisfied he had enough to work with. Brushing off his pants, he headed back into town. The trick rolled around his mind but no solution came to him. Not that he expected it. One thing he learned well from Pappy — when it comes to magic, a magician never makes it easy. The mystery and the challenge were all part of the show.

Even with an audience of one stranger trying to get an "in" with a magic club.

As the town appeared ahead, Duncan realized he had a more immediate problem than figuring out the magic trick. He had no place to stay. Of course, he had a pocket full of cash and Vincent had mentioned a hotel, so he wasn't worried.

That sense of security didn't last long, though. Big round headlights cut into the darkness. A car stopped at least a hundred feet away and idled. Duncan stood in its beams and waited. No point in running. It was too dark and he didn't know the area at all. Chances were he'd break his ankle, run around in a circle, or head straight to wherever he didn't want to go.

He heard the car door open but couldn't see much beyond the headlights. A figure stepped in front of the car, lit a cigarette, and started walking up the street. Duncan saw a large, wide-shouldered man. He moved at a steady clip, jingling the change in his pocket. A few feet closer, and Duncan's stomach dropped. It was Freddie — the big guy from the card game. He wore a trench coat and a fedora. Sweat dribbled down his face and he huffed with his final steps.

"I've been looking for you," he said, his voice low and cold.

It took all of Duncan's drunken will to keep from laughing. Freddie sounded like a thug from an old black-and-white movie. But when he wrapped his meaty hand around Duncan's bicep and squeezed, the humor vanished.

"You're real lucky I got orders, 'cause I'd like to give you a taste of my knuckles."

"Sorry," Duncan said. "Maybe some other time." Normally, self-preservation would have kept him from saying such a stupid thing, but alcohol and nerves got the better of him.

"Real smart," Freddie said and yanked Duncan closer, their noses nearly touching. Duncan could smell a mixture of cigarettes and beer that made Freddie seem even more dangerous. "You won't be so cute when Mr. Walter is done with you."

CHAPTER 9

By the time the car rolled up in front of The Walter Hotel, Duncan had sobered extensively. Though not fully free of alcohol, he could walk straight and, he hoped, think straight, too. Freddie had jammed him in the back seat, sandwiching him between two equally large thugs. They reeked of cigars and sweat, and nobody said a word the entire trip.

For Duncan, the whole experience felt a bit surreal. When would Edward G. Robinson pop up? And like a movie, this would all end. Once he found the door home, none of this would amount to much. Just an amazing, bizarre experience. He would love to come back for a visit and spend time playing cards with Vincent, but he didn't have to worry about Nelson Walter and his thugs. Yet at the same time, a twinge of apprehension formed in his gut. Cavalier could only go so far. He had to be a little careful. After all, if he got injured or beaten badly, he'd have a difficult time getting back to the 21st century. And worse, if he got himself killed …

Before the valet could take three steps toward them, Freddie stepped out of the car and pulled Duncan along. He kept a firm hold on Duncan's arm and steered him through the hotel. "I won't run," Duncan said, but Freddie grumbled and shoved him along.

The Walter Hotel would have made Donald Trump weep. Marble floors and crystal chandeliers, nude statues and groomed servants, and wherever one looked — gold-trim. An enormous fountain graced the lobby while a string quartet played near a sweeping staircase.

People mulled about, all wearing their finest clothes, all abuzz with anticipation for a wonderful evening. Some looked uncomfortable as if they only spent such sums once a year and didn't know all the etiquette involved in an opulent place such as this. Others looked bored at yet another evening of drinking and eating and reveling. Most, however, smiled and laughed and tried hard to let some of the gold glimmer upon them.

Guess not everybody suffers during the Depression.

Freddie escorted Duncan through a curtained archway and into one of three cavernous restaurants. The place hopped with activity. All the tables were occupied. The moment satisfied diners left, busboys hurried in to clean and set up. Before the diners had exited the room, new diners were seated and giving their menu orders. All of this danced to the infectious tunes of the house's twelve-piece big band.

Two couples used the dance floor that gleamed like ice from extensive polishing. Most people appeared more interested in eating. For further entertainment, a few men in long-tails and top hats worked the tables, performing close-up magic.

Duncan thought of the soup line from earlier that day and that people might still be waiting for an evening meal a few blocks away. It was like a science-fiction story — two parallel worlds co-existing in the same space.

"Over there," Freddie said, indicating a bank of three elevator doors. All the doors were open, and each housed an attendant dressed in a double-breasted uniform with a pillbox cap on top. Freddie pointed to the one on the end and the young operator straightened at their approach.

"What floor, sir?" he said, his voice still cracking with puberty.

"Mr. Walter's floor."

The boy paled but otherwise remained calm. "Right away,

sir. Watch yourselves as I close the doors." With a practiced motion, he slid the main door closed and then an accordion gate. He glanced at Duncan before pulling the lever that engaged the elevator, and Duncan swore he caught a look of pity in the kid's eyes.

The elevators of 1934 left much to be desired. The start and finish lacked the smooth grace of a modern elevator, and no form of noise reduction had been employed, so Duncan suffered through listening to every creak and moan the machinery emitted. He had to keep reminding himself that the chances of the cable snapping and the elevator plummeting to the ground were remote. Yet each time a cable twanged, it reverberated through the walls, and Duncan's heart twanged with it. Making matters worse, there was little room inside. Duncan had to press against Freddie a bit, and neither man appeared to enjoy the experience.

When they reached the penthouse, the elevator operator opened the door and stepped out. "Mr. Walter's private floor," he said with a slight bow and a flourish of his hand.

Freddie stomped into the hallway, yanking Duncan along. As an afterthought, he tipped the boy a dime, and then waited until the boy rode the elevator back down. Voices echoed from the right end of the hall — a woman and a child.

"This way," Freddie said, pushing Duncan left toward a heavy wood door at the far end. On either side of the hall, statuettes of nude females posed in small recesses like devilish imps laughing at the approach of a fresh victim.

Freddie pushed open the door with one hand and shoved Duncan through with the other. He pointed to a high-backed chair with gold arms and grapevines carved into the wood. "Sit."

Duncan settled in the chair which was far more uncomfortable than it had appeared. It had been set in front of the most ornate desk Duncan had ever seen. The legs and edges were a mixture of silver and gold sculpted into a design of playing cards fanned out around the corners. The cherry wood top held two glass panels. A lamp with cloth tassels hanging from the shade sat on the far right corner. On the left corner, Duncan saw a phone — a more modern one than he had seen anywhere else since his arrival in 1934, one in which the speaker and receiver had been combined into one handset. Most importantly, he noticed two decks of cards. It was difficult to make out from the chair, but it appeared to be one deck on the edge and another fanned out on a felt cover as if someone had been practicing card tricks.

Like the desk, the office was a peacock's exercise in display — substituting wealth for plumage. Marble, gold, crystal, ivory — all of it spoke to power and money. *Possibly insecurity, too,* Duncan considered out of habit — his well-trained brain sought out an angle on every person he met, trying to locate the weakness to exploit.

Freddie stood by a small table on the left side of the room under an oil painting of a buxom woman hiding only half her body beneath a crumpled, red sheet. Duncan watched him for a moment but Freddie no longer appeared interested now that his task was complete.

Two other items caught Duncan's attention, and neither one made him feel good about meeting Nelson Walter. The first was the door behind the heavy-handed desk. Unlike everything else in the office, this door was plain. A simple, wood door with a boring, round knob. No paint on the door. The knob — black-painted metal. It was wrong, this door, and the fact that it had been given such an important position in the room — directly behind Walter's desk — Duncan had to wonder what kinds of things went on back there.

The second thing he noticed answered that question with sickening clarity. An empty umbrella can stood next to the simple door. Dark splotches covered the rim. Duncan knew dried blood when he saw it. His nostrils flared as he tried to keep the rest of his body from reacting.

When the door opened, however, Duncan flinched. A middle-aged man wearing brown slacks and a white shirt with the sleeves rolled-up entered. He was short and heavy, at least 200 pounds, and brown suspenders strained against his bulk —

no Depression-era starvation for this guy. He slicked back his hair to cover the balding circle forming at the crown. In all, he looked like an overweight, middle management-type. Until he faced Duncan with his startling blue eyes and his thick-lipped wolf mouth.

He stared at Duncan for a moment before thrusting a golf club into the umbrella stand. From the desk chair, he lifted a suit jacket, rolled down his sleeves, and slipped it on. Duncan couldn't help but notice the golf club had been put in with the club head sticking out of the stand. And the club head glistened crimson.

"You're Duncan, right?" the man said, his voice deep and dangerous. Duncan nodded. "I'm Nelson Walter. I hope we can work well together." He extended a hand.

"Pleased to meet you," Duncan said, surprised to hear the nervousness in his voice seeping out. He shook Walter's hand, choosing not to fight back when Walter crunched down on his fingers. It reminded him of how Pappy would shake hands — as if he were in a contest to see who could hurt the other more. As Walter let go, Duncan saw two little red specks on the man's white cuffs.

Duncan knew enough to stay quiet. Men like Walter wanted to be in control and the only way to control them was to make them think they ran things. Besides, for the moment, Nelson Walter did control things. Duncan had no choice but to ride this out until he had more information.

Walter lit a cigarette, sucked in the carcinogenic smoke, and blew it out with a long, satisfied breath. His mouth opened into a wide grin that sent a shiver through Duncan. "Freddie here tells me you're something special with a deck of cards. Is that true?"

"Wait, is all this because he lost money? Really?"

"You didn't answer my question," Walter said, his grin looking colder with each passing second.

"I'm okay, I guess."

"That's not what he said. He told me he couldn't catch you cheating all night, but he knew you were doing it."

Trying to regain his composure by looking relaxed under the scrutiny of this intense man, Duncan leaned on his elbow and crossed his legs. "If he didn't see me cheating, then what makes you think I was cheating?"

"Freddie?"

Freddie smirked. "Because I was cheating."

Walter spread his fingers in the air. "Wha-la. If Freddie set the cards one way but they kept coming out another way, that suggests that you were manipulating the cards. Is that what happened?"

"If you're after getting your money back—"

Walter slammed his open hand on the table top, his cuff with the two drops of blood fully visible. Duncan sat up involuntarily. "When I ask a question, you answer it. Got it?"

"I'm sorry."

"I said, *Got it?* That's a fucking question. Answer me."

"Yes," Duncan said, his sense of mental balance thrown awry. "Yes, I got it."

"Good." Walter sniffed back hard. He took a long drag on his cigarette before regaining a calm demeanor. "I don't want your money. You cheated it off a guy trying to cheat you. That seems fair to me." He nodded to Freddie who responded by leaving the office. Walter studied Duncan's face until Freddie returned with a glass of scotch on the rocks. After handing it to Walter, Freddie went back to his post by the card table.

Walter swirled the glass, the ice cubes tinkling against the side like a haunting wind chime. "You know, not all magicians are card cheats, but all card cheats are magicians. It's true. They may not think of themselves as magicians, but the skills they possess go hand-in-hand with good magic. You are clearly a card cheat, and I think you know you're a magician, too."

"Okay," Duncan said, crossing his arms unconsciously. It was a weak, defensive bit of body language, but once he noticed it, he didn't want to rapidly pull out of the move which would only betray his rising nerves more.

"That fellow you were playing with. What was his name?"

"Vincent. But I only met him today. If you got a problem

with him—"

"He runs a little magic club. Did you know that?"

"He mentioned it."

"I'll bet he did." Walter's face twisted up for an instant. "Well, here's what I want you to do. I want you to get into that club and bring back to me every trick, every cheat, every oddity of magic knowledge you can find. You do that, and we'll forget about the money you owe Freddie."

"Hold on a sec," Duncan said, real confusion nibbling at him. "What's with everyone's interest in magic? I mean, I understand it's entertaining, but you're strong arming me to spy on a little magic club. Why?"

Walter's eyes lifted in surprise, shriveling his forehead in a mass of wrinkles. "Why did Houdini explore the magical arts? Why Dai Vernon? It's more than just ripping off a few bums at cards or making a seven-year-old boy laugh in amazement. Magic is about unlocking secrets. And let me tell you something — Houdini was no fool. He was on to something. And Vincent Day knows more than he lets on, too. Why the fuck do you think I came to this craphole in the first place? Do you know who I am?" It had been the fastest Walter spoke so far, and the man wheezed for a moment before washing his congestion away with his scotch.

He pointed a stubby finger at Duncan and spoke with a new urgency. He paced behind his desk, smoking, drinking, and spouting off his words like a mad poet. "I come from New York City. That's the real world. I don't know where you're from, don't really care, but I can see on your face that you spent many years playing with your blocks and sucking your Mommy's teat. Me? I got started running numbers when I was an orphan and I didn't look back. I've had women and booze and money like you couldn't even dream. Make those stupid Hollywood features look like table scraps. So now why would a successful guy like me ask his boss to send him out into this little nothing town in Pennsylvania? You get it yet? I asked to be here because magic, real magic, is far more important than anything else. Because guys like Vincent Day know things.

Secrets. And only through those secrets will we uncover the truths that are going to protect us. I live in a dangerous world. A lot of people try to kill a man like me. I can't have that happen. You understand yet?"

Duncan nodded. He had no clue what Nelson Walter really meant by any of this, but he knew enough to agree with the crazy man. Besides, he wanted to join that club. Perhaps some of what Walter had said was true — not the mystic crap, but the idea that Vincent Day was a talented magician and knew things others didn't. That seemed like the kind of guy Duncan needed to help him find a truly magical door. Then he could walk through back into 2013 and forget all this.

And if none of that convinced him deep inside, Duncan had another strong motivation to play along with the crazy mobster before him. If he didn't, he would find himself on the wrong end of a bloody golf club.

"I'll do it," he said. "I'll help you."

Walter opened his arms wide and practically sang the words, "Wha-la." He sat in his big chair and patted a handkerchief on his sweaty forehead. "I know you're new to this town, so Freddie'll do whatever he can to help you settle in."

"Thanks, but that won't be necessary. I can manage—"

"I insist."

"Then it'll be a pleasure."

"Don't worry about him crowding you. If Vincent Day saw Freddie and you together, he'd never let you in the club. But Freddie'll be watching you. To help you, of course."

"Of course." And to Duncan's relief, his brain finally kicked into gear. "There is one thing I need."

With a magnanimous smile, Walter said, "Name it."

"I don't have a place to stay."

Walter broke into a hearty laugh. "Then it's a damn good thing I own this hotel."

Duncan smiled, but he couldn't muster even a chuckle.

Chapter 10

Duncan stared at the ceiling and listened to a clock tick along the night. He had never traveled well, jet lag dogged him in even the most minor time zone changes. Heck, daylight savings required a week to adjust. Apparently time travel would be worse. The night crept like a sloth and Duncan endured every ticking second of it.

Walter had him dumped in one of the worst rooms because "Hey, it's a roof over your head" and even if he hadn't been suffering from lag, Duncan's mind refused to settle down. Thoughts of magic doors, card tricks, Vincent, Freddie, and Nelson all swirled in a befuddling mess that only cleared long enough for him to be plowed over by the fact that he actually was lying on a bed in 1934.

He tried to keep calm about the whole thing, keep his mind focused on finding the door home, but waiting for the humid July night to end only served to rattle his nerves. The sounds of 1934 cars and 1934 drunks and 1934 life drifted in through the open window. Worse, sometimes no sound drifted through. Silence unlike anything he had experienced in 2013. A true absence of sound. No whirring laptop fan, no hum of a fluorescent light, no constant noise of traffic. Nothing.

Duncan grabbed a pencil and paper from the bedside table

and worked on drawing the symbols on Pappy's door. Some came easily, some he struggled to recall. After a half-hour, he had an approximation that satisfied him. It still needed work, but at least he could see it again. The exercise had the added benefit of occupying his mind for a little.

When dawn finally arrived, Duncan found his way to the kitchen via an employee entrance that Freddie strongly advised he used. Walter didn't want any of the paying customers to know about Duncan. A black chef (probably another person Walter didn't want the paying customers to see) fried up some eggs, bacon, and threw on two slices of toast. He handed it over without a word or a smile. He hardly had time to blink considering the speed of orders ramming through.

Back in his room, Duncan ate his breakfast and thought over Vincent's card trick. After washing down the toast with a small glass of orange juice, he shuffled a deck of cards and ran through a few ideas. Nothing worked out but it killed time. By nine, Duncan decided the Magic Emporium had probably opened. Freddie provided an address, so Duncan cleaned up and made his way the few blocks over to the shop.

A bell jingled overhead as he stepped into the small store, a welcoming sound that cleared Duncan's head and brought a smile to his face. A glass counter ran along the right side of the store, displaying cards, gaffs, and all manner of basic illusions. Behind the counter, Vincent leaned close to a gangly, ginger-haired fellow wearing a suit with the pants hiked up high in the common fashion of the day. Round tables dotted the floor and a cash register sat on a little wooden table in the back. Behind the table was a blue door with a white handle.

"This is him," Vincent said with a clap of his hands. He hurried around the counter and wrapped an arm over Duncan's shoulder. "Gentleman, this here is the guy I was telling you about. Duncan Rose."

The ginger-haired man put out his hand. "I'm Ben. Good to meet you."

Before Duncan could respond, two other men approached. They had been seated in the dark back corner, but as the came up, Duncan saw he had nothing to fear. They were happy fellows — one a bit sloppy but full of energy, the other droopy-eyed and serious.

Vincent pointed to the sloppy one. "That's Morty, and the other guy is Lucas."

Morty tucked in his shirt before offering to shake hands. "Welcome, Duncan. We sure are glad to see you." He spoke in a wet, sloppy manner that Duncan liked. He half-expected a punchline followed by a rim-shot every time Morty said anything. Morty went on, "Vincent's said you got some talent. Boy, that's great. Really great. We need fresh blood in our club. If I have to sit through another one of Ben's stale tricks, I'll wish The Big One started again so I could join up."

Everybody laughed, including Ben. It took Duncan a second to realize Morty had referenced World War I, and then all he could think was how in less than a decade, Morty would get an opportunity to fight a big war after all.

Lucas flicked his tongue under his bottom lip. "He ain't passed the test yet."

Morty deflated. "Do we have to bother with that? If Vincent said the guy is good, then the guy is good."

"My friends," Vincent said, "I'm sure Duncan won't have much trouble figuring out that trick. He probably already has it done. Right?"

All eyes turned on Duncan. He squirmed under their scrutiny. "Not quite yet," he managed.

"Oh, well. Nothing to worry about. You'll get it. Of course, until you do, you'll have to stay out here in the main part of the store. Only club members get to go through the magic door."

Duncan perked up. "Magic door?"

Vincent made a grand gesture to the blue door with the white handle in the back. "Beyond there is where we do all our big stuff. But we can still have fun out here."

"That's right," Morty said. "Here's a trick for you." He scurried back to the table he had been sitting at and swiped his hat — another Fedora. When he returned, he pulled out a deck of cards and made a show of letting anybody shuffle the deck that wanted to do so. He then had Duncan pick a card while he turned his back. Finally, Morty turned the hat upside down and tossed the deck into the hat with three shakes of his hand. "Now for the amazing part."

"Good," Ben said, "because the boring part has sure been swell."

"Ignore them. They don't understand real quality when they see it." Morty held the hat in one hand and began to bounce it around. Cards popped over the brim and flipped around. After a little of this, Morty concentrated on the hat, reached in and pulled out Duncan's card.

The whole group burst into applause and laughter. Duncan joined in. "That was good," he said, and he had no idea how it was done. He suspected Morty had forced the selection, a technique every magician learned early on. There were tons of forces, each one designed to make the spectator select a specific card, but how Morty got the card to stand out in the hat while being tossed about was strange. Something deep within sparked — a memory of those first years when Pappy would show him something new and amazing, when the joy of tackling the trick matched the joy of pulling off the trick once he had figured it out.

"Morty," Duncan said, "I like you."

"That's because you've got good taste." Morty placed his hat, cards still in it, on his head. As the cards cascaded down, Duncan led the laughter.

"How's it done?" Ben asked.

Lucas put a hand on Morty's head before the man could swipe the hat down. "We don't explain tricks out here," Lucas said.

"Nonsense. This isn't a big secret trick. Just a little party thing. Right?"

Morty swiped his hat from under Lucas's hand. "That's right. This is a little nothing of a trick. Why I'd show this to my little nephew if I had one. And don't worry like that. I won't reveal any real important stuff. I know what's secret to the club and what isn't."

"But we agreed—"

"It's fine, Lucas," Vincent chimed in. "Duncan is going to be part of the club very soon. It won't hurt us to show off one secret."

"Thank you," Morty said with a half-hearted scowl at Lucas. Then his face animated with delight as he turned the hat over. "You guys are going to hate yourselves when you see how simple this is. Now I suppose you could do it with most any hat, but it's easiest and natural with a Fedora. All I did was let the cards fall to one side of the fold in the hat. Then I put the selection on the other side and with my fingers I can literally pinch the selection card so it doesn't go anywhere when I jostle the whole thing." Morty demonstrated by holding the hat in his right hand, his fingers reaching up into the folds of the Fedora to squeeze one card tight while the others were free to be tossed around.

Duncan felt that old thrill again. "That's great. Simple but very effective. I like it."

"As well you should, my friend."

"Okay, okay," Ben said. "I'll show you a trick."

"Come on," Morty said. "I haven't finished my breakfast yet. You're going to ruin my constitution for the whole day."

"I'd feel sorry for you if you actually had anything to eat."

"You got me there. Just don't do that Thurston trick again. He may have been called the King of Cards, but you are most decidedly not. I can't stand to see a good trick botched."

"This is a new one I've been working on." The gang moved in again as Ben pulled out his own deck of cards. "Now, I need two volunteers. Vincent, Duncan. Vincent, I want you to think of a number between ten and twenty. Go ahead and tell us."

Vincent leaned back against the counter as if he knew this trick already and would play along to amuse his friends. "Fifteen."

"To make this really interesting, add the two digits together. Fifteen is a one and a five, so we got six. To make it even tougher, take your number, fifteen and subtract six from it. That gives us nine."

Morty elbowed Duncan. "Yeesh, I thought I finished math class years ago."

"Patience," Ben said and gave the deck of cards to Duncan. "Now I want you to count off nine cards and remember that ninth card, but Vincent, you can't watch."

Vincent turned around as Duncan counted down nine cards and ended with the Four of Diamonds. He showed it to Morty and Lucas before putting it back in the deck.

"Okay, Vincent, turn back." Ben bent over a black satchel and pulled out a small crystal ball. He handed it to Vincent. "Take a look in there and see if the mystic forces tell you the name of the card."

Vincent played along, looked in the ball, and his eyes widened. "I see a Four of Diamonds."

Duncan and the rest applauded, and while Morty and Lucas tried to look at the crystal ball which Ben had returned to his satchel quickly, Duncan had an idea. He had a suspicion about how the trick worked, and he hoped it might help him with solving Vincent's trick. He stepped closer to Ben to ask him a question when the blue door opened and Duncan's brain shut down.

A young gal, no more than twenty-three, stepped into the shop. Duncan had never seen such a beautiful woman before. Her individual features were nothing unique or even desirable — she was short, wore her brown hair bobbed, and had a small scar on her upper lip — but combined she formed an exquisite sight that left his mouth dry and his chest tight. When she looked up at him and smiled, he understood the spell a woman could put on a man.

Luckily, Vincent snapped him back to the world with a simple sentence. "Duncan, I'd like you to meet my sister, Lucy."

Duncan cleared his throat and tipped his hat. "Ma'am," he said, hoping he hadn't committed a 1930s faux pas.

Lucy smiled and the room became warmer. She placed a stack of papers on the counter and winked at Morty. "So what do you think of Vincent's latest find?"

Morty hiked up his pants. "Oh, he's all right. But we ain't yet seen what he can really do."

Duncan turned to the man. "I've got to admit it's been a long time since I performed tricks. Mostly I play cards."

Lucas wrinkled his nose. "You're a gambler."

"Boys," Vincent said. "A gambler is the best kind of magician there is."

Morty pushed Lucas back. "That's right. Why would you want to go spoiling this?"

"Fine," Lucas said, crossing his arms. "Let's see what he can do. Let's have a cheat off."

Like a schoolboy on Christmas morning, Morty rushed to clear a table. "Great idea, Lucas ol' pal. Now, you're talking my language."

While the men brought out paper and a pencil, poker chips and cards, Vincent offered Duncan a chair and a deck of cards. "The rules are simple. We play poker with chips for no real money. Everyone tries to cheat as much as possible without getting caught. If you get caught, you get a point. Winner is the one with the most chips and the least points at the end. That's it."

"Sounds fun," Duncan said, and he meant it. He had never encountered a group like this, wasn't sure such things existed anymore, but here in 1934, he tasted a group dynamic, a level of friendship, entirely new. It was like a group of friends out of a sitcom — always horsing around, cracking jokes, and entertaining each other without burying themselves in iPhones, tablets, and texting. Except this was no television show. These were real people.

"Wait a minute," Ben said. "I know we're doing this to check out Duncan, but we still need good stakes. We can't play without something to win or lose."

"Yes, yes, excellent point," Morty said as he distributed twenty blue chips to each player.

Vincent laced his fingers behind his head. "How about the loser buys lunch for the rest of us?"

The other men groaned. Morty said, "You only say that

'cause you won't be the loser. Besides, I'm lucky to afford my own lunch. How am I going to pay for everyone else?"

"Don't lose."

Lucas counted his chips. "I think everyone should buy the winner lunch."

"I like that," Ben said.

"Why?" Morty asked. "You ain't going to win."

"Oh, boys," Lucy's said in a sing-song voice. "I sure could use some help cleaning up the mess you're making. So, how's this: you buy the winner lunch, and whoever loses the most stays here to clean up."

The men agreed to this which left Duncan conflicted. He had to prove his worth to these guys but he also wanted to lose so he could spend a little time with Lucy.

Don't be stupid, he scolded himself. She may be the greatest woman in the world but when he got back home, she'll have been dead for a decade or two. All of this world had died long ago in relation to him. There was no point to thinking any other way.

"Okay," Morty said, "ante up. I'm dealing first."

"Actually," Ben said, laying a hand over Morty's. "You just dealt seconds."

"Point against Morty," Lucas said.

Morty raised his hands. "Starting out with an easy one is all."

Vincent gathered the cards and dealt a hand. They played through with Lucas winning the pot. Duncan watched but failed to see a cheat. The others also missed any cheating, so the deal shifted to Duncan.

He knew this element of card handling well and had no trouble hiding an ace on the bottom of the deck for his own use. He won the hand. Then Ben and Lucas each had a turn. Ben fumbled a false riffle shuffle, sending cards fluttering across the table and onto the floor to Morty's delight. Lucas attempted to stack part of deck.

Duncan saw it right away but said nothing. He caught Vincent's attention who inclined his head with the unspoken question — *Aren't you going to call that?* But Duncan remained silent. He watched Morty and Ben, waiting for one of them to say something. But Lucas's deal went through unchallenged and his eyes lifted slightly in self-satisfaction.

As the game progressed, it became more and more evident that except for Vincent, the magic club consisted of amateurs. They were all good guys and had a love for magic, but Duncan knew he could wipe the floor with them if he had to — and although there was no real money involved, he had to show them he was worthy for their group. Especially because he had a nutcase mobster watching from afar.

When the deal came around once again, Duncan decided to put the game to rest. He pulled in the cards with a blatant move to stack the deck with the two aces from the last hand. Then as he shuffled, he found the other two aces and positioned them so that he'd win with four aces. With that done, he placed the deck on the table and paused long enough to allow anyone to call him on his cheating. Nobody said a word.

"Let's make this one count," Duncan said, and pushed all his chips into the pot.

Morty's infectious laugh erupted and he pointed at Duncan as if the others hadn't met him yet. "Get a load of this guy. I love it. You, Duncan, are a pickle. And I'm in."

Lucas put his chips in and grumbled. "Well, he's certainly got us in a pickle."

"Not at all," Vincent said, also calling the bet. "Nobody's forcing you to play this hand."

Ben folded his arms. "You all play."

"See that," Morty said. "That's why Ben ain't ever going to be anything big. Always got to play it safe. Not in this world, bub. The real winners risk it all."

"Couldn't agree with you more," Duncan said and picked up the cards to deal.

"Don't I get to cut?" Vincent asked.

A chill hit Duncan. "Of course," he said and watched as Vincent cut the cards. He didn't see a cheat but now he had to nullify the cut with a cheat of his own. This meant using one of several techniques to return the deck to the stacked position he wanted while making it look like the cut had been handle fairly.

With a partner, this could be done easily but Duncan was playing solo. He decided to go with a simple move — misdirection. He turned to Lucas. "What's the score going into this hand?"

While Lucas grabbed the tally sheet, all eyes would involuntarily glance at him for at least a second. That's when Duncan put the half deck that Vincent cut back on top instead of on the bottom. When the focus returned to Duncan, all anybody saw was him placing one half on top of the other, and it all looked clean.

Lucas said, "You and Vincent ain't got no points. Ben's got four, Morty's got two, and I got three."

"Okay, here we go," Duncan said and dealt out the cards. He had expected all the men to play, but because Ben stayed out, the stack was off by one player. It required some extra counting for Duncan and a difficult maneuver to slip off the extra card between the ones he wanted, but he managed to do it without getting caught. Twice he thought Vincent had seen the cheat, but the man said nothing.

After the deal, Duncan lifted his cards and he understood. He had a pair of twos and the rest was junk. He glanced up at Vincent.

"Something wrong?" Vincent said with a smug grin. "Were you looking for this?" He laid down four aces.

Duncan replayed the deal. He knew he had counted right. He knew he had nullified the deck. How did this happen?

"Good game, everyone," Vincent said.

Ben grabbed the tally sheet, "Looks like Lucas is the loser. You all have no money except for Vincent and Lucas has the most points."

"Hold it," Vincent said. "This deal isn't done yet. I've got a few cheats to call Duncan on. One, he stacked the deck when he pulled in the cards. Two, while shuffling, he riffle stacked until he could complete the stack to his satisfaction. Three, he controlled the deal so that he'd get all four aces. Ain't that right?"

Duncan nodded.

Ben pointed to the tally. "Then it's a tie with Lucas, each with three points."

"Oh, one more thing," Vincent said. "He also cheated on the cut. Tried to restore it. But he didn't count on me. See, Duncan used Lucas and the tally as a distraction, but he had to address Lucas for a moment to get us all looking at him. And when you did that, I switched the decks." Vincent produced Duncan's stacked deck from under the table.

"That makes four points for Duncan," Ben said. "Guess you're staying here to clean up."

Morty slapped Duncan on the back. "Don't worry about it. You did a great job. Even grumpy Lucas has got to admit you're everything Vincent said. A real talent with the cards. So clean this up fast and go figure out Vincent's trick so we can all have a good time party together."

"And don't play cards with my sister," Vincent said. "She cheats."

The gang laughed as they crowded out the door and off down the street.

CHAPTER 11

LUCY CHUCKLED — A GENTLE but knowing sound. "Vincent isn't lying, y'know. He taught me how to play cards."

Duncan shook his head, his mind still on the last hand. He had looked at Lucas for no more than a second. How had Vincent duped him so fast? And why? With a frustrated sigh, he collected the dirty glasses and brought them over to the counter.

"Don't feel bad," Lucy said. "My brother always likes to show up people, especially a new guy. It's his way of keeping everybody in their place. And you're good. Much better than those clowns. So he doesn't want to lose his standing as the best in the magic club."

"Then why even invite me in?"

"Because Vincent admires talent when he sees it. One look at you shuffling the cards and I could tell you knew what you were doing. I'm sure Vincent fell in love with your hands right away. Besides, he always wants to get better. He wants to be challenged. You think Morty challenges him? Or Ben?"

Duncan stacked the chips and put the card decks back together. He glanced at the blue and white door. He would have to figure out Vincent's little trick. No other way around it. But he felt it deeper than that. He didn't simply want to join the club to use it as a base from which to locate the magic door, and he didn't simply want to appease Nelson Walter to avoid a golf club to the brain. Some ember of the kid practicing his pass while sitting by Pappy warmed within his gut — he wanted to show Vincent just how good he could be with a deck of cards.

"You like it here, so far?" Lucy asked, her voice shaking Duncan from his thoughts.

"It's ... different."

Lucy cocked her head as if giving the idea serious attention. "It's nice, though, don't you think? I mean, it's big for a small town, and there's lots to do for a guy and a gal."

"I don't know." Duncan wondered if he should finish cleaning fast and try to track down the guys. "I suppose it's like anywhere."

Lucy hopped onto the counter, spun to the other side, flashing a bit of leg in the process, and then put on a cute pout. "What's the matter? Did Vincent hurt your feelings?"

Duncan looked at her directly with the intention of dismissing Vincent and the magic club in order to maintain control over the way she saw him — but he froze. Gazing upon her, he felt a quiver in his chest. Something about this girl moved him unlike any before. Maybe he should be thanking Vincent.

"I'm sorry," he said. "I've been rude."

"That's okay," she said, breaking into a blinding smile. "My brother gets that way too when he's working on a trick or a cheat. Very focused."

"But I shouldn't be. Not with such a lovely lady in my presence."

She pushed his shoulder as if to deny the sentiment, but at the same time, she said, "I was wondering how long it'd take you to notice. And now that you have ... let's get back to cleaning. Mr. O'Neil usually stops by at lunchtime to check on the store."

"Who's he?"

"He owns this place. Doesn't really know much about

magic, but his brother told him he could make good money selling tricks, so he opened the shop."

"Does he really make good money?"

Lucy tossed him a rag and walked to the merchandise shelves with a duster. "Some. I don't know why he keeps at it though. No passion for the job, you know? Still, we get a free place to stay, so I'm not going to question it."

Duncan got to work wiping down the counter. He took the time to enjoy looking at all the old rope illusions and coin effects under the glass as he cleaned. There were gaff cards — specially made cards used to pull off unusual effects — and Svengali decks, loads of Svengali decks. In a Svengali deck, every other card was the same but cut slightly shorter than the regular cards in the deck. Riffle the deck one way and you'd see a normal flashing of various cards. Riffle it the other way and you would see only a single card over and over. Loads of tricks had been designed around this simple deck, and even in 2013, Duncan had owned a few. But to see these old 1934 versions amazed him.

He moved down the counter and spotted an autographed photo of Cardini — a big name performer of the time. Lucy's stack of papers blocked his view, so Duncan slid them aside and in doing so, jostled one particular page to the floor. He bent over to pick it up, and the world stopped.

On the page, Lucy had sketched out a drawing of a wooden door with unique markings on it. Duncan's mouth dried up. They weren't exactly the same markings as the magic door in Pappy's living room, but they were clearly of the same type.

Lucy walked toward him with another rag. She halted when she saw his face. "What's wrong?"

He lifted the paper off the floor and held it like treasure. "Where did you see this door?"

"That?" she asked with a dismissive tone. She walked right up to him and snatched the paper from his hand. Placing it on the stack of papers, she squared them up, and held them against her chest. "It's nothing, really. Just a little project I'm working on with Vincent."

"Project?"

"It's nothing. Don't worry about it."

"But that door. Where did you see it?"

"It's just a doodle. Honest. I've never seen that door for real." Her brow furrowed with worry, and she took the papers with her through the blue and white door. When she came back, she had a big smile on her face. "I guess that's enough cleaning for today. Don't you think?"

Duncan's brain kicked on the turbo. He had a few seconds to make a big decision. She knew something about the magic door, that was clear, but if he pressed her any further, chances were he'd find out less than if he held back. But if let the opportunity go now, he might have to wait many days before another chance came. Unless he tried to break into her room one night. But thieving had never been his strong suit. Yet the longer he stayed in 1934, the more a tiny voice niggled inside him, suggesting that he had really screwed up going through that door, that he might never find the door again, that he might be stuck here. He'd be damned to let that happen.

"I was wondering," he said, buying another half-second for his mind to find a solution.

"Hmm?" she purred.

And it clicked. Simple, easy, and sure to give him plenty of chances to learn more. "I heard a rumor that this town is rather big for a small town. In fact, there's quite a lot to do for a guy and a gal."

"Oh, you heard that, did you?"

"And I'm new here, so I was hoping maybe a lovely gal like you might show me around."

With mock surprise, Lucy said, "Why, Mr. Rose. Are you asking me on a date?"

"I believe I am." He smiled, and to his delighted surprise, he felt genuine about the offer even if the door had proved to be the instigating factor. "I thought perhaps I could take you out to a respectable dinner tonight."

An amused light covered her face. "That sounds agreeable, Mr. Rose," she giggled. "Vincent and I live in the apartment

upstairs. You may call on me tonight, say around seven?"
"Seven it is."

Chapter 12

The remaining hours of the day crawled by at a languid pace as if the universe knew the importance of Duncan's upcoming date and wanted nothing more than to torture him by halting time. Considering that he had walked through a door and emerged on the other side almost eighty years earlier, he didn't put it beyond the realm of possibility. In fact, the more he pondered it, the more he thought that the universe loved messing with him. But the universe had nothing compared to the war waging between his brain and his heart.

Stay focused, his brain commanded as he lay in his hotel bed. This date was reconnaissance — find out all he could on the door and why Lucy had drawn it, where the door was and how he could get to it. Nothing else mattered.

But his heart countered with images of Lucy smiling at him while a gauzy filter of sunlight shined around her. He pictured her disrobing in a graceful motion, her dress fluttering to the ground as she stepped closer to him. Making love on clouds.

Who the hell are you? his brain countered. This wasn't the man he had lived his life as. He never had fallen hard for a girl before and now certainly wasn't the time to start. *Go on the date, find the door, get your ass home.*

Sliding the bedside table drawer open, Duncan brought out

a deck of cards he had stashed there and tried to recreate Vincent's trick. Earlier in the day, when Ben had performed the trick with the crystal ball, Duncan thought he might be able to use the same principle on Vincent's trick. It was called the 10/20 split because no matter what number the mark picked, the math always worked out the same. There were many variations on the idea but the basic mathematics of it all never changed.

He tried to recall every word Vincent had said when performing the trick. There hadn't been any calculations involved, he never asked Duncan to add or subtract or anything like that. But he did have Duncan count out a specific number of cards. Perhaps that set the card order up in a way that couldn't be changed.

Duncan shuffled his deck and made several attempts to count out specific card orders. None of them worked. He ended up with a different card every time and he had no clue what the card would be.

He rose from the bed, crossed the room, and poured some whiskey into a glass. As he sloshed it around before drinking, he smirked. He'd only been in 1934 for a day-and-a-half, and he had already taken to drinking as hard as the locals. Besides having lived with Prohibition, everybody had to deal with The Great Depression. It's a wonder they all didn't become alcoholics. But he hadn't been hit by either of those major historical events. He was a wealthy tourist to this time period, yet the stress of not knowing when he'd get his return ticket seemed to be drying his mouth out more often than not.

He shot back the whiskey and returned to his cards, but nothing he tried solved the problem. With a disgruntled moan, he threw the cards onto the bed and flicked on the radio. Thank goodness he still had that pleasure. Though television and the Internet were decades away from creation, good old radio existed to fill the gaps of time with lovely voiced harmonies and jazzy big bands. Even the news breaks were entertaining. Announced in that old time radio voice that, Duncan had to remember, was not old time at all but merely the way they did radio.

"... of sadness and strife when the National Guard was ordered by California Governor Merriam to end the chaos at San Francisco's waterfront area after the organized strike that began May 9th deteriorated into violent riots," the broadcast went and Duncan let another half-hour slip by to these oddly comforting voices.

When the show "Believe It or Not" kicked in, Duncan had to laugh. "Well, Mr. Ripley, I believe a hell of a lot more now." He pulled out his sketch of the door and worked on it for most of the show. He closed his eyes, imagined the door leaning against the wall in Pappy's cluttered apartment, and then checked his drawing. This line needed shortening. That symbol had more swoop. He would close his eyes again — definitely more swoop.

The universe continued to play with Duncan, though, for when he glanced at his watch, he discovered that he suddenly had only twenty minutes to clean up and get to the Magic Emporium or he'd be late. He had picked up a few toiletries and a clean shirt earlier in the day, and now learned just how far toothpaste flavor had come since 1934. Straight baking soda might have been preferable, but he pushed through the process, got dressed, and hurried down the street for his date.

A scrawny woman wearing a brown, patched overcoat stood on the corner selling flowers for a penny. She had a meager selection, probably plucked from somebody else's garden, but Duncan picked out a dozen yellow daffodils and gave the lady a dime and a nickel. "Keep the change," he said, garnering many thanks and praise from the poor woman.

When he arrived at the apartment, he discovered a lightness in his step that energized his heart. Just because this was about the business of getting home did not have to preclude him from enjoying the quaintness of the evening. After all, never before had he stood at a woman's door with flowers in his hand. Other than some girls from high school, he'd never dated anybody worth the effort. It wasn't that he scorned such encounters, but rather that the kind of women who sought out card cheats were never the kind of women who wanted flowers. Yet in 1934, things were different. At least, they were treating him different. As he rapped his knuckles on the door, he had to admit, he kind of liked the change.

Vincent opened the door, a cigarette dangling from his mouth. "You're so sweet. I'm more for roses myself, but I'll take these."

"You touch them and you'll have to answer to Lucy."

"And no man wants that." Vincent clapped Duncan on the back. "Come on in." Then with a raised voice, he said, "Your date's here, sis."

"I'll be right out," Lucy called back.

Vincent shrugged. "She'll be right out. Come in, have a seat."

Once more, the difference in era hit Duncan. The sparse apartment consisted of a single open space with two windows overlooking the street above the magic shop. A card table with four unmatched chairs occupied the center of the small room. Just off the front door, the floor switched from wood to tile and a long counter with a sink and shelves denoted the "kitchen." A stained cloth curtain hid the workings under the sink and a heavy looking box stood at the side of the counter. The far end of the room had a brown-and-white striped curtain that ran from ceiling to floor. From the sides, it was evident that a bed and dresser were on the other side. The only other actual room in the apartment, one with walls and a door, formed a corner several steps in from the front. This was the bathroom, and Duncan could hear Lucy humming from inside.

"Ready to show me how I did the trick?" Vincent asked as he straddled a chair at the card table.

"No," Duncan admitted. "I'm getting close, though."

"I must say I thought you'd have figured it out already."

"I've had quite a lot on my mind lately."

"I suppose so." Vincent glanced at the bathroom door. "Do I need to play the big brother with you? You know to treat her better than a princess, right? She's had it hard. I mean, who hasn't? But she's been stuck traipsing around with me, so I'd like to see her happy. She deserves to be happy."

"Don't worry. I'll be perfect."

With a stringent look, Vincent watched Duncan. "What's that supposed to mean?"

"You know. I'll be a gentleman. A perfect gentleman. Relax. I won't do anything a big brother would disapprove of."

"It better be that way. I'm going against my good judgment by allowing her to date a known card cheat. If I didn't like you so much, I'd have kicked you in your ass for asking her out. So, don't make me regret my decision."

Duncan forced out a jovial spirit and picked up a deck of cards off the table. "Will you relax already? It's going to be fine. She'll have a wonderful evening, but not too wonderful. Okay?"

Vincent winked and took a long draw on his cigarette.

The bathroom door opened and Lucy walked out wearing a light, summer dress. She had done her makeup to accentuate her lips and cheekbones, and the result proved quite effective. Duncan stared at her, stunned into silence, knowing that he had seen this beauty before but feeling like he witnessed her for the first time all over again.

"Well, I can't argue with a reaction like that," Lucy said. "Has Vincent done his big brother duties and made you feel like you can't even smile at me?"

Duncan chuckled. "He certainly has."

"Good then. You have my permission to ignore everything he said. Shall we go before he tries to stall us with a magic trick?"

"That sounds like a wonderful idea."

Lucy bent down and kissed Vincent's forehead. "Don't wait up for me."

"I better not have to," Vincent grumbled but Duncan could see that it was all a familial game.

Cooler by at least five degrees, the downstairs air had a slight breeze that made it seem even nicer. Duncan put his arm around Lucy's shoulder. "I thought we'd have dinner at The Walter Hotel. Does that sound good?"

Lucy scurried ahead, getting out from his arm. She turned around, her brow drawn down. "Now, look. I don't know what kind of girls you're used to dealing with, but I won't be hung on like you're a sailor just arrived into port. Have some manners, please."

Duncan pulled back. "I'm sorry. I didn't mean to offend you. Um ... forgive me here but I'm not that good at dating in the 1930s."

"Did you get a bump on the head or something? Forgot how to date after the Crash?"

"Something like that." Duncan glanced around the sidewalk to see if they were causing a scene, when he noticed how all the couples strolled together. "Oh. Of course." He put out his arm, bent at the elbow. "Would this be better?"

Lucy relaxed into her easy smile and wrapped her arm around his. "That's much more appropriate. Especially if you managed reservations at The Walter. I hope we're going to the cafe, though, because we are not dressed up enough for the formal dining room."

"The cafe's all I could get a table for on such short notice, but they do maintain a few for hotel guests. From the way the person taking the reservation sounded, she was mighty upset at having to deal with me."

"All the more reason to go there."

She couldn't have said anything more right. That kind of spunk hooked Duncan hard. They quickened their pace, excitement mounting as they neared the hotel.

Like the previous night, business at The Walter Hotel boomed. One would have been hard pressed to believe an economic depression, let alone The Great Depression, had taken the country into a stranglehold. Perhaps it was the holiday crowd, but Duncan found it difficult to buy that as a reason. After all, who would choose this nothing town as a holiday destination.

"Is it always like this?" he asked as they entered the lobby and headed for the outdoor cafe.

Lucy's eyes drank in every sight — all the finely dressed

people, the gold and marble decor, the giant chandeliers. "I wouldn't know. This is the first time I've ever been here."

"Still, this is not that big of a town. Doesn't this hotel seem a bit too much for the town to support?"

"It's Mr. Walter's money, isn't it? And the place employs a lot of people, so I'm pretty sure the Reedsburg mayor would marry Mr. Walter if that's what was required."

Duncan grinned. No doubt, this hotel would be depositing a lot more cash than it took in from lodgers and the restaurants. With the local government turning a blind eye, Walter could launder most of the money for his New York City connections as well as his own.

From the main restaurant, simply called The Club, the big band finished a raucous number that had the showgirls jiggling their feathers and the audience applauding wildly. The Club's doors had been left open supposedly due to the summer heat, but Duncan suspected it had more to do with enticing those in the lobby than anything else. It worked, too. Many people stopped a moment to peek over at the door, trying to glimpse a bit of the excitement inside.

Though the Walter Cafe lacked the atmosphere of The Club, it had an intimacy Duncan appreciated more for a date. Outside and cooler in the night air, they were taken to a table farthest from view by a disapproving maitre'd. A waiter poured water in glasses as if it were the worst chore of his life. All of this greatly amused Lucy.

Duncan, on the other hand, took offense. "You know, I'm staying at this hotel. You'd think they'd be nicer to the people paying their bills."

Lucy waved it off. "There's always going to be idiots in the world. They take a look at my dress and make decisions as to what the rest of me is like."

"I think they're judging my ability to tip more than your dress."

"Either way, it's all appearances with rich folk. You can't let it get to you."

Though still miffed, Duncan tried to take on a bit of Lucy's calm. "I don't like to be disrespected like that. For nothing, I mean. I'll bet you anything there's a card game going in the back and I could clean out all those snooty waiters in an hour."

"I bet you could. But then you are a cheat."

Duncan couldn't help but laugh. The waiter returned, and Duncan ordered filet mignon with a baked potato and steamed broccoli. Lucy, however, stumbled around the menu.

"Is there a problem, madam?" the waiter said as if he might be called upon to read for a clearly uneducated, illiterate girl.

"I don't know what to get," she said, looking to Duncan for help.

Duncan understood right away. "You want a steak, too? It's okay. Anything you want. Don't look at the prices."

She leaned closer to him, speaking barely above a whisper. "It's two dollars. I could buy a pound of hamburger for ten cents. I could feed Vincent and myself for weeks on what that steak costs."

"But it wouldn't be half as delicious. Come on. Live a little tonight. Besides, it's not your money. It's not even my money. I won it at cards."

That settled it for her. With renewed confidence she ordered the steak and asked for a bottle of wine as well. She lowered her head with a conniving grin. "I feel so criminal."

"It's really okay. I don't mind spending the money on a beautiful woman like you."

Lucy laughed. "That's an awful lie. Do women swoon for you when you say that?"

"I don't know. First time I've tried it." Duncan joined in the laughter. It felt good to laugh at himself with her.

This strange territory kept getting stranger. Growing up he had never really understood dating. For years, he blamed his father. The guy never really did much for him, after all, and so he never saw how to treat a woman right. His real tutor came in the form of Internet porn and from Pappy's DVD collection of old '80s sex comedies. Neither proved very useful other than to guide him into thinking that the whole point of dating, the only point, was to get laid in as athletic a manner as possible.

Cheating cards made more sense and so he stuck to that. When his physical needs took hold and he couldn't think straight, he knew his way around dive bars well enough to find some woman willing to screw the night away and forget it all the next morning.

But sitting with Lucy brought a whole different set of concepts into his brain. He'd be lying if he said he didn't think about bedding her, but that wasn't the sole thought surrounding his actions. Even finding information on the door took a backseat for a few moments while he simply bathed in her presence. Her gorgeous smile, her bright eyes, her soft voice — all of her seemed to exist for no other purpose than to melt him.

"Are you planning on spending the whole evening staring at me or are we going to talk about something?" she asked.

Duncan coughed, trying to hide his embarrassment, and then coughed for real. "Sorry," he said, taking a glass of water. "I'm fine. Why don't you tell me something about yourself?"

"Me? Oh, I'm not all that interesting. Mostly I try to help Vincent get his career going. He's been trying to become a professional magician for a long time. And he's good too. You've seen that. But no matter how close he gets, he can't seem to catch that lucky break."

With a sage nod, Duncan said, "I see now. That's why he cheats at cards. To keep paying the bills without having to give up his dream."

"What else is there? He's got a real passion for magic. It's all he thinks about all the time. I can't even recall the last time I saw him without a deck of cards. And what's worse is that people have told him, people who are in the know, who have the right connections and such, they've told him how good he is. They say they love what they see him doing, love his creativity and his card handling and his showmanship. But then they don't book him for a show. It's maddening."

"I'm sure. But this was supposed to be about you, not Vincent. What's your passion?"

"It is about me. We've been looking out for each other

forever. I mean, who do you think takes care of paying off the people who figure out they were cheated by him? Who do you think makes sure he stays focused and doesn't give up? I've got my whole life invested in him. Besides, he's my brother. I want to see him happy and successful."

"These are hard times."

"And that makes it both worse and imperative."

"But what if it wasn't like that? What if times were better and Vincent had a better career? What then? Would you still be taking care of a magic shop? Would you—"

"Dancing." Lucy's eyes sparkled. "I always wanted to be a dancer. You know, a showgirl or in the movies or anything like that. That's how I ended up helping Vincent. I was his stage assistant back when he did big stage kind of stuff. Before he discovered sleight of hand."

"Now that is something all about you. Dancing, huh? I wouldn't have guessed."

They smiled at each other. A waiter arrived with salads, and as Lucy dug into the food, she said, "What about you? Tell me something."

Duncan came close to choking. He had been so wrapped up in this charming woman, that he forgot the conversation would go both ways. Except he couldn't tell her anything — at least, nothing she would believe. She would probably have him locked away in an asylum before the night finished, tears running down her face as she convinced herself it was for the best. But he didn't want to lie to her either. Not that it should matter — he'd be gone soon enough and all of this would be a bizarre, faded memory. Yet part of him, that same part that had awakened to the very idea of a real date, that part didn't want to hurt her.

"I'm nothing special," he finally said. "I've traveled a far way, I suppose."

"Travel sounds exciting. Where have you been?"

Duncan rolled his tongue along the backs of his teeth, wincing at the strain of choosing each word as if testing a landmine. "I'm sorry. I'm not really comfortable talking about this — about me."

"Oh." She poked at the croutons in her salad. "I didn't mean to pry."

"No, no," Duncan said, but he couldn't take it back either. With no light to guide him out of the mess he made, he decided to push forth for the information he needed. At least with that, he could be on his way and lessen the damage he might have done. "So what's with the door drawing?"

"The door? Oh, that. It's something I'm working on for Vincent."

"It looks interesting."

Lucy hesitated, debating something within, before putting her fork down. "I'll tell you this much, and I'm only doing this because like everybody else in the club, I know you'll be a member soon. So, it's not really that big of a secret because I can tell other members. But don't you dare let on that I told you."

"Your secret is safe. You can trust me."

"Vincent is working on a book. A book that explains in clear, simple language all about being a magician. And not just the how to do this trick or that trick, but the history and the reality of how hard it is to make a career and all of it. There's nothing like this book out there. I'm helping illustrate the different tricks and edit his grammar, proofread his spelling, and that kind of thing. But I won't divulge any of the particulars until you join the club. Understand?"

Duncan leaned back and sipped his wine. Pappy had introduced him to all the big texts that had been written on the subject of magic — *Expert at the Card Table, Royal Road to Card Magic, Stars of Magic,* and even Professor Hoffman's *Modern Magic.* Nowhere could he recall having seen the name Vincent Day. "I think that's wonderful," he said because Lucy's eager eyes looked like she believed this was their ticket to money and a better life. "You and your brother have my sincere best wishes. I hope you can change things."

"Change things? Like what?"

"Oh ... just ... that your book will help people who think

magic is all glamour and success and a blast. It can be, of course, but it's hard work, too."

"Exactly. All these kids come in thinking they can learn how to pass a card or palm one and that's it. Instant fame. It isn't like that at all."

"Never has been."

"And that's why we're doing this book."

"So how's the door fit in?"

Lucy wagged her finger. "I told you — no particulars."

"But the door isn't a trick. I'm not asking for its secret."

"Good, because it is a trick and I haven't the foggiest notion how it's done. I'm only putting it in as a historical reference."

"Well, then tell me. It's not a particular trick that you're divulging."

"Nope," she said, smiling now that she had some playful leverage on him. "You have to solve Vincent's trick first."

Duncan had a playful smile of his own but it trembled away when he caught a glimpse of the man two tables over. A big man with a square jaw and a distinctive, flat-nosed face. Nelson Walter's main thug — Freddie.

He didn't seem to be watching Duncan, though. In fact, a lovely lady with a long cigarette holder and an outrageously large hat sat with Freddie. She looked thrilled to be eating at the hotel, to be eating at all, and Freddie's attention appeared to be entirely on her. Yet Duncan couldn't help but think that it was a ruse, that Freddie attended the restaurant in order to spy on him. Walter said he would be watching. Perhaps he truly was watching.

The rest of the delicious meal (Duncan couldn't recall a better tasting steak in his life) went by with an edge digging in his back. He tried to focus on Lucy's words and questions and chatter, on the way she savored each bite of her steak and saved half to bring home for Vincent, but his eyes darted upon Freddie continually. When they finally received the bill, all seven dollars of it, Duncan squirmed to get it paid fast and be on their way.

The walk back to the apartment lacked the vigor of their

earlier conversation, and Duncan had to restrain the desire to peek back over his shoulder numerous times. By the time they reached Lucy's door, Duncan's paranoia had reached a fever pitch. He kept sneaking glances in all directions and stumbling his sentences as he struggled to both speak and search at the same time.

"It's the steak, isn't it?" Lucy finally said. "You said to order anything but you didn't think I'd actually get the steak, huh? I'm real sorry. If you want I can pay you back. I mean, I really can't right now, but I'll pay you back in installments. Would that be okay?"

"What?" Duncan said as snippets of her words penetrated his head. "No, no. You didn't do anything wrong. I had a great time with you."

"Oh, yeah? I just thought ... well, you were a bit distracted and ..."

"Sorry about that. I shouldn't have been so rude."

"No, it's okay."

They continued to sputter out apologies and forgiveness until finally Lucy managed to say goodnight. Originally, Duncan had envisioned a firework-inducing kiss to end the evening, but instead, he watched her awkwardly back into her apartment, leaving him alone and confused in the hallway.

As he climbed down the stairs, he shook his head to clear it. He headed back to his hotel room, no longer worrying about Freddie. *He can follow me all he wants when I'm not with Lucy.* And as he thought those words, it hit him hard in the chest — he really liked this girl. Maybe he could convince her to join him in the future. If he could walk through the door into 1934, surely she could walk back with him into 2013.

Such dreams wouldn't matter if he failed to find that door, though. That had to be the first, most crucial step, no matter the allure that 1934 had gained. And finding that door still meant solving that damn trick of Vincent's.

"Then that's what I'm doing tonight," he announced, garnering an odd look or two from those walking by. He never noticed, though. He already had the cards shuffled in his mind.

CHAPTER 13

BY TWO-IN-THE-MORNING, Duncan had to admit that he had come no closer to a solution. He had tried every permutation of the 10/20 force he knew. He attempted to pull the trick off with a Svengali deck. He cut up a piece of cardboard to act as a gaff card and played out the trick with this extra, fifty-third card in the deck.

Nothing.

What crawled along his nerves, what caused him to swear and throw cards around the room, was that the solution had to be simple. He knew this in his bones. Pappy had taught him that most tricks relied on the participants thinking things were more complex than they actually were. Even the difficult tricks were often simple in concept — they only required the dedication to practice an insane number of hours in order to master a small set of skills.

But this trick had been one that, presumably, Morty and Ben and Lucas had all figured out. So all the highly skilled tricks couldn't possibly be the way to go. It had to be even simpler than what he had tried so far. But what could be simpler?

A knock at the door startled Duncan awake. He stared for a few seconds, his brain unable to process what had happened. Slowly, he came to understand that he had fallen asleep, that he had a deck of cards spewed across his chest, and that somebody knocked on his door at four-thirty a.m.

"Yeah?" he said, his voice scratchy and low.

"Open up," the distinctly unpleasant voice of Freddie the Thug said, and he pounded on the door again.

"Hold on, hold on." Duncan shuffled to the door and fumbled with the old lock until it opened. "What do you want?"

"Mr. Walter wants to see you."

"Now?"

"You got your lady friend in there or something?"

"No. And that's none of your business."

Freddie let his shoulder drop onto the door frame, and he crossed his thick, muscular arms. "While you're working for Mr. Walter, everything you do is my business. And I don't like it when dames get caught up in business."

Duncan combed his hair with his fingers as he stepped into the hall. Freddie moved out of the way. It was a small victory, but Duncan took what he could get. When he saw Freddie crook his neck to peek in the room, he said, "She's not in there. Let's go."

"Shame. She's not bad looking."

The urge to defend her honor raced up Duncan's throat like flames on gasoline, and it took enormous effort to keep his mouth shut. Not only did Freddie possess the strength to cause serious injury, but Duncan did not want to alert Freddie or Mr. Walter to Lucy's importance. Better that they think she's a fling.

Once more, Freddie led the way to the elevators, and once more they took an unpleasant ride to the top. When they stepped into Walter's hall, an enticing aroma of eggs, toast, and coffee surrounded them. From the right, a light shone through the edges of a door and the clatter of an active kitchen could be heard. But as with before, Freddie guided Duncan to the left, to Walter's office.

Duncan took his stiff-backed seat and Freddie stood to the side. Duncan looked at the door behind the desk and though he had no desire to picture it, he could not stop his mind from drumming up images of Walter bashing some poor fool's kneecaps with a golf club. The uncomfortable chair only heightened the pain he imagined Walter's victims suffered.

From behind, he heard Nelson Walter's heavy footsteps. Duncan kept his eyes forward. Then he saw stars as he felt a sharp pain on the side of his head.

Walking to his desk, Walter had smacked Duncan hard on the ear. "What the fuck are you doing going out on a date when you should be getting in that club? You think I'm joking around here? You think this is a game?"

The words would have sounded cliché if not for the burning on the side of Duncan's head and the fact that this was 1934. The guys Duncan knew who said crap like this had been mimicking guys like Walter, but Walter, for all Duncan knew, might have been one of the first to utter these mobster lines. Either way, Duncan had heard similar words before and knew what could happen to him if he responded in the wrong way.

Looking at the door behind Walter's desk, Duncan said, "Believe me, I take this very seriously."

Walter leaned over and posted his arms on the desktop — a hulking, perspiring brute. "Do you know what they called me before I moved out to this craphole?"

Though Duncan knew the answer, he also knew to keep his mouth shut.

"They called me 'Thumbs.' And you sure don't want to find out the reason. Not if you like doing card tricks."

"Please, Mr. Walter, allow me to explain."

Having blustered enough to make his point, Walter settled back in his chair and lit up a cigar. He threw on the face of a gracious benefactor but still bared his teeth like the Big Bad Wolf ready to eat up a kid and her grandma. "I'm all ears."

"You must already know that it's not as easy as just showing up and saying you want to join the club. If it were, you wouldn't be screwing around with me. The way I figure it, my best move is to try to infiltrate the group from more than one angle. I've befriended the guys, but I also thought I'd try to use the girl."

"Oh, I bet you thought about using her." Walter snickered enough to get a chuckle out of Freddie.

"I didn't mean like that. I meant—"

Walter slammed a hand on the desk. "I don't believe a word of this crap. We watched you on your date. It didn't look like any infiltration of the magic group at all." Walter got up and lifted his golf club from the stand by the door. "In fact, it looked a lot like the two of you were swooning over each other so much that you weren't thinking at all about the things you should be thinking about."

Even as Duncan's skin prickled at the sight of the golf club, a part of him warmed at the idea that Walter's spies thought Lucy had swooned for him. "There's no need for that club. I'm telling you, this is a real way to get what you want."

Walter's face reddened as his lips tucked in. He clenched and unclenched his grip while a vein pulsed on his forehead. Duncan thought the man might have a heart attack. "Prove it," Walter said. "What great information have you got? Tell me. How are you going to use this dame to get yourself in the club?"

"It's working already. I'm not even in the club yet and I've got a trick to show you. They like me. They show me stuff."

This caught Walter's attention. Though he kept the golf club in hand, he sat back in his chair and puffed his cigar several times. "Show me."

Duncan paused for two seconds, but those seconds stretched out before him as if they would never end. He had to present something to Walter, but it couldn't be any old card trick. It had to be something that Walter would believe came from the magic club, something those guys were capable of but also something that led Walter to believe there was value in continuing his pursuit of the club.

Ben's 10/20 force trick came to mind. It certainly came from a club member, but it wasn't special enough. Besides, Duncan thought Walter probably understood a 10/20 force already.

No, the club's magic that Duncan had seen would not

suffice. He needed to draw on his own repertoire, but that meant he had to be extra careful. He had some flashy tricks he knew, but many had been developed as late as the 1970s or even the 2000s. If he tried to show one of those tricks, Walter would think Duncan to be a magical genius. He would probably see massive dollar signs. He might even try to tie Duncan into a performance contract and manage his career. What would definitely happen, though, was that Walter would no longer have an interest in the magic club, would attempt to take over Duncan's life, and Duncan's line to finding the door home would be severed.

As time returned to normal, a memory flashed in Duncan's mind — a rainy, Sunday afternoon with Pappy, and a challenging trick he had spent the whole day working on. "I need a deck of cards," he said. Walter snapped his fingers toward Freddie, who quickly provided a new deck.

Duncan shuffled it up and placed the cards down. "Do you believe in a higher power?" Before Walter could get upset, Duncan put out his hands. "Please, I'm trying to show you. So, do you believe?"

Rolling his shoulders and uttering an impatient sigh, Walter said, "Yeah, of course."

"Of course. And because most people believe like you do, most people believe everything happens for a reason." Duncan picked up the cards. "It sounds good enough. Well, let's put that idea to the test."

Walter leaned forward, only this time his face bore a hint of boyish excitement. Duncan knew the look well, had worn it many times in front of Pappy — this was the look of a man who had a great passion for magic, love for learning new tricks, and a desire to master the skills needed. Those same hands that bashed in skulls with an iron stick rubbed together in anticipation of Duncan's performance.

Duncan cut off about a third of the deck into one hand, a third onto the table, and the last third in his other hand. He then put the deck back together and casually counted off a six card packet. "To be completely fair, you'll make all the decisions here." Duncan dealt two cards face down next to each other. "Which one do you want? Either one. It's up to you. Pick one and slide it over to yourself."

Walter thought for a moment and then picked the left card. Duncan knew that thoughtful look, too. Walter wasn't deciding between cards. He was trying to figure out what the trick might be.

Duncan dropped the packet on top of the right card, picked the whole thing up, and then dealt two more cards. "Once again, pick whichever card you want." Walter picked the one on the right this time. Again, Duncan reformed the packet, shuffled, and said, "One more time." As before, Walter paused and replayed the trick up to this point, his eyes sparkling as he rocked slightly in his chair. Then he chose the card on the right.

"Okay," Duncan said and recapped that Walter had made three selections without any influence upon him. While he said this, he picked up the deck with his left hand while his right scooped up the unselected card on the table and brought it all together. "Now, for the rest of this I'm going to need the help of two assistants."

Time for a flashy move he knew Walter would eat up. Holding the deck in his right hand, he tossed the whole thing into his left but pinched off the top and bottom cards so they remained in his right. Easy to do with practice and it looked fantastic. He then turned over the two cards — the two black Jacks. "These fellows will do fine."

Walter chuckled. "I like that part." The glee radiating off him made him seem younger by the second. If not for the golf club on his lap, Duncan could have forgotten the kind of man Walter was — at least, for a moment.

"These two guys are very important." Duncan placed the Jacks face up on the deck. "They're going to help us out. One goes on the bottom, one stays on top." He moved one Jack to the bottom of the deck. "Now, if I just do a little toss," he said and once again tossed the cards to his opposite hand, pinching the two Jacks. Except this time, a face down card was caught between the Jacks. "Looks like my assistants have found something for us. Let's see what it is." Duncan turned it over to reveal the Five of Spades. "That's all well and good, but of course, we have to ask the question — Why did the Jacks capture the Five of Spades? Well, remember, everything happens for a reason. Please, Mr. Walter, turn over the cards you chose."

One at a time, Walter turned over his cards — the Five of Diamonds, the Five of Hearts, and the Five of Clubs. Duncan spread the remaining deck face up. "You can examine the deck if you wish. You won't find any other fives."

"Son of a bitch." Walter stared at the cards wide-eyed. "I like that. Oh, yeah, I like that one a lot. Now, show me how it's done."

"Of course. That's the whole point here, after all."

Walter nodded to Freddie. "I told you this guy was going to be good. I told you."

"First thing you want to do is stack the top of the deck with any four of a kind, we'll use the fives again, followed by the two black Jacks. The rest of the deck doesn't matter. We give a little speech on how everything happens for a reason and I cut the deck in thirds, but when I put it back, even though it looks like I cut the deck, I make sure the top third, the part with my stacked deck, remains on top."

Walter scrunched up his face in concentration. "I thought something looked fishy there."

Sure you did, Duncan thought. "Next I count off six cards — my stacked cards — and we go through the charade of having the spectator choose cards. They choose one, and you set the packet on top of the unchosen card and do it again. Now I've got the two Jacks up top and that can't work, so I set the packet on top of the unchosen card and look like I'm doing an overhand shuffle."

"But really you're reversing the order, getting the two Jacks to the bottom, and the last two fives to the top."

"That's right. Now, we let the spectator choose a third time. Remember, every time they've chosen, it doesn't matter which card they pick because both cards are fives. Then comes the flashy part." Duncan paused a little to let the anticipation build. This was another performance, and he wanted to milk it for all the goodwill he could get. With a man like Nelson Walter, goodwill was gold. Especially considering the alternative involved a blood-stained iron golf club.

"Watch close," Duncan said. "This takes practice. First thing you do is drop the Jacks on top of the deck and pick up the deck with your left hand. With your right hand, you're going to lift off one of the Jacks and slide it under the remaining five card on the table while you scoop it up."

"So it looks like you just picked up the five? They don't see the Jack."

"Exactly. Scoop up the cards and place both five and Jack under the deck. Understand?"

"Yeah, yeah. You got a Jack on top, and on the bottom is the five and the other Jack."

Duncan nodded. Walter actually made a good student — eager, excited, and involved. As long as Duncan ignored the gnawing fact that Walter could, at any moment, kill him, this would be an enjoyable experience.

"Next thing you do is give a little talk about needing two assistants, at which point you hold the deck in your right hand with the thumb on top and the fingers below. Toss the deck from your right hand to your left, and the friction from your right-hand fingers and thumb will hold back the top and bottom cards so you can appear to pinch out the two Jacks. All you do now is put the Jacks face up, one on top and one on the bottom of the deck, in your left hand. But this time, when you put the Jack on the bottom you leave it side-jogged to the left."

"Side-jogged?"

"So that the card sticks out a bit to the left. The spectator won't even notice it. You do the toss again, this time left to right. The friction in your fingers keeps back the Jack on top and on the bottom, both the five and the Jack. After the deck is tossed, you've got three cards in your left hand — the two Jacks sandwiching the Five. Reveal the Five and have the spectator turn over his cards which will be the other fives. And that's it."

Walter stared at the cards on the table. "And Vincent Day showed you how to do this trick?"

"He showed off the trick. I figured out how to do it. Been working on it all night."

Walter lifted his head and stared straight into Duncan. All the humor and joy drained from his face. Duncan tried not to blanch at the sight but knew he had failed. It took all his will not swallow against his drying throat. If Walter suspected a lie in any of this, Duncan knew he'd be taken to the other side of that door.

At length, Walter stabbed the cards with his index finger. "Get me more of this stuff. And get in that damn club. If this is the crap Vincent's willing to show outside of the club, then the really good stuff, the things I most want to see, will be on the inside. And they'll be amazing."

"I'm trying."

"Try harder. I got my interests here but they won't last forever. And when they're gone, then so are you. You understand?"

"Yes, sir." On instinct, before his brain could process a thought and override his mouth, Duncan added, "If you really want me in there, then I could use a favor."

Walter looked to Freddie in disbelief. For the longest pause, Duncan waited, expecting a bullet to pierce the tall back of his chair and slam in his skull. But the bullet never came. Instead, Walter lifted his cigar and puffed. "What favor do you want?"

Chapter 14

When Duncan splashed into the Magic Emporium, his wide grin lighting the room up, the whole gang sat around a table hot and bored.

"What's got you so happy?" Morty asked.

"Vincent, my friend, you and I have jobs."

Vincent sat up in his chair, his face paling as he looked to Duncan. "I never said I wanted a job."

"If you got a job, you take the job," Lucy said from behind the counter.

Duncan had not noticed her until she spoke, but when he finally did, his eyes lingered upon her lovely form until Ben spoke up. "What about the rest of us? You got jobs for us?"

"Sorry, fellas, but this is a job performing magic tableside at The Walter Hotel."

"Oh." Vincent brightened. "You didn't say this was a magic job."

"You didn't let me get that far."

"We can perform magic, too," Lucas grumbled.

Morty rolled his eyes. "Lucas, the day you and Ben and I can do magic well enough to perform at The Walter is the same day you'll pay for lunch. In other words, it ain't happening." To Duncan, Morty added, "Feel free to use my fedora trick. I'll bet those rich folks will eat it up."

"Thanks," Duncan said. "And if I can get you guys jobs, too, I will."

"Look at him," Ben said. "Gets a job and suddenly he thinks he can throw out bones to us all."

"It's not like that. Look, Vincent and I played poker with this guy who knows Mr. Walter and they wanted some tableside magic for the club. That's it. I didn't mean to sound like—"

"Relax," Morty said. "He's just being a screwball. We're all happy for you guys."

Vincent stood up on his chair with grandiose flare. "Of course you're happy for us. Why what could be better for our club than to have its senior member being a working magician? And if loverboy over here ever figures out our little trick, we'll have two members working as magicians. That's great stuff for us. That'll make us more legit." He snapped his fingers. "We need to be dressed for the part. When's our first gig?"

"Tonight," Duncan said, taken aback by Vincent's sudden enthusiasm.

"Well, we need some new clothes. Some mystic-looking robes."

"No," Morty kicked in. "You need to be wearing a couple of sharp-looking suits."

"He's right." Vincent's eyes danced with the idea. "Can you see it, Duncan? You and me, dressed to the nines as we impress all those fine folk with our magic. It'll be wonderful."

Lucy said, "Yup, real wonderful. Only one problem, big brother."

"And what's that, sis?"

"You ain't got any money. How are you going to afford two suits?"

Morty laughed. "She's got you there. A new suit for you has got to run, what? Twenty dollars?"

"At least," Lucas said. "A fine suit would be more like thirty."

"Okay, okay." Vincent stepped back onto the floor. "So we need forty, maybe fifty dollars for two suits." Cocking his head toward Duncan, he asked, "You think Mr. Walter would give us an advance against our first paycheck?"

"Are you crazy?" Lucy said and hurried over to Vincent. "You cannot screw this up. And I don't mean just because we need the money. This is a job performing magic. This is what you want, isn't it? It's a big step forward. So, don't go worrying about advances or buying fancy new suits. Just show up on time and do a good job. And as for trying to smooth talk Mr. Walter — I'll kill you for trying, if he doesn't do it first."

Vincent hesitated and then broke out his charming smile. He hugged Lucy tight before facing the gang. "You see, fellas, this is why I love my sister. Perspective."

"Yeah," Morty said. "The perspective of her foot in your rear."

"Well, I for one think this is great," Ben said, digging into his coat pocket. "I got three dollars here and I'm donating it to the boys to help them make a good impression. What about you two?"

Morty and Lucas shared an uncomfortable look. Begrudgingly, Morty pulled out a five dollar bill. "I was saving this, but I ain't letting Lucas make me the last one in. Here you go."

With a scowl that forced his droopy eyes to darken more than normal, Lucas threw in two dollars more. "There," he said without enthusiasm. "I'm in."

"That's really kind, but you can't do that," Duncan said.

Vincent swiped up the cash. "Of course they can. They want to help out the club as much as we do. Besides, after we amaze the audience and they're clamoring for more, we'll get moved off the floor and onto the stage. That's where the real money is. And when we got that much cash rolling in on us, we can pay these fine gentleman back, and throw in some extra, too."

"You've only got ten dollars. You can't get a good suit for that much."

"We know plenty of places to go that'll have nice suits cheap. They may not be the best but they'll be better than anything we got now."

The rest of the guys stood up, grabbed their hats and headed out. Ben said, "Oh yeah, we know places. You don't worry about it, Duncan. You got the jobs, we'll get the clothes."

"That's right," Morty added. "You've done enough. You stay here and we'll take care of everything."

Before Duncan could protest, Vincent and the gang hurried out the door. Even Lucas left without so much as a furtive glance back. Morty and Vincent led them away, giddy and laughing like two teenage boys rushing off to a party.

Lucy laughed. "I swear I wish they were drunk. Then they'd sit around too tired and woozy to go off like that making trouble."

"Do I want to know where they're going?"

"Probably some friend of a friend who happens to have a bunch of fine suits to sell down an alley. Don't worry about it. And anyway, thanks. Vincent could really use this job."

"It's my pleasure. Frankly, I didn't even do anything."

"You didn't have to share the job with Vincent."

Duncan rested an elbow on the counter. "Maybe I did it to impress you."

Lucy smiled, a mixture of disbelief and embarrassment — Duncan loved that smile. To hide her reddening face, she tossed a rag onto the counter. "If you're going to stick around here, might as well make yourself useful."

"Wouldn't have it any other way." As Duncan started cleaning, he caught a slight curve rise on Lucy's lips.

"You know I was thinking about you earlier today, and it occurred to me that even though we had a date together, I still don't know anything about you. Vincent asked me what we had talked about, and I couldn't think of a thing."

Duncan focused on extensively wiping a spot on the counter. If he looked up, if he saw her eyes, he knew he would lose any resolve he had maintained. He would open up about everything — who he was and where he had come from, the magic door that resembled the one she had drawn and how he had to find it in order to get home, and how he wanted her and how he hoped she would join him in the future, even if it meant leaving behind all she had known.

He could picture them in 2013. A new world for her; a fresh start for him. With Lucy by his side, he thought he might be able to walk away from the crazy life he had led. And he knew in his bones that it had been crazy. Seeing Vincent and the boys and Lucy and all of 1934, he had no doubt that his previous life had been as shoddy as his father feared. Pancake was proof enough of that.

But as much as he wanted to tell Lucy everything about himself, everything in his heart, a primal instinct prevented him from doing so. Something deep inside told him that it would be cruel to tell her, that it would break asunder her entire concept of reality to the point of madness. After all, if someone popped into 2013 saying they were from 2102, it would be hard enough, but at least the modern world was a bit like living science-fiction anyway. Cell phones, tablets, voice recognition, robots and space travel — a time traveler from the future would not be so outrageous. But here in 1934, every aspect of the modern world would seem impossible.

Yet Lucy struck Duncan as a strong-minded person. Assuming she even believed him, she might be able to accept the changes, maybe even embrace them. Still, who was he to play with her life like that?

"What's wrong?" she asked, standing closer to him than he had realized.

The other problem was Nelson Walter. If Duncan told Lucy the truth, he'd have to admit that he was sort of a spy for Walter. Though technically he had failed to do any real spying, he knew that the time was coming when he would either have to deliver or face serious injury. Lucy should be able to understand that. That he had no choice. Except whenever she looked at him playing cards with Vincent, he saw a special joy, a happiness for her sibling's growth and maturity. If she knew that their friendship had been born from a desire to use the magic club, she would hate him forever.

She placed a hand on his arm. "Please. Let me know you. Even a little bit."

Still with his eyes down to the counter, he said, "I don't know what the right thing to do is."

"Sure you do, silly. There's no big secret here. I've seen the way you look at me. And you did take me out on a date. You like me. Don't be afraid. I like you, too."

She placed a finger under his chin and raised his head with the lightest touch. When he looked upon her, the world whirled around him. His pulse quickened. Warmth flashed through his body. His hands hovered over her shoulders, trembling with the desire to touch her, grip her, clench her close against his skin.

He shook his head and turned away. Never before had he suffered this kind of emotion over a woman. Was this what people always were talking about when they went on and on about *Love?* He certainly thought about Lucy in more ways than just sexual. He wanted to hold her, smell her, hear her voice. He imagined her crying just so he could be the one to comfort her. More than all, though, he wanted to be in her presence. She calmed him despite the stressful position Life had put him in, and that calm held great allure.

When he turned back to her, she searched his face for some clue to his thoughts. "What is it? Please, don't close yourself off from me. I can help. Even if it's just to listen."

Duncan stepped closer to her and inhaled her sweet scent. "You're intoxicating," he said, not caring that he would have laughed at anybody else saying such a corny line.

Lucy did not laugh. In fact, she looked startled. "Oh ..." she whispered.

His heart hammered fear straight through to his bones. He closed his eyes, afraid to see her reaction, afraid that the only woman he had ever felt strongly for might not share the emotion. His hands wrapped around her waist and he pulled her in. Pressing his mouth against her, his mind exploded in a pleasure far beyond any simple kiss.

The kind of women he had been with in the past would kiss him, but it had been a soulless experience. When Lucy kissed him, he felt the same urgent need he had experienced. Magic coursed between their lips, striking the nerves in his body like an electric jolt. He pressed harder against her mouth, wanting every motion of his lips to translate those wordless sensations causing his heart to beat for her. And he could feel breath as she kissed him back, wanting him, too. Not his charm, not his cleverness, not his money, not his bravado. She simply wanted the man within.

When the moment faded like a deflating balloon, Duncan pulled away and allowed his eyes to open. His heart collapsed. She stared at him aghast — her lips quaking, her eyes filling with tears. Her hand shot up to cover her mouth as she spun and rushed for the stairs.

"Lucy, wait!"

But it was too late. She disappeared upstairs, leaving Duncan standing alone.

"Shit," he said to the empty store.

Chapter 15

Backstage at The Club, Duncan stood next to Vincent waiting for the band to finish its set. The tableside magicians, there were four, went on while the band got a rest. Vincent looked sharp in his new suit, black coat with tails and gray trousers plus a gimmicked top hat. It cost most of the money the gang had pooled leaving little for Duncan's costume — a sequined robe and matching turban.

"I feel like an idiot," Duncan said.

Vincent kept his eyes on the showgirls powdering their bodies a few feet away. "Relax. We're going to do great."

Duncan wanted to ask about Lucy. That moment in the store had haunted him the rest of the day. Where had he screwed up? She liked him. She even said it. And while he would admit that this kind of relationship was utterly new to him, he found it difficult to accept that he was that far off base on how to treat a lady. After all, he did okay on their date. How had he misread her signals so badly that she had to run away like a schoolgirl getting her first kiss on the playground?

Unless ...

"Hey, Vincent. Has your sister ever dated anybody besides me?"

Vincent picked lint from his suit, caught the eye of a lovely brunette dancer with too much up top to get any further than The Club, and winked. "You work here long?" he asked.

"Vincent," Duncan pressed.

"What?"

"Your sister."

"Yeah, yeah, of course she's dated. Which is what I'd like to do with you. What's your name, doll?" And that was it. Vincent walked over to the brunette, sat on her make-up vanity and stared at her breasts while trying to pick her up for a date after the show.

A harried fellow wearing all black and carrying a clipboard, dashed by, whispering aggressively, "Five minutes, magicians. Five minutes."

On stage, a trumpet player stood and belted out a fast-paced solo while the rest of the band backed him up with a pounding rhythm. Duncan's heart had felt the same way only a few hours earlier. He knew he should be focusing on the upcoming performance, yet all he could see was Lucy running up those stairs. If he had a reason, if he understood what had happened, he would feel better. He would have a direction to go in, some idea of how to patch things up. But the not-knowing was excruciating.

Vincent tucked a piece of paper into his pocket and stepped close to Duncan. "Nice girl. Her name's Edith, but I like her stage name better. Trixie."

"You're kidding me."

"You don't like that? I thought it was playful and fun. Like I hope she'll be later tonight."

The eagerness in Vincent's face struck Duncan. Of course Vincent would be excited. He might get to have a great night of heavy petting. Edith did not appear to be so loose of morals as to sleep with him. In the twenty-first century, nobody would care about these two hooking up for the night. They could go to a convenience store, pick up some condoms, and do whatever their lust required. But here — Duncan had no idea how one procured condoms. And the pill hadn't even been invented yet, so the risks were far greater. But more so, people here noticed when a dancer left on the arm of a magician. Even if nothing happened, Edith would be treated as if it had. Unless she really had fallen for Vincent, Duncan guessed that by the time the show ended, she would change her mind and stand Vincent up.

That was 1934. No matter what he did, Duncan didn't belong here.

As the band poured out its final, stomping flurry of notes, Vincent adjusted Duncan's turban. "You better be ready. It's show time."

The band filed backstage, heat radiating off their sweaty suits, and the magicians headed to the diners. Each magician had an assigned section to work — Duncan's was next to Vincent's. They walked out as people milled about — talking, ordering, drinking, laughing. It all brought back memories of growing up.

Pappy had finagled a job for Duncan working tables at a local restaurant. He was only fifteen but Pappy convinced the owners that nobody would ever know. Duncan did look older than his age, so a deal was struck for a small payment and any tips he could earn.

Duncan hated it. The restaurant owners contributed nothing to promotion and stuck him on the floor Monday through Thursday. They reserved the weekend for live music. This meant that Duncan had to perform for people who had no idea that a magician would be appearing at the restaurant and on a night when people were not seeking entertainment. They wanted to get their food so they could be home in time for their favorite sitcom then slump off to sleep before starting another grueling day.

Though most of the tables were tolerant, people tended to be polite for a trick or two, the bad tables always stayed with him like burping up an acrid meal from hours earlier. There were the families that decided Duncan's "little magic show" would be a perfect way to entertain the kids while the parents huddled in a little conversation, soaking in the few minutes of respite. There were the drunks who thought they could outdo the magician, would ultimately fail in some embarrassing manner, and then wait out back ready to start a fight. And there were the religious folk who were offended even at the mere suggestion that they would be near the evil arts. He even had a man once forcibly take him by the arm and say through gritted teeth, "Leave us alone." No, tableside magic was not for the faint of heart. One needed confidence, a touch of arrogance, and a skin thicker than a rhino.

Vincent and the other two magicians rushed out to greet their audience but Duncan hung back a step. He wanted to scope out the most approachable table in his section before bumbling into the lion's den. In case the management asked them to switch section, he gave advice to the others rather than let them fall flat and ruin the audience for him later.

The two magicians had brought along some gimmicks that would work great one time but then require a complicated reset. "There's no time for that," he told them. "You need to keep things simple and clean. Card tricks, coin tricks, maybe a ball or two. Nothing more. You don't want to be searching for props while these folks are losing interest." He told them to watch their time. Nothing was worse than being in the middle of a trick when the waiter showed up with food. All their interest in the magic would transfer to their stomachs, and the show would be over. He tried to tell them a few more important points, but one of them said, "Look, I don't know who you are and I don't care. I been doing this long enough to know how to do it right. So maybe you should clamp it and watch how a real professional works."

Duncan said nothing more. Watching them approach the tables, he had to admit they did seem at ease in the situation. Even Vincent had little trouble with his approach.

He walked right by the table he wanted, stopped and picked a coin up off the floor. He offered it to the patrons who shrugged, so he made it disappear before their eyes. They laughed, and he had them.

Duncan scanned his own tables now. They were tiered booths like a mini-theater and a half-moon, upholstered couch formed each booth. The other half opened out so diners could watch the show.

He passed over the nearest table. A middle-aged couple sitting as far apart as the booth would allow. The next table consisted of a husband, wife, and little brat splattering mashed potatoes on Mommy's hand. No, thank you. The third table at the nearest tier had a young couple mooning over each other, longing to lie down on that half-moon couch and see if it had any spring to it. Not the best choice, but he could work with it.

"Good evening," he said as he approached the table.

"Oh, look, honey. He's a swami," the perky woman said.

Duncan used all his strength not to react. Forcing a smile to his lips, he pulled out a deck of cards and launched into a classic ace cutting routine. Since the man's perturbed brow and crossed-armed body language told Duncan more than he cared about, Duncan focused on the woman. He had her cut the deck into four piles, and then he turned over the top card of each pile. Amazingly they were all aces.

Perky clapped her hands like a performing seal. "Oh, do another, do another."

"Of course." With a flurry of his robes, Duncan swiped up the cards and pulled out a coin. He then went into a series of hand motions to make the coin disappear and re-appear all over the table. He segued this neatly into the classic "coin under the salt shaker" trick in which the coin appears under the table's salt shaker that he then magically smashes through the table so that it ends up on the floor.

As Perky wound up into another seal impression, Duncan bowed, thanked them, and moved on. As he walked up to the second tier, he caught sight of Vincent performing an assembly routine in which four kings are shown, placed down in a row, and three cards are put on top of each king. With a magical wave of the hands, three of the card packets prove to be empty of kings because they all jumped to the last packet. Vincent's diners went nuts for it. They applauded and laughed and wanted more.

Duncan had never seen such a reaction before — and these

weren't even impressive tricks. Maybe it was all the alcohol the people of 1934 consumed, maybe it was because television and the internet hadn't been invented yet. Drunk and starved for entertainment might be a winning combination. Whatever the reason, though, this was the best audience Duncan had ever experienced.

With more bounce to his step, he went up to the next table, bowed, and put on a show. "Ladies and gentleman, I have come from the far reaches of the globe to bring you this seemingly simple but truly rare and difficult magic. You, madam, please name any card."

The woman at the table, a wrinkled woman with bad teeth yet beaming with enthusiasm, touched her forefinger to her chin and thought. "I think I'll go with the Ten of Diamonds."

"And what lady wouldn't want diamonds to go around such a charming neck."

"Oh." She blushed.

Her husband, an equally wrinkled and dentally challenged man, frowned. Duncan decided to ease back a little on the false compliments. He pulled out another deck of cards and started searching through them, making a big display of the difficulty he had in finding her card. Finally, he spread the deck on the table. "Please, help me. Do you see the Ten of Diamonds?"

Together they looked amongst the cards but could not find the woman's selection. "Wait, I remember now," Duncan said. "It's in your hat."

"My hat?"

"Please, may I?" Duncan lifted her hat from the booth and pulled out the Ten of Diamonds. The woman loved the trick and the man softened at her happiness. For the briefest moment, Duncan felt a sense of excitement and even pride in being able to shine that light upon her. He even wondered why he had given up performance and settled for cheating instead. Never had a successful cheat felt this good. And had the night continued in this manner, Duncan may have followed an entirely different path — one that would have led him to fulfillment and joy through performance. But as he turned to go to the third tier, he once more glanced at Vincent, and what he saw changed everything for him.

Vincent stood before an eager, young couple. He fanned a deck of cards in front of him and said something about making a prediction. He then wrote on a piece of paper and folded it up.

"Ma'am, I'd like you to think of a secret number," he said. Duncan heard the sheer delight in Vincent's voice. "Okay, I'm going to turn my back and I want you to quietly deal down the cards until you reach your secret number. Look at that card. Okay? Now, place the rest of the deck on top." Vincent turned back to the couple. "Go ahead and cut the cards. Good. You know, one prediction is actually quite easy. Let's make it interesting. I'll make a second prediction." He fanned the cards again, thought, squared up the deck, and wrote on another piece of paper and folded it up. He then handed the deck to the young man. "Please have your lovely lady here whisper the secret number to you. Now, deal down to that secret number and look at the top card of the pile you dealt. All done? Let's look at the predictions."

From where he stood, Duncan could not make out the individual cards, but he could tell by the astonished laughter that Vincent had predicted correctly. As Duncan turned to the nearest table, he realized he knew that trick. It was called *Twin*-something. He had read it described in a magic book. Or maybe it was one of Pappy's old issues of *The Sphinx* magazine.

To be sure, he decided to do something a magician should never do. He decided to perform the trick unprepared. An older couple sat at the table, and as he shuffled up the cards, buying some time to think, he made a little small talk.

A splinter of worry slipped under his skin until he fanned the cards. The trick rushed out of the recesses of memory and into his hands. He had to note the top and bottom cards of the deck during the fan. The Five of Spades was on the bottom and the Queen of Clubs sat on top.

With a pen and paper he had stashed in his robes for another trick, Duncan wrote "The man will get the Queen of

Clubs." He folded the paper and told the woman to think of her secret number to count with. As he led them through the procedure, he knew all he had to do was remember that the Five of Clubs was on the bottom.

After the lady had cut the deck, he made a show of thinking through his next prediction, but really he searched for the Five of Clubs and re-cut the deck at that point, sending the Five of Clubs back to the bottom of the deck. He fanned the cards and noted the card on top — this would be the card that the lady had stopped on when she counted down whatever number she had picked. In this case, the Two of Hearts. Duncan took out another piece of paper and wrote "The lady will get the Two of Hearts."

He handed the deck to the man who would simply count the cards back to their original order and end up where the whole thing had begun. When Duncan revealed the correct predictions, the couple applauded.

"That's a real peach of a trick," the man said and tipped Duncan a quarter.

"It certainly is," Duncan said, his mind replaying Vincent's challenge trick.

There was still more time in the performance, but instead of moving on, Duncan bowed to his section and scurried offstage. He rushed over to an empty section at the makeup table and ran the Twin trick one more time to be sure. When he finished, he fell back into a chair with a triumphant grin.

He had the answer.

The secret to the Twin trick was that the two selected cards were separated by the "secret number" which cleverly forced both cards on the spectators. He still had to work on Vincent's challenge trick a few times back at his hotel room to get the specifics, but the principle behind the Twin trick and the challenge trick had to be the same. In his head, it made sense enough and as he ran it over yet again, his confidence in the answer grew.

Tomorrow, he would be joining the magic club.

CHAPTER 16

WHEN DUNCAN TOLD VINCENT he had solved the challenge trick, Vincent had the gang assembled early that morning like a gaggle of eager toddlers told there would be candy. They surrounded Duncan at a table in the back near the blue door. The energy sparked around them — even Lucas managed to show true interest. From behind the counter, Lucy watched in silence.

Duncan tried to read her eyes, tried to see if she was still angry with him, but either she had superior skills at hiding her emotions or he had yet to be able to understand the complete catalog of 1930's facial expressions. While Ben unwrapped a fresh deck of cards and Morty made sure every man had a beer for the expected celebration, Duncan stepped over to Lucy.

"Look, I'm sorry. I don't know what else to say, but—"

"What are you sorry for?" she asked, genuinely confused.

"For whatever I did that sent you running upstairs."

"I was just being stupid. Forget it." But nothing on her face agreed with her words.

"Flirting time is later," Morty said. "Get over here and show us some magic."

Unable to get a clear read on Lucy, Duncan turned back to the card table and focused on the trick. "I have to admit," he said, taking the deck of cards from Ben, "this had me stumped for quite a bit longer than I had expected."

"We all thought you were a bit slow on this one."

"I have a lot on my mind, so it was hard to concentrate."

"Hear that, Lucas? He's going to end up just like you — got an excuse for everything."

Vincent shushed everybody before they could get rolling with insults. "Let's all pay attention and see what Duncan's come up with."

Shuffling the cards, Duncan said, "The secret is that the two key cards are separated by a specific number of other cards. That's it. The rest is simply manipulation."

"Show me," Vincent said, his shoulder blocking Ben from a clear view.

"Then you'll be my spectator."

"Wouldn't have it otherwise."

Duncan started to deal cards into a pile. "You know how this goes. Stop me when you want." As he dealt the cards, Duncan silently counted them out. They stopped on the twelfth card.

"Now what?" Vincent asked.

"I've counted out twelve cards."

Morty clapped Duncan on the back. "You're counting. That's good. That's right."

"And Vincent's trying to screw me up by stopping on an even number. But it doesn't matter. With an even number of cards, I simply take the thirteenth card and make that the card I turn up and call the 'magic card'. If you had stopped on an odd number, I would've turned over the top card on the dealt pile." Duncan took a card from the deck and turned it over — the Eight of Hearts. He then dropped the rest of the deck on top, just as he had when performing the Twin trick. Now, like the Twin trick, Duncan turned his back and let Vincent deal out a selection card, return it, and place the rest of the deck on top.

"I now deal alternating piles and the key is the secret number — the number of cards I dealt out at the beginning. You had me stop at twelve. So there are twelve cards between the selection and the 'magic card' and as I deal out the deck, I have to pay attention to where the 'magic card', the Eight of Hearts winds up. There it is on my left." Duncan finished dealing out the deck. "I pick up the packet on the left and count off six cards because that's half the secret number and we've split the deck in half. I show them to you with some crap about these not being your cards, but the real reason is so I can move them to the bottom of the packet. If the Eight of Hearts had been on the other side, I'd do the reverse. I'd pick up the right packet and count of half the secret number plus one from the bottom and put them on the top. Either way, this forces the 'magic card' and your selected card to be in line with each other. Now all I have to do is keep turning over cards from each pile until I reach the Eight of Hearts. All based on a simple force using the number of cards between selections." Duncan turned over Vincent's selected card and folded his hands on the table. All eyes shifted to Vincent.

Vincent scratched his chin before breaking out a wide smile. He slapped Duncan on the back. "Welcome to the Club."

"Woo!" Morty yelled, hugging Duncan around the shoulders. Even Lucas raised a bottle for Duncan.

Ben held back a beer belch and nodded toward the blue door. "Let's show him the club."

With a flurry of his hands, Vincent produced a key out of the air. He bowed before Duncan, and in a magnanimous voice, said, "You have earned the right to unlock the secrets behind the magic club door."

Duncan took the key and went to the blue door. He felt the others crowding behind him, and despite their hokey moment, Duncan had to admit a bit of pride sprung inside him. Placing the key into the lock, he turned the knob and peered in on what he hoped would be a major step toward home.

The clubroom consisted of a space large enough for a single table and four chairs. An icebox sat in the back corner next to a storage closet. A half-open door revealed a dingy bathroom. Old show posters adorned the walls — Houdini, Cardini, and Holden. Along the back wall, Duncan spied a beaten couch —

the leather torn open on one cushion, and a box filled with decks of cards.

As the rest of the group filed in behind, Duncan did his best not to show his disappointment. Perhaps it had been false hope, or perhaps it had been a bit of Nelson Walter's desire, but something had set Duncan up to expect a grand room of secrets and mystery — or at least, an attempt to create such an atmosphere. Instead, he got the boys' poker room.

Vincent sat at the head of the table with Lucas to his right. Morty kicked back on the couch while Ben leaned against the bathroom door frame. They all fit comfortably in their chosen spots. Duncan suspected they always ended up in these positions.

"One last thing before we can reveal the club secrets," Vincent said. "The oath."

"Oh, yeah," said Morty. "I almost forgot about that."

"It's a simple oath. All we want you to do is swear on anything you consider holy that you will never divulge the secrets of any tricks you learn here at the club and that you will do all you can to protect these secrets from being revealed by others. Will you make that oath?"

Duncan put his hand over his heart. "I make that oath." The guilt inside churned his stomach. Soon he would have to break this oath or face the ugly end of a golf club.

"Well then," Morty said, "let's have some fun."

For several hours, they traded tricks — performing and explaining for each other until they grew tired and hungry. Lucas and Ben left for their homes. Morty decided to catch a bite at a street diner down a few blocks and Vincent joined him.

"You coming along?" Morty asked Duncan.

Vincent must have caught the look on Duncan's face because he said, "Just you and me, Morty. Our new club mate has my sister on his mind."

Duncan winced a bit at the phrasing but did not deny the statement. He wanted to clear everything up with Lucy. The idea that he might soon be traveling back to his time and not have made things right unsettled him. So, after locking the blue door, he climbed the stairs to her apartment.

She answered on the first knock. Her smile warmed him more than the July sun. "Congratulations. You're in the club."

"Was there ever any doubt?"

"Vincent can come up with some tough tricks to crack. With you, I'm sure he gave something extra hard. So, yeah, I had my doubts."

Duncan stared at her, unsure how to take her comment. Was she merely stating a fact or was she trying to put some distance between them? At least she stepped back and allowed him to enter the apartment. He had to believe that was more than mere courtesy.

"You want a drink?" she asked. "We don't have much but Vincent has some beer in the icebox. I'm sure he wouldn't mind."

"I had a beer to celebrate joining the club."

"Oh."

An uncomfortable silence formed between them. Once more, Duncan faced the uniqueness of Lucy, the way every experience with her landed him in unknown territory. And though card cheating required him to pretend to know the answers even if he didn't, he decided that would not work in this case. Even if it did, he didn't want to treat her like a mark.

"I tried to say this downstairs. I'm sorry."

"You did say that downstairs."

"I'm just trying to—"

Lucy put a hand on his arm. "It's okay."

"No, it's not."

With a sigh, Lucy sat at the table and waited for Duncan to sit, too. She examined her hands, glanced out the window, and finally said, "I'm the one who should be apologizing. I didn't mean to make things so strange between us, and really, everything is okay."

"Then what happened?"

"Nothing happened."

"Something happened."

"We kissed."

"I know. I was there."

"We kissed ... and ... oh, this sounds so stupid now."

"Please stop judging this for me. Tell me what's going on and let me decide for myself how it sounds."

Lucy took a shaky breath. "When I was five, my brother would go off fishing at the pond. It was a big pond about a half-hour walk from our house. During the summer, he'd stroll out there, be gone all day, and when he returned, he'd have fish for us to eat. Daddy worked all day and sometimes into the night, and I was stuck at home with Mother. I hated it. I absolutely hated it. It was boring and dusty and in the worst of the summer, it was sticky hot. And of course, fishing sounded like a heck of a lot more fun than cleaning house. So, I begged to be allowed to go off with Vincent.

"Vincent didn't want me to go along. He liked his freedom back then almost as much as he does now. What did he want with a whiny five-year-old? But whiny prevailed through sheer stubbornness, and when I went with him the next day, he punched me hard in the arm. Left a big bruise there, but I refused to cry about it.

"The problem, though, was that Vincent didn't know a thing about how to handle a little kid like me, let alone actually look after me. We couldn't have been at the pond for more than ten minutes before I had a fishhook stuck through my top lip."

Duncan chuckled. "I wondered how you got that."

Lucy lifted a hand over her mouth before consciously putting it back on the table. "I got teased a lot growing up. It's not so bad now, but the scar looked a lot worse on my growing face. It's faded a bit now, too."

"Was that what this was about? You were afraid what I would think of that scar?"

"A bit."

Duncan reached across the table and clutched her hands. "I don't care about a scar."

"But doesn't it feel wrong to you? When we kissed, your mouth made a little motion, like it disgusted you. And I wouldn't blame you. I've had boyfriends who said kissing me felt weird."

"Kissing you felt wonderful. Whatever motion my mouth made, it was only trying to get more of you. Honestly."

Lucy allowed a smile to crack through her lips. She raised her head. "Really?"

Duncan couldn't believe this was what had caused the problem. Was a woman's life so limited that such a minor thing like a facial scar could cause her so much strife? It never occurred to him before that the reason women fought so hard against an inequality he never noticed was because throughout history their lives had been reduced to worries like this.

He kissed her hands. "You are incredible. Don't worry about your scar. I don't care."

"I'm glad to hear that. Because when I got to thinking about all of this, the scar and growing up and all, I realized I needed to tell you. Not only because of what happened but because it's important for you to know about me. And when I realized that, I knew we had a problem because I don't know anything about you. Every time I start to get close to you, you pull away. You're so full of secrets."

"I'm a magician," he said but chastised himself for his earlier thoughts. While he didn't doubt the plight of women in the 1930s, he should have given Lucy more credit than he had. She had a feisty quality that wouldn't let something as ridiculous as masculine standards get in her way. Nor would she accept his lame attempt at misdirection through humor dissuade her. One glance at her stern eyes told him that. "It's not that I'm trying to hide from you. I simply don't want to hurt you."

"And knowing even a little detail about you is going to hurt me? That doesn't make any sense."

"Ice cream," he blurted out.

"What?"

"You want to know about me, right? I don't like ice cream. Never have. Cake, pie, chocolate are all good but not ice cream. Don't know why. It's not like my sisters tortured me with ice cream down my pants or anything. I just never had a taste for it. So, now you know something about me."

"Now I know two things about you."

"Oh?"

"You don't like ice cream, and you have sisters."

Duncan forced a smile. This was why he had held back saying anything. He never knew what might slip out.

But Lucy did not give him time to regret for long. She launched into his arms and they began kissing in earnest. She smelled lovely, and he held her tight on his lap, his hands roving along her legs and up her side. She surprised him by using her tongue in the kiss, driving his mind to focus on nothing more than his mouth and his hands. But when he cupped her breast, she slid off his lap with an embarrassed grin.

"Didn't you want know about that door trick?" She smoothing her summer dress as she regained control of her breathing. "You're in the magic club now, so I can tell you all about it."

No other words could have sobered Duncan faster. As much as he wanted her to return to his lap, he wanted to get home more. He understood life back there. Good and bad, he understood it. This life he had led for the last few days felt more like a vacation than reality. A trip to 1934 as a break from the daily grind. But he needed to get back home to feel normal.

Thinking about it all in these terms also helped put his feelings for Lucy into perspective. It was a vacation fling. They didn't belong together. They both knew it. When the excitement, the danger, wore off, they would no longer desire each other. Better to go back to 2013 and have the fond memory of Lucy than bring her with him and watch her fall to pieces at the changes in the world. It had been strange enough for him coming back in time. He couldn't imagine how she would cope with the future.

"Please," he said, zeroing in on the only thing that should matter. "Tell me all about the door."

Lucy nodded and got out the papers for Vincent's magic book. She sat on the opposite side of the table from Duncan. He knew what she was thinking — that his words had been a signal that he had regained his composure, that she did not have to fear him trying to get more kisses, and more everything.

She handed him the paper with the sketch of the door. "It's called the Door of Vanishing trick and, according to the legend, it was perfected by The Amazing Verido. He started out young as a close-up, sleight-of-hand magician working out of Virginia. Barely had whiskers but he fooled a lot of seasoned professionals. When he was eighteen he hit the road with a traveling show and started performing all kinds of illusions. This, the Door of Vanishing, was his greatest trick. It baffled everyone who ever saw it."

She handed him another paper — an advertisement for The Amazing Verido. Covered in writing about how unbelievable and talented Verido was, the ad went on to say that he would be performing at the Pennsylvania State Fair and don't miss the Door of Vanishing. Artwork below depicted Verido in a fine suit bowing to a happy, young woman as she stepped through a doorway. Her leg was far enough through that it should have appeared on the other side, but, of course, nothing came through.

"The story goes that Verido would wheel out a door on a small platform. After spinning it around to show no trickery, he would open the door and pass through it fine. A little bow on the one side and then he'd step back through to the other side and bow again. At this point, he would find a volunteer from the audience and bring her to the stage."

"Was it always a woman?"

"There wasn't a plant in the audience, if that's what you're thinking. At least, the best we can determine was that the volunteer was truly a stranger. That person was warned that if they stepped through, they might never come back. And then the person would walk through and disappear."

Duncan's stomach sank. "Did they ever come back?"

"Of course. Well, except the last time."

"What happened then?"

"I don't really know what went wrong, but in some backwoods county in the middle of nowhere, he sent somebody through the door and they never returned. The police were called in but by the time they showed up, The Amazing Verido added escape artist to his list of accomplishments. Though no evidence of foul play ever arose, most people think Verido is a murderer."

While Duncan stared at the two papers in his hands, Lucy added a newspaper clipping. At the top was a photograph of two policemen standing on a stage with a suited-man, and the headline read: POLICE CALL MAGIC EXPERTS IN VERIDO CASE.

"The police had no idea what was going on," Lucy said.

"And these experts did?"

"Not one of them came up with a plausible solution. At least, not plausible to Vincent and me. To the press and the public, their answers would suffice. They said that Verido had a trap door in the platform and this would 'vanish' the volunteers. The fall, if substantial enough, would either kill or incapacitate his victims. The platform did have a secret door but it only opened into the platform itself. Just enough space to curl up in if you're small. The fact that there was no large drop for a victim to fall through didn't seem to bother anyone. The police decided Verido killed these people, and they tried to hunt him down. But he never resurfaced. It was his ultimate vanishing trick.

"Vincent thought it would make a great story for his book, and if we can figure out how the trick worked and what went wrong, the piece would be a big selling angle. Might even be able to sell the story to the movies. Wouldn't that be something? Especially if they included the story about how we figured it all out. They could get Spencer Tracey to play Vincent, and Janet Gaynor to play me."

Duncan stayed quiet. He looked at the drawing of the door. "This was what the door looked like? You're sure."

"Not entirely. There aren't any clear photographs, but that's what I think it was like based on what I've read."

"You read about all this? Just these newspaper articles or something else?"

"Well, books of course. We may not be a big city but we do have a respectable library."

Duncan lifted his head and stared straight at Lucy. "You want to know something about me? One of my secrets? Well, I'm going to tell you one right now."

Leaning forward, Lucy said, "I'm all ears."

"I'm going to find this man, Verido, and you're going to help me."

Lucy smiled.

PART III
1934

Now you'll perform a Duck and Deal.

With the packet face down, lift off the top card
and slide it under the packet (duck),
deal the next card to the table,
duck the next card,
deal the next on top of the first, etc.

Repeat until one card remains in hand.

Deal this on top of the rest and pick up the packet.

Chapter 17

The Reedsburg Library was on the corner of Main and Elm, and it looked as generic and old-fashioned as the names of its cross-streets. Two pillars rose in Greek-inspired architecture and marble steps lined the way to the front door. Inside were two floors filled with books upon books. This particular library housed an unusually large collection on the subjects of illusions and card magic — mainly because an influential resident held that interest.

I don't imagine many librarians would stand up to Nelson Walter over what to stock a few shelves with, Duncan thought as he waited by the front door for Lucy to arrive.

A lone man, white-haired with thick glasses, sat behind a circular desk in the center of the main room. Three tall cases filled with little drawers formed a wall nearby. Duncan knew this was a card catalog, but he also had no idea how to use one. Any library he had ever visited (and he had visited one or two before) used a computer system to search for books. He could have asked for help from the librarian, but he figured the less people who knew what he searched for, the better. It also didn't hurt that his need allowed him to call upon Lucy for assistance.

She came in carrying a large bag over her shoulder. He

pointed at the bag. "I don't think we'll be taking that many books."

"This is for later. Let's get to work."

All his plans for the card catalog turned out to be wasted. Lucy already knew where to find the books they needed because she had done the research once before. She led Duncan to the second floor and into the back. There they located an entire musty stack devoted to magic.

"I've read most of these before," Lucy said, "but I wasn't specifically looking for information on the Door of Vanishing until recently."

"Start with the ones you researched the Door in already. You'll know exactly where to go in those books, and I'll start with the others."

Hours passed. Duncan had never enjoyed research of any kind, but his desire to find Verido kept him planted in a chair reading tedious page after tedious page. He longed for the ability to plunk Verido's name into Google and have the computer spew out links to every last detail of the man's life. Instead, his eyes were the search engine, scanning index after index and page after page for any glimmer of Verido's name.

By the time noon arrived, Duncan thought they had accomplished little. He learned that *Verido* was a stage name. No surprise there. And he learned that Verido had a fear of water based on a story he circulated that he had almost drown at the age of eight. If that story turned out to be true, then they could assume he wouldn't be living near any large bodies of water — the ocean, lakes, and such. But magicians loved to promulgate the air of mystery surrounding them — especially magicians in the 1930s. Every bit of information they found in these books could be nothing more than the continuation of a hoax or publicity stunt originating from the magician himself.

"Hungry?" Lucy asked as she stretched her arms.

"Very much. May I treat you to lunch?"

"Nope."

Duncan turned his head to the side and raised an eyebrow. "Ms. Day, do you have something planned?"

"Have you ever seen me carrying such a big bag before? I made us a picnic lunch. There's a lovely park across the street, and it's a beautiful July afternoon. Let's go outside and clear our heads, fill our tummies, and breathe some fresh air."

Duncan snapped shut the book in his hand. In a ridiculous, pompous voice, he said, "That sounds like a splendid idea, my dear."

Lucy giggled as they packed up their things and headed to the park. Turned out, she was right. The day was gorgeous, a bit humid but wonderful for July, and he found the experience of sitting on a large blanket eating cheese sandwiches delightful.

As the sun warmed his face, Duncan watched over the small oasis of trees and grass and a pond that made up the center focus of the park. Three children sprinted by laughing and shouting. One threw down a can and they all went off to hide. A flash of sheer amazement hit Duncan — they were playing Kick the Can. They were actually playing Kick the Can. And they played it with such unbridled enthusiasm one would think the game had been newly invented.

Maybe it is new, he thought. He knew so little of the minutiae of the time. *That's because I don't belong here.*

It always came back to that. Before Verido had come to his attention, he could play this back-and-forth in his mind about Lucy and 1934 and all of it. But no more. He didn't belong here and he didn't want to belong. There were plenty of aspects that he had warmed to, but in the end, he wanted computers, modern toilets and showers, Xbox and cell phones, and all the amenities of life to which he had been accustomed.

Lucy opened her bag and pulled out two cheese sandwiches and a container of beans in butter. Duncan leaned back on one elbow and took a bite. Amazing — a simple sandwich from a meager lunch on the right day with the right gal in the right place had surpassed the steak dinner they had on their first date.

He wanted to let her know how much he appreciated this, and before he could stop himself, he said, "Things are going to get better. Soon, too. I mean there are hard times ahead, war even, but in the end, you won't have to struggle like you do."

"What are you going on about? What war?"

Trying to hide the shock on his face at his own misstep, he said, "Forget it. I'm just babbling."

"The Big One's done. Nobody's ever going to do that again. After what we've all been through, any President would have to be crazy to start another war. He'd be impeached before he could say word one. So, it's already getting better. And times are hard, but that's life. Sometimes it's good, sometimes it's bad. We get through it. You don't have to worry so much."

"That's not what I meant."

"Then what?"

Duncan gazed on her sweet, inquisitive face, but he could only offer a smile and a regretful shake of his head.

Lucy stayed quiet for a time. They ate their sandwiches and enjoyed the warm air. He could feel her frustration mounting — a wire-thin tension ready to snap. When she did speak, he could hear the trepidation shiver her voice. "I was thinking that since I'm helping you with Verido, you might tell me a little about why we're searching so hard for him. I know Vincent can get single-minded when it comes to learning a big trick like this one, but I don't get the feeling you're after this man's trick." Duncan shifted uncomfortably, and Lucy quickly said, "I'm not trying to make you betray your secrets. I just think that if I knew what I was looking for, it might help in our search."

Duncan tightened his face and thought. "Did you ever see *The Wizard of Oz?*"

"See it? Like in a movie? Are they making a movie of *The Wizard of Oz?* I'd love that. You know I love the movies. I've seen *The Thin Man* three times already. And my favorite ..."

Lucy's nerves caused her to ramble which suited Duncan fine. It gave him a little time to regroup his approach. He had no idea when *The Wizard of Oz* had been made into a movie but clearly it had not happened yet.

"Forget the movie," he said, snapping her attention back to him.

"Do you have something to do with Hollywood? Are you

looking for magicians for some kind of movie? Is that why you've been so secretive?"

"No. I misspoke. That's all. Really. I just meant that you've read the book, right? *The Wizard of Oz?*"

"When I was younger."

"There are these two completely different worlds. Kansas and Oz. Dorothy, she's kind of stuck between the two. Because part of her wants to stay in Oz even though a stronger part wants to get back home. And in the end, she's given the choice." At least, he hoped that was the way the story went. He barely remembered the movie. "I mean she could've taken those ruby slippers and just held on to them, stayed in Oz, and lived with her friends and—"

"I suppose, but I don't understand. What are you saying?"

"I think I'm asking what you would do if you were Dorothy."

Though clearly befuddled by Duncan's odd behavior, Lucy gave the question serious thought. "I think I'd go home."

"You would? You'd turn away from all the excitement and adventure of Oz and go back to a life of suffering on a farm?"

"First off, life on a farm isn't so bad, and no matter how hard it might be for Dorothy, that's where her real family is. And if it were me, I think I'd miss the world I knew and understood too much. Oz is a magical land, there's no doubt, and like you said, filled with all kinds of excitement and adventure. There's part of me that would love the experience. But that's a fleeting moment. Eventually, the excitement would lessen, and I'd realize that I'm living in a world that didn't make any sense. I mean if I had grown up in Oz like the Scarecrow or the Tin Man or the Lion, well then a world of flying monkeys and strange fields and cities made out of emeralds would all seem normal. But it's not. Frankly, it's the same reason I would love to go visit some far off country in the Orient, but I wouldn't want to live there."

"You're sure?"

This gave Lucy pause. He could see on her face that she understood they were talking about something more serious than a children's book and a fanciful question, but she did not know what exactly and that made her question her own answer. In the end, though, she nodded. "I don't know if it's the right thing to say, but it's the truth. I wouldn't want to live in Oz."

Duncan felt the tightness in his chest loosen. "Thank you," he said. Despite how much he had come to care for her, he knew that his fantasy of her coming to 2013 with him was nothing more than that — a fantasy. He simply had to enjoy the time he had left with her while he focused on getting back to Oz.

Sitting up, he glanced off to the right and saw Freddie standing by a tree. His skin chilled and he looked away.

"Who's that?" Lucy asked.

"Nobody."

"Isn't he one of Nelson Walter's men?"

"Maybe. I think so. I'm done eating. Let's get back to the library and see what we can find."

"Don't do that. We were having a nice time, and you were actually talking with me. I didn't understand all of it but you were talking. Why should seeing that man change anything? Unless you're tied up with him?" A cold look came over her face. "How exactly did you get those jobs for you and Vincent?"

"Lucy, we're not going to talk about this."

"Don't you dare shut me off. We're talking about my brother. Is he in serious trouble? What did you get him caught up in?"

"Vincent's fine. He's not caught up in anything."

"Then what is it? Tell me."

Duncan's eyes narrowed on Freddie. He hated closing off Lucy but what else could he do? He had to stay focused — find Verido, get home, don't screw up.

Lucy threw the picnic back into her back and stood. "Duncan Rose, you're horrible."

"Please, Lucy—"

"I've given you every chance and you still act this way. You think I'm going to judge you because of Nelson Walter? I don't care about that. I want to protect Vincent but I don't care about a hoodlum like Walter. Every day people are losing all that they have. We've all got to do whatever we can to survive. But what I do care about is the fact that you seem to like me yet you turn cold on me as fast as you turn warm. I'm not the kind of girl who takes that kind of nonsense. So, Mr. Rose, make up your mind. Figure out what it is you want, and if it's me, then tell me." She stomped off four paces, halted, and turned back. "Don't take too long. I won't wait forever."

Duncan watched her leave, wishing he could explain. But a broken heart for her would be better than breaking her entire concept of the universe. Some pains were never meant to be handled.

"Okay, Freddie," he said, knowing the brute had to have approached. "What do you want?"

"Mr. Walter would like to see you."

"Of course, he would."

CHAPTER 18

WHEN DUNCAN STEPPED OFF THE ELEVATOR, he looked to the right out of habit. A woman stood in the doorway at the end. She had a classic, old world weariness about her as if she had only just arrived in the United States. She carried a child on her hip and stared at him with pity. As he turned away, heading toward Walter's office, he heard the woman speak softly in Italian.

His instincts fired off warnings with machinegun speed. Things were bad and he wanted to heed the warnings in his head, but he failed to see how he could avoid any of this. If he could take on Freddie, break free, and catch the elevator before the operator sent it down, he would buy a little time. Freddie gave a firm push forward — enough to smother any illusions Duncan had of a heroic escape.

When Freddie opened the office door, he kept an iron grip on Duncan's shoulder. It was a smart move because what Duncan saw made him want to risk everything to get out of there. He even stepped back, but Freddie had no trouble pulling him into the room.

Nelson Walter filled up the open doorway behind his desk. He rested a golf club on his shoulder. His jacket had been hung on the coat rack along with his hat, and his shirt sleeves had been rolled up, revealing hairy, gorilla arms. Dark, cold eyes narrowed in on Duncan.

"Congratulations on joining the magic club," Walter said, sheer rage tapping underneath a stoic exterior. "I knew you could do it."

"Thank you." Duncan's voice died before he finished his few words.

"I wanted to say I'm proud of you, but instead of coming over here and reporting in to me of your success, I have to send Freddie looking all over town for you."

"I'm sorry about that. I didn't mean any disrespect."

"That's funny, because you've done a lot of disrespectful things. You didn't come to me when you were supposed to, you haven't given me anything but one card trick, and you went out dating that girl again even though you knew I didn't want you distracted by her. Or are you going to suggest that even after you got in the club, you somehow were using her for even more secret club information?"

Walter walked around the desk in a deliberate pace. Each step closer filled Duncan with an urge to rush for the door.

"Please, Mr. Walter, I was following a lead on a trick, and I wanted to be sure about it before—"

Walter's hand moved so fast, Duncan did not even realize he had been struck until he hung over the edge of the chair and his face stung. Blood spotted the floor. Duncan's nose throbbed and a quick touch proved that this was the source of the blood. He tried to stand but the room swirled around him.

"Help that bastard," Walter said.

Freddie got under Duncan's arms and hoisted him up. It took another half-minute before Duncan could stand without assistance.

With his head clearing, Duncan said, "I have a trick to show you."

"Really? You suddenly have a trick?"

"Please. I'm trying to co-operate."

Walter grabbed Duncan by the chin and looked upon him with dead eyes. "This better be a good trick, or I'll have Freddie beat you while I get warmed up in the back room. Then you'll find out the other kind of tricks I know."

As Walter strolled back around his desk, Freddie escorted Duncan's unsteady body into the stiff guest chair. Duncan needed a trick and none of the ones Morty and the gang knew would suffice. This had to be better than the trick he had shown Walter before but it couldn't be something so advanced as to be near-impossible for the time period.

"I'll need a deck of cards," he said. While Freddie obliged, Duncan's mind raced through one trick after another, rejecting them as fast as he could think of them. This had to be impressive enough to save his life. His numbing nose promised as much.

A new deck of Bicycle playing cards thumped on the desk. Walter slid the deck closer to Duncan. "I'm waiting."

Duncan picked up the deck and fumbled with the seal on the flap. "I-I'm sorry. I'm having a little trouble here." Nerves, not brilliant stalling, caused this, but he took advantage of the extra time. Walter signaled for Freddie to open the deck. Freddie produced a switchblade from his coat and let it snick open in front of Duncan. After he cut open the deck, he made sure to linger the blade under Duncan's bloody nose for a moment.

Walter's thick arms crowded the desk as he leaned in. He looked like he would whisper a threat, but a sliver of his anger shot out, instead. "Now show me a fucking trick or so help me on a stack of King James, you'll regret it."

The name *James* hit Duncan's brain with lightning. It connected with the name Stewart James, a magician from the 30s who had a trick that fooled many magicians back then. He developed it around 1936, but Duncan figured a couple years earlier wouldn't matter — especially when considering the alternative.

"Oh, I forgot," Duncan said. "I also need paper and pencil. I'm sorry." He pulled out the deck and made a show of shuffling the cards up while waiting for Freddie to handle this latest request. Normally the trick required a tiny bit of prep before presenting it to a spectator, but Duncan doubted he would be given an opportunity alone. However, Freddie came to the rescue.

The big thug did nothing more than place the paper and pencil on the desk, but his bulk blocked Duncan from view for an instant. Without any difficulty, Duncan palmed the cards he needed, and he was ready.

"I'm going to write a prediction on this paper." When he had finished, Duncan folded the paper. "I'll put this right between us, so there's no way I can change what I've written. That's my first prediction." He then handed the deck to Walter. "Go ahead and shuffle as much as you want."

Walter hesitated, but Duncan saw the spark of interest ignite. The man might be ruthless, but he also loved a good trick. He wanted to see this.

"We're going to play a little game," Duncan went on. "One of us will get black cards and the other gets red. You decide."

Walter continued shuffling. "I'll take red."

"Red it is. I'm black. Now, you keep the deck, and I want you to turn over the top two cards. If they're both red, you keep them in a pile in front of you. If they're both black, you put them in a pile in front of me. And if they're one of each, just hand them to me and I'll put them back in the card box. Keep doing that until you reach the end of the deck. Okay?"

Walter nodded as he watched Duncan's hands carefully. "I do all this?"

"Yup. I won't touch the deck."

With an impressed nod, Walter began. The first two cards were the Ace of Hearts and the Seven of Diamonds. "These are mine, right?"

"Correct."

The next two cards were also both red, so Walter kept those. Then came one of each color which went in the box as a discard. A pair of black cards went to Duncan.

About halfway through the process, Duncan said, "By the way, if you want to reshuffle the cards you have left, you're welcome to do so. Anytime you want to shuffle more, you may."

The right corner of Walter's mouth lifted. This little addition had him hooked. He shuffled the cards and continued through the deck, shuffling every so often. When he finished, he looked up at Duncan with a challenge in his eye — *make this good.*

"Please pick up each pile and count how many cards are in the red pile and how many are in the black pile."

Walter did so. "Fourteen red and ten black."

"Interesting," Duncan said and unfolded his prediction. The paper read: *There will be four more red cards than black cards.*

"Is he right, boss?" Freddie asked. That gave Duncan a burst of confidence. Getting somebody observing from the sidelines interested was always a good sign.

"Yeah, he's right. But there's lots of ways he could've done that."

"I'm not done yet," Duncan said. "We're going to do this again. And I'll make a new prediction." He put the red, black, and discard piles together into one deck, and asked Walter to shuffle them up while he wrote and folded the next prediction. Once the paper sat between them, Duncan indicated the deck. "Go ahead. The same trick."

Walter went through the entire deck, separating out the cards. When he finished, he counted up the red and black piles. "I got eighteen in each pile."

"Wow," Duncan said. "That's a lot. And it's a tie. Both our piles have the exact same number of cards. Let's take a look at my prediction."

Walter snatched up the paper and unfolded it. Duncan smiled as Walter read: *There will be the same number of red cards and black cards.* To Duncan's relief, Walter nodded in pleasure. "That's good. That's real good. So, how's it done?"

"All you have to do is take out four black cards at the beginning and place them in the card box. That's it. Then when you get the unmatched discards, you put them in the box. The spectator has no idea they aren't playing a full fifty-two card deck, and no matter how many times they shuffle, no matter how many matches they find, in the end, the first time through there will always be four more reds than blacks. Then when you do it the second time—"

"You dumped all the cards out of the box, including the four black cards. So now I've got a full deck and the result will always be even."

"That's it. Simple, elegant, and very effective."

"And one of those idiots at the magic club showed you that?"

"Vincent did. He's no fool."

Walter's smile dropped as he lifted his heavy body off the chair. "I'm no fool, either. It's a good trick but is there anything else you want to tell me about? Any other tricks you learned about since joining the club?"

"I've only just joined and most of our first time together was spent celebrating. I haven't had time to see anything else."

"You've had time for a date."

"I meant that I hadn't had time—"

Walter jutted his chin toward Freddie. Without thinking about it, Duncan looked in the same direction. Freddie's fist cracked into the side of Duncan's head, knocking him out of his chair.

His sight shimmered with pinpricks of light, and he felt the skin near his cheekbone swelling. Freddie grabbed him by the shoulders and forced him back to his feet. Though the world rose and fell around him as if he were clinging to a buoy on rough seas, he saw the back of Walter as the man walked deeper into the office.

"No, no, no," Duncan mumbled. "We don't need to go in there."

Freddie got behind him and lifted him off the ground. Duncan kicked, but Freddie only tightened his grip. They went through the door behind Walter's desk and down a dimly lit corridor. Though it could only have been a few feet, it felt like they were traveling down an endless, ever-constricting tunnel.

Duncan burst into a clammy sweat as his heart raced. He could only manage rapid, shallow breaths. Fighting down the urge to vomit, he tried to focus his thoughts, but panic had seized his mind. "Don't do this. Don't do this!"

At the end, Freddie threw Duncan into a wooden chair with leather straps on the arms and legs. The chair had been bolted into the floor. Freddie slapped Duncan's face and used his disorientation to strap him down. Walter watched from the other side of the room, leaning against a brick wall. His harsh eyes glared like a hawk judging the best time to strike.

"Please, Mr. Walter." The whine in his voice hurt as much as the side of his face. "I don't know what you want. You said you wanted card tricks, I brought you card tricks."

Nelson Walter closed in with the golf club in hand. "You really think that's the reason I'm out here? You really think that's the reason I went through all this trouble with you? To learn a few damn card tricks?" He jabbed the golf club into Duncan's stomach. Duncan wanted to double over but could only lean at a slight angle. The straps kept him from moving enough to relieve the pain. Walter used the end of the club to shove Duncan straight back against the chair. "Don't misunderstand me. I love magic. That should be obvious. And I appreciate the things you've shown me. One magician to another, I've found these tricks to be as you said — simple, elegant, and very effective. But that's not why I bothered with you. I got enough people who'll steal all the card tricks I want."

"Then what do want from me?"

Walter's face screwed up tight as he swung the golf club down onto Duncan's thigh. Duncan screamed out and tears streamed from his eyes.

"What the fuck do you think I want? The same damn thing you want? The Door of Vanishing."

Though pain burned in his leg, Duncan could not hold back his astonishment. It deadened his panic and awakened him — he had to think.

With his hand, Walter slapped the side of Duncan's face. "I told you from the start that we would be watching you. You really think Freddie was the only guy out there paying attention? I got people everywhere. I got the damn librarian reporting to me. You understand, you moron?"

"I don't know about a Door of Vanishing."

Crack, crack. Walter struck him twice in the ribs. As fire burned inside his gut, Duncan glanced up long enough to see Walter's fist pop him in the forehead.

Duncan's head lolled. He caught sight of a blood stain in the corner, and any last threads of bravery left him. He had to say whatever worked to appease Walter. He'd never get home if he were dead, so if Walter wanted to learn this trick, Duncan would happily pretend that the trick existed. "I don't know where the Door is yet, but that's a sophisticated trick. Very advanced. I don't know if I'll be able to figure out how it works."

"Wrong." Duncan cringed as Walter swung the club again. A blaze of pain ignited in Duncan's arm. He yelled as sharp jolts raced down to his fingers. "I'm not talking about the legendary trick. I'm talking about the same thing you're after — the *real* Door of Vanishing. I've followed the story close for years. I know about those people who went through the door but were never heard of again. And you know, a lot of magicians talk about the spiritual world in their acts, but to them, it's nothing more than an act. But you take a guy like Horace Goldin. Back in '29, he wrote an article that talked about some of his great illusions. And in it, he also talked about the fact that he had been chatting with his dead mother and that he got visions of new tricks and all kinds of stuff like that. Reading Goldin, listening to Houdini, and following Verido taught me that there's more than tricks and illusions out there. There's an authentic magic. We only have to be brave enough to find it. The Door of Vanishing — that's the real thing. I don't know how this door works, and frankly, I don't care. But it does work. So, you're going to find me that door."

"If that's what you're after, then why me? Why not just grab Vincent yourself?"

Another swing of the golf club into Duncan's stomach. Sweat beaded on Walter's head. He dabbed at it with a handkerchief. "How many times do I have to tell you that I got people watching all the time? The second you arrived in town, I knew about it. This is Reedsburg, for crying out loud, not Chicago or New York. It's a small town. Easy to control. Suddenly a well-dressed guy like you shows up out of nowhere, and suddenly you're best friends with the only magician that's the closest thing this town has to a pro, and suddenly you're researching Verido in the library — that's too many *suddenlys* for me. I don't know who you're working for, and that's another thing I don't care about. I get that door, and you'll have only one boss in your life — me."

"I don't work for—"

"You need to learn to shut up. You keep talking and I'll keep beating you. See, when I first talked to the bosses about coming out here, they thought I was nuts. I had to build this money laundering Mecca in order to get the go ahead. But I figured eventually they'd send someone like you along to check it out. To check me out. After all, they watch me as close as I watch everyone else."

"I never—"

"They don't understand, though, do they? They think I want these tricks so I can make money off selling them or something. They think there's an angle that fits in with the way they see the world. But you and I know there's a lot of power to be had from owning that door. I mean, why the hell do you think I came to live out here? If I find the Door, I can take out anybody and there won't ever be a body to be found. Capone? He's nothing if nobody can find him. I'll take over Chicago in a month easy. You understand me? I'm talking about being the most powerful man alive. And you know what? It'd be good for everybody. With me being the only one in power, all the family fights, the old rivalries, the boss hits, the street wars, the senseless bloodshed — it all goes away. We could have peace and prosperity for our kids."

Walter punched Duncan in the nose and continued punching with each word he spoke. "So, you will get me that door."

"I'll get it for you," Duncan said. He would say almost anything to escape that chair. "I just have to find Verido."

"You sure you don't want to argue some more? I'm having fun." Freddie snickered from the back.

"I'll find Verido," Duncan said, sweat dribbling into the blood on his face.

"One more thing." Walter leaned in close enough for Duncan to smell the man's hot breath. "I don't trust you anymore. If you try to get out of this, if you try any kind of trickery, that little gal you're sweet on is going to pay for it. And believe me, there's plenty of worse things I can do to her in this chair than I've done to you."

"I'll find him. Don't do anything to her. I'll find the Door for you. I promise."

Duncan repeated these words like a mantra while Freddie released him from the chair.

Chapter 19

Duncan stumbled up the stairs from the Magic Emporium. Clutching his side and breathing hard, he headed straight to Lucy's apartment. He banged on the door several times but nobody answered. With his face pulsing in pain, he wasted no time breaking in — a 1934 lock proved to be easier picking than he had expected. Even if it had been too hard, he knew he could have kicked the door open with ease. Thin wood frame and only one lock meant it would splinter open with one strong kick.

No guilt plagued him as he rifled through the room, searching for Lucy's notes. If she walked in on him, he didn't care. Her life was in danger now, and that trumped all else as far as he was concerned. He could handle a lot on his shoulders but not that — not knowing that Lucy suffered because of him.

In the few minutes it took to cover the room, he found nothing useful. Standing in the center, he scanned the area with his eyes while his mind tumbled over the possibilities. Where would she hide the notes?

"Why would she hide the notes?" he asked the empty room. She wouldn't. She would put them together and hand them to the person she had done all the research for — Vincent. And Vincent would, without a doubt, hide the notes.

But not in his apartment.

Duncan raced back downstairs, unlocked the blue door of the magic club, threw it open, and began his search with the back corners of the small room. Sweat dribbled down his frantic face, stinging the cuts and bruises along his cheek and jaw. He had suffered beatings before — it went with the territory of being a card cheat — but he never experienced ferociousness like Nelson Walter. He had never seen such animal rage held in check by one simple idea — Walter needed Duncan alive and functional. If not, Duncan would have been dead hours ago.

Flipping through books and knocking down stacks of card decks, he could feel the rising panic in his chest. Somewhere in this room, Vincent had to have stashed his sister's notes on Verido. For his book, of course, but he would want to take a crack at figuring the trick out, too. After all, if Vincent solved the Door of Vanishing, he could possibly gain notoriety as great as Houdini.

After going through the bits of cards and papers on the table, Duncan plopped down in a chair. He exhaled in frustration. Rubbing his face, careful to avoid the tender cheek, he tried to organize his thoughts.

In order to protect Lucy, he had to find Verido and the Door of Vanishing. Though Walter's beliefs about the Door's power were not entirely false, Walter appeared to have no real concept of what the Door was, and that gave Duncan an advantage. When he found the Door, he would have to use it right away or else Walter might get hold of it. If that happened, Duncan might never get home. And when he did use the Door, he would have to take Lucy through with him. She might end up feeling worse than Dorothy in Oz, and she would certainly miss Vincent and her friends, but Duncan could never leave her behind to be abused and possibly murdered by an enraged Nelson Walter.

"The question is: Where did Vincent hide his notes?"

Could Duncan have missed them in the apartment upstairs? No. This crappy room was the magic club, the place where

Vincent ruled. He might even have taken some pleasure in knowing that this great trick sat under the noses of the club members while they had no idea.

Unless he didn't write any notes down? Vincent was a magician of the 1930s, after all. Duncan's world was one of recording everything and plastering it across the world via the Internet. But Vincent's world had privacy. Vincent's world didn't wear its heart in the open. He may have read Lucy's report, filed it away in his head, and tossed the papers away.

He never wrote it down. This is too important. He's kept it all in his head until he's in a position to make the most out of the information.

"Damn," Duncan whispered.

"Something the matter?" Morty asked from the doorway. When Duncan looked over, Morty's face dropped its customary glee. "What happened to you?"

"What's it look like? I got beat up."

Morty pulled over a chair and inspected Duncan's injuries. He poked Duncan's swelling cheek.

"Ow! What the hell are you doing?"

"I don't know," Morty said. "I ain't a doctor. But you should be seeing one, I can tell you that much. That looks really bad."

"Thanks. I couldn't tell from the pain I'm feeling every time I move my face."

"No need to be nasty. I'm trying to help. You want, I'll get the guys together and we'll get them back, whoever them is. Who is them, anyway? Who did this to you?"

Despite the pain, Duncan smiled at the ridiculous image of Morty, Ben, and Lucas fighting Walter and Freddie. But thinking of Walter beating Morty with a golf club erased all amusement from his mind. "You seen Vincent around?"

Morty shrugged. "Vincent's here. Vincent's there. Who can keep track of a guy like that? I'm sure he'll come by later today when we have a club meeting."

"I need to speak with him now," Duncan said with too much force.

Morty looked at him closer. "What the heck's going on?"

There was no way Duncan could tell the truth, but he had learned long ago that telling lies was easier when mixed with bits of truth. "I'm sorry. I did a bad thing. But I did it for a good reason. At least, I thought it was."

"Slow down. Tell Morty what happened."

"The jobs I got for Vincent and me, working the tables at The Walter Hotel, they didn't come free. I made a deal with Nelson Walter to get those jobs."

"Oh, Duncan, no. You never make deals with the Devil. Don't you know anything?"

"He only wanted a card trick. I figured I could give him any old trick that impressed him and that would be that. Vincent would get some steady work and Lucy would be happy."

Morty nodded. "I see. This is about Lucy."

"But then Walter wanted another trick and another. And now he wants this famous Door of Vanishing trick that he said Lucy and Vincent have been working on but I never even heard of it. Morty, you got to believe me. I never wanted to get them in trouble, and I certainly don't want them getting hurt like me. I was trying to help them."

"Why wouldn't I believe you? You think you're the first bum to ever get caught in a mess trying to make a buck? Look around you. Who wants to end up on a soup line? Everybody's doing whatever they can to make a buck."

"Yeah, but not everybody has Nelson Walter threatening to break Lucy apart if he doesn't produce."

"That's true. But you're one of the club now. So not to fear, you got me on your side."

"I appreciate your loyalty," Duncan said, and he meant it. He learned long ago the great value of guys like Morty. "I don't know how you can help, though. Unless you know how to do the Door of Vanishing trick."

"Can't say I know that." Morty lit up a cigarette. "There's probably only one guy who knows that — The Amazing Verido."

"You know about Verido?"

"What kind of magician would I be if I didn't know one of

the greatest legends of our profession?"

"I think Vincent was trying to figure the trick out. If only he kept notes."

"Notes? Vincent?" Morty chuckled. "That's too much like work. Heck, take a good look at him. He's got his sister doing all the work on a book he plans to put his own name on as the author. I mean, he's a stand-up guy and all, but he ain't going to be making notes for anybody."

Duncan slouched. "There's got to be something I can do."

"Oh, I didn't say you were out of luck. Your pal Morty knows lots of folks. And I happen to know someone who claims to know where to find The Amazing Verido. I always thought the claim was bunk, frankly, but I'd hate to think that if Lucy got hurt, it was on account of me not sharing everything I knew. Don't get too excited, though. Probably is a loon, and we probably shouldn't even bother. Still, there's always a chance, right? Oh, I almost forgot to mention — we'll have to go to a real bad part of town, one of the worst."

"I think Lucy's worth risking the bad part of town, don't you?"

"That's not what I'm saying. I just mean that maybe we should wait for Vincent. I'm sure he'll be back anytime soon. It's his sister, after all. And that way we can go to this place with numbers on our side."

Duncan stood fast and waited for the lightness in his head to subside. "Morty, I'll go alone, if I have to, but I'm not in the best condition at the moment. So make a choice — come with me or wish me luck. Either way, I'm going now."

"Okay, okay." Morty waved his hands as he stood up. "No need to turn this into a big stage show. I'll get you there. You'll need some money though."

"Right, for bribes."

"Bribes, maybe. But, see, my friend works at Lady Lane's Cat House. Nobody does anything there unless you pay."

Chapter 20

Lady Lane's sat deep in the recesses of town, accessed via a narrow back alley far removed from the daily life of the regular streets. The fact that a steady stream of gentlemen found reason to stroll down this dark alley bothered many of the proper souls (or at least those wanting to be seen as proper), but that never stopped the strolls from happening. In fact, when Duncan and Morty made their way to Lady Lane's, a portly police officer led the way.

"Getting a lunchtime snack, eh, Morty?" the officer said.

Morty acted confused. "Just going to talk with a friend."

"Me, too. And let me tell you, she's a very good friend."

Duncan smirked as the officer hurried his step. To Morty, he asked, "Been here before?"

Morty shrugged. "Once, maybe. This isn't the way I like to do things."

At the end of the alley was a plain metal door painted black with a tiny square peephole at head height. Morty knocked on the little square and it slid open. A square-jawed, unshaven face filled the opening. The man took a hard look at Duncan, especially his wounds, then shifted his eyes to Morty and nodded.

"Hey, Morty. Who's this?"

"He's Duncan. A friend who wants to talk with Forrest." To Duncan, Morty added, "Okay, I've been here more than once. Maybe three times. That's it."

The doorman eyed Duncan once more before admitting them into the building. Morty led the way up a flight of stairs and into a low-ceilinged, low-lit lounge filled with overstuffed furniture. Three tired women clothed in frilly feathers and little else were draped over the furniture. Duncan caught sight of the police officer exiting down a hall with a buxom girl leaning against him, her hand cuddling his backside. A radio big enough to be considered a piece of furniture in itself sat in the corner playing big band jazz to drown out the squeaking beds, deep moans, and false squeals of pleasure that cut through the thin walls.

Though Duncan had never visited a whorehouse before, he had spent plenty of time in gambling parlors and other places of poor reputation. He recognized the smell of desperation coating the air. He knew the false sense of frivolity that layered the somber loneliness below.

In sing-song unison, the three women said, "Hi, Morty."

Duncan raised an eyebrow, and Morty reddened. "Maybe I've been here quite often. Who can remember?"

One woman wearing a slip that showcased her prominent nipples over her anorexic-thin body sauntered up to them. She glanced over Duncan's bruised face but knew her job well — never point out something the customer might not want to talk about. She rolled her shoulder toward Morty. "You looking for something special or is your friend wanting a gal all to his own?"

Morty shook his head. "Sorry, Mary. We're actually looking for Forrest."

"Oh. A nancy, huh?" The other girls giggled.

"Very funny. Is he in?"

Seeing there was no money to be made, Mary headed back to the couches, making sure the men received a good look at the bottom they should reconsider. Over her shoulder, she said, "You know how it is here. Go talk to Lady Lane if you want to go back."

To Duncan, Morty said, "I was hoping to avoid this. You brought money, right?"

"Some."

"Lady Lane don't let anyone do anything in this place without charging you."

Morty led Duncan down the hall the police officer had used shortly before. A small square opening on the left side of the hall cast out the only light. A narrow counter formed the bottom of the square. Resting his arm on the counter, Morty rapped his knuckles against the wood. "Ms. Lane?"

Lady Lane entered from behind a curtained archway, cigarette poking from the corner of her painted mouth, and glanced at Morty with eyes that had seen plenty of the world's seedier side. She must have been in her late-fifties but retained enough of her beauty that Duncan imagined she might still service select clients should she choose. The way she winked at Morty, Duncan wondered if he could be one of those clients.

"Who's your friend?"

"Duncan, may I introduce you to Lady Eunice Lane. Ms. Lane, my good friend Duncan Rose."

Duncan kissed her hand. "It's a pleasure to meet you."

"Cute. You going to defend my honor now, too? Don't waste your time. I ain't got any left." She hacked a sound that Duncan suspected was laughter. "So, what're you fellas looking for? Morty knows all the usual girls, and if you can afford it, I got a new gal upstairs that would be perfect for whatever celebrating you're looking to do."

Morty raised a hand to stop her from going into any details. "My friend wants to talk with Forrest."

"Forrest? You a nancy, Duncan?"

"Duncan just wants to talk."

"That knucklehead can't say anything worthwhile."

"Got a few questions for him, that's all. Then we'll be gone."

"You sure? While your friend asks his questions, you could wait with Patty. She hasn't had a customer yet today. You'd be first."

"Please. Just Forrest."

Sighing, Lady Lane put out her hand. "Ten dollars."

"Ten dollars? That's crazy."

"So is wasting my time."

"You want to charge us ten bucks to talk with a guy who—"

"This is my house, Morty. I'll charge you for breathing my air, if you don't watch it."

Before Morty ended up ruining his regular haunt, Duncan placed ten dollars on the counter. "Where do we find Forrest?"

Lady Lane swiped the money with startling speed. "He's in his apartment. Basement."

"I swear," Morty said as he walked further down the hall, "I don't come here nearly as much as they make it seem."

A narrow servant's stairs led down to the basement. Duncan followed Morty. "I really don't care what you do. Everybody's got their secrets. Don't worry. I won't tell anyone."

"Thanks. That's a swell thing to say."

They reached a wood-slat door, but before Morty knocked, he turned to Duncan and whispered, "You should know that Forrest isn't really right in the head anymore. I mean, he can think fine and if he knows anything, he'll tell us, but he's a special case here. Lady Lane acts like she don't care about him, but she does. See, he used to be a regular customer here. You think these gals know me well? They all knew Forrest — really, really well. Anyway, as I heard it, one night he's sitting around the lounge, relaxing with a cigarette and a beer after having been with one of the gals, when a group of soldiers on leave come in. They were rowdy and drunk and everything you'd expect. Now I don't know exactly what started it — I've heard everything from that it was an accidental bump in the arm to that Forrest was protecting a girl one of the soldiers was getting rough with — but I do know for sure that these men hauled Forrest out into the alley and beat him bad. Shook his brain loose or something. He was never exactly right again. Lady Lane felt responsible and terrible, so she hired the doorman to stop from letting just anybody in. Then she hired Forrest to be a jack-of-all-trades around the building. Gave him this place to stay, too."

He looked like he wanted to say more but ended up turning away and knocking. When the door opened, Duncan saw a scrawny man wearing stained brown pants and no shirt. Scruff grew in patches on his pale face, and his ginger hair reached out in all directions. He had an odd look to him — simultaneously empty and thoughtful. As if he strained to form a thought but lacked the ability to express it. He took one hollow look at Morty, nodded, and walked back into his apartment.

"Good to see you, Forrest," Morty said, forcing a festive tone as he entered.

Turned out the apartment was nothing more than a single room slightly larger than a maintenance closet. It may have been a maintenance closet at one time. Forrest had a cot to sleep on, a box for his belongings, and a bucket for — well, Duncan did not want to think about things that far. From the ratty condition of the army green blanket on the cot and the stale odor in the air, Duncan guessed there was no maid service.

"How are you?" Morty sat with Forrest on the cot.

"Okay, Morty," Forrest said but it sounded like *oo-kahy Mo-ordee*.

Duncan had wondered how they would sweet talk Forrest into giving up what he knew about Verido, but it turned out to be easy. Being the resident charity case at a whorehouse proved to be quite lonely. Forrest eagerly launched into his story with a simple question from Morty.

"Forrest, my friend here was wondering if you knew anything about The Amazing Verido. Do you?"

"Yup, yup, yup," Forrest said, and though Duncan found the young man difficult to understand, he pieced the words together well enough. "I met him. The Amazing Verido."

"You met him?" Morty asked.

"Yup, yup, yup. When I was a little boy. Sweet and innocent like an angel. That's what my Ma would say. I was her little angel. And once, we heard about the traveling show coming to town. We heard about it and I was so excited." Forrest rocked on his hands while he gazed at the wall, peering through it into the depth of his memories. "I loved the magic shows. I loved them." He grew quiet and his bottom lip drooped.

"Forrest?" Morty prodded.

As if nothing had happened, Forrest continued. "Ma said I'd have to work hard all week, do all my chores, and then she'd take me to the show. Just like Ms. Lane. I do all my work each week and Ms. Lane takes me to a show, but Ms. Lane takes me to the pictures. I like *The Thin Man*. You seen *The Thin Man?*"

"Not yet, but I hear it's really good."

"It is. It's really good. Ms. Lane took me to see it because I worked really good." The way Forrest spoke and moved, Duncan thought he might have had been born with some type of genetic issue like Down Syndrome. But then maybe a severe beating to the head could do the same. He had no idea. Forrest went on, "But it ain't live people. It's just a movie. When I was little I saw that show with live people. I worked hard all week and Ma was real proud of me and she gave me a big hug and said we could go see the show. The Amazing Verido."

"That's right," Morty said. "Tell us about The Amazing Verido."

"There were lots of people at the show. Lots and lots. And all kinds of neat stuff — jugglers and sword-swallowers and music. Oh and I got a balloon but I let it slip away and it flew so high. So high. Ma and I watched and watched until we couldn't see it anymore. But I wasn't sad or anything. I was having so much fun."

Holding back his tongue, Duncan rested against the wall and listened. He figured it would be best to let Forrest tell this in his own way. Though part of him wanted to pressure the damaged man into getting to the point, he feared Forrest might have a fit or shut down or worse. And it wasn't just because of the obvious mental problems Forrest suffered. Duncan sensed a tension growing underneath the story. His card-cheater's sense told him to be wary — something wasn't as it seemed.

Forrest popped to his feet as he spoke, gesturing with his

hands held at awkward angles. "The man came out of a tent and he had a big cone he spoke into and his voice grew bigger. *'Come on in! See the show!'* I ran ahead of Ma, ran right past people in line so I could get to the front but everybody was laughing so I guess it was okay. And they even let Ma join me up front which was good because I didn't like being alone." He froze and his face twitched.

"And this was The Amazing Verido?" Morty asked.

"Yeah," Forrest said, his voice losing all sense of life. "This was The Amazing Verido. This was him. Not the man with the cone. That was the money man you had to pay to get in. We sat in the front row and Ma bought popcorn and we sat there eating and eating and eating and I ate so fast my belly hurt. And then the show started."

While Duncan knew to be patient, Morty barreled onward. "Yeah, tell us about the show. Did Verido perform the Door of Vanishing trick?"

Forrest turned to Morty and nodded like he feared he might wet himself.

"And?" Morty said.

Duncan said, "It's okay, Forrest. Tell us when you're ready."

Forrest nodded, visibly torn between the desire to please his new audience and the fear of telling this next part of the story. Struggling with his words, he said, "The show was real good. The Amazing Verido was the best. He wore a cape and top hat and he had this girl assistant who was so beautiful, so beautiful. And they did the tricks, all kinds of tricks. He made birds appear in his hat and they were real and they flew over our heads. He had a special bag that you put things in and they turned into other things. Ma and I were so happy. Then the girl brought out a door." Forrest took a deep breath, his bottom lip shaking, and spoke the next part as fast as he could get it out. "It was on wheels and she put it sideways and Verido walked through it and it was just a door in a frame and then he turned it facing us and he had the girl go through and close the door and then he said magic words and when he opened the door she was gone but then he closed the door and opened it again and she was back." Forrest jumped onto the cot, knocking into Morty without any care. In a booming voice, he said, "*I need a volunteer from the audience! I need a brave soul to help me astound you all.* I raised my hand and Ma raised her hand and he picked us. He picked us!" He stepped back to the floor, the tension within him dropping into a sad energy. "And while he talked with us, the girl wheeled the door away and I was sad because I thought it would be fun to disappear in a magic door. I told him that and he smiled. He asked the audience if they wanted to see it, and they cheered. So the girl wheeled the door out again only this time she put it sideways. Then he did the trick. He had me stand on one side of the door and Ma on the other and he had Ma walk through the door to me. And ... and she vanished."

Forrest looked straight at Duncan. "She was gone."

"Aw, kid, that's terrible," Morty said. "I'm sorry. I didn't know."

"I waited. All the people left and they were quiet and scared and I waited. But she didn't come back. The man came to me and said he was sorry but I had to go. But what about my Ma? He said he had to move the show on and I had to go. But what about my Ma? He said The Amazing Verido sent her home and I should go check there. Okay. I'll check home. I ran and ran and ran home. I never run so fast in all my life. But she wasn't home. Ma never came back. Never ever. When Pa got home, he looked and looked and he couldn't find her too. He took me back to the show but the show was gone. It was an empty field again."

He stopped talking.

Duncan waited for him to continue but Forrest simply stood in the middle of the cramped room and stared into the distance as if he expected his Ma to show up at any moment. Crossing his arms, Duncan said to Morty, "I thought this guy knew who Verido is?"

Morty bristled. "Be a little sensitive. You heard his story."

"It's a terrible thing that happened, but I can't change that. I'm trying to make sure nothing terrible happens to Lucy. So does he know Verido or not?"

Forrest whirled around and stuck his hand in the box next to his cot. "I got a picture of Ma," he said and pulled out a rolled up piece of canvas. He unrolled it to display a mediocre painting of a heavyset, stern woman with gray hair tied up in a bun.

Duncan jumped forward. Not because of the painting but because of the paper that unrolled with it. It was a long paper filled with writing in numerous sizes and fonts.

COME SEE THE MOST ASTOUNDING
THE MOST ASTONISHING
THE MOST AMAZING
MAGIC!
COME SEE THE AMAZING VERIDO!
ONLY AT THE
WILKINSON'S WONDERS TRAVELING SHOW!

Duncan read it over three times before he asked, "Who's Wilkinson?"

Morty checked out the paper. "I don't know, but I'll tell you who will. Lady Lane. There's no way this guy's traveling show came through this town without a visit to Lady Lane. Forrest, thank you. You've done real good."

Morty hurried back upstairs. Duncan hesitated. He watched Forrest for a little. The young man gazed at the painting of his mother, his mind locked in an event that would never stop haunting him. Had he never been beaten, he might have learned to cope, to get on with life, or at least to make some sort of existence palatable. But the beating had ruined him and appeared to have left his mind capable of only two modes — Lady Lane and Ma.

"I'm real sorry," Duncan said, his voice dead in the quiet room. "I ..." But there was nothing he could say.

By the time he reached Morty, Lady Lane was writing down a name and address. She handed it over with a wink. "Don't you forget me, now. I got needs too, you know."

"My dear," Morty said, "I promise I'll see you the first chance I get."

Lady Lane glanced at Duncan. "You come back, and I'll set you up with a real pretty girl. I'll even give you a deal on account of you being Morty's friend."

"Um, thank you," Duncan said, heading straight for the exit, his mind troubled by Forrest and his tragic story.

Outside, Morty caught up and waved the paper in his hand. "I told you Lady Lane would know. Claude Wilkinson is the guy and he lives in Gettysburg."

Duncan took the paper and continued walking. "Let's get out of here."

CHAPTER 21

BY THE TIME DUNCAN AND MORTY returned to the Magic Emporium, the sun had set. Lucy was closing up the store when she heard them approach. Before Duncan could say a word, she rushed over to him.

"What happened to you?" Her fingertips brushing across his bruises. "Are you okay?"

"I'm fine."

"But where were you? Who did this to you?"

"I need to speak with Vincent. Where is he?"

Lucy pulled back, her mouth drawing a thin line. Then with a flippant toss of her hand, she said, "Who knows? He's always done this, gone off for days at time, leaves me for his secret ways. Sound familiar?"

Duncan turned to Morty. "See if you can find Vincent."

Morty took one look at Lucy's face. "Right. I'll get going." To Lucy, he added, "Just don't kill him. I don't want to help you hide a body."

After he left, Lucy returned to the counter. "Notice I didn't make any promises."

"I know this bothers you, and I understand. I do. But you've got to see that I'm being secretive to protect you."

"I find that when people say they're trying to protect me,

they're usually trying to protect themselves."

Duncan frowned. "Maybe you're right."

Lucy wrinkled her forehead at this unexpected answer. She paused. "Do you even care about me?"

Duncan could hear in her voice that she was not seeking a compliment but rather she was leading up to something. "Very much."

"Then you better listen to me real hard. I'm willing to take a lot from my brother because he's my brother, but I won't take it from you. Life is too short for these kinds of games. I mean one day everything's going fine and the next the day it's the Crash and everything we knew ended. You aren't invulnerable, you know. Something could happen to you to take you away forever and then you'll be stuck without ever having had a chance to know me, or for me to know you. I'm sure you're trying to do the right thing by keeping your secrets, but they do more harm than you realize. So, this is it. You say you care about me so much, then tell me something. Otherwise, it's all a farce."

Duncan shook his head in amazement. "The way you speak — you're a woman ahead of her time."

"That's the nicest way anybody's ever called me a bitch before."

"I wasn't calling you—"

"It was a joke."

He watched her in silence as she finished closing up. She did her work with one eye on him all the time. Twice he opened his mouth and she instantly halted to listen, but then he clamped up. Though her anger simmered — she pressed so hard on her cleaning rag, she came close to cracking the glass counter — worse was her disappointment. It showed in the seconds her eyes turned away from him. He knew he was letting her down, and his throat tightened as if he were in grade school and about to cry.

"Damn," he muttered under his breath. For the first time in his life, he understood what it meant to be spellbound by a woman. Because despite all the dangers and worries and fears that held him back, he knew he could not deny Lucy what she needed from him.

"My family," he began, and his voice startled her. "My family is not very close. At least, not close to me. My sisters and my dad all talk with each other, but I'm the outcast. I got along well with my great-grandfather but he's so old that he's not all there in his head anymore. Besides, they're all so far away now, it's easier to forget about them — better than pining away for some bond that won't ever come. I've watched the way you are with Vincent, the way you talk about him. Your pride, your desire to see him succeed and thrive. That's real special. Me, I barely know my sisters. They have their lives and they don't let me in. So, I don't really have a life back home with my family. And then I ended up here, but I don't really belong here either. I mean, I've only been here a few days and already I've messed everything up."

"What have you messed up?"

Duncan decided not to tell Lucy about Nelson Walter. If he played that out right, she might never have to know, never have to worry or fear for her life. "I wish I could explain everything to you, but my life is complicated."

"All lives are complicated and messy and oftentimes a little ugly, too. You don't have to be perfect for me. I don't expect it. I hope you don't expect it of me."

Duncan looked out the store window and watched people hustle along the sidewalks in their brown suits and various hats. "I don't belong here. And I don't belong from where I came. I'm a man without a home."

Lucy locked the store door and stepped in front of him. She inched up and kissed him gently on the mouth. "Let me be your home," she said before climbing upstairs to her apartment.

Trying to act cool and collected, Duncan walked to the stairs and watched her. It took a tremendous effort to not rush up. He climbed three steps and stopped.

He wanted her, of course, but what if being with her messed him up even more? She had his head spinning when he should have been focused on getting home all this time. And how far should he expect things to go between them? Back in 2013, this little scene would have easily played out with a romp in bed, but could he expect the same from 1934? He didn't want to hurt her or upset her, and he had certainly done that before. What were her expectations? Even worse, what if they did take things that far and she got pregnant? Duncan recognized that he had been rather cavalier about being in contact with people from the past. Every time travel story he knew suggested he might be screwing up the future. But most of his actions were in an attempt to get the Door and get home. Fathering a child, however, would have to be catastrophic to the future. And yet, if he had already destroyed the future he knew, then what did it matter? Not to mention that at the rate things were going, Nelson Walter would have him killed long before he could get back to 2013. So why not be with the woman he cared so much about?

Come now, Duncan — it's more than just caring about her a lot. Isn't it?

Stunned by his thoughts, he gazed upward. Lucy had returned to the staircase and looked curiously at him. "Are you coming up?"

He swallowed hard and tried to speak but his voice had abandoned him.

She moved in closer, a shadow of fear crossing her brow. "You okay?"

"I ... I ..."

She reached the bottom of the stairs and held on to the railing as if it could protect her. "What is it? Please, tell me."

Her scent overwhelmed him, and he said something he had never said to a woman in all in his life. "I love you."

Lucy's smile faltered. Her chin quivered, and she lowered herself to the floor, keeping a tight grip on the railing. "You are nothing, if not surprising, Duncan Rose."

He hurried to the stairs and clasped her hand. "I mean it. I love you. I don't care about all the mess around my life. No matter what it does to the world or the universe or Time itself.

I love you, and I want to be with you."

She looked into his eyes, and he saw an emotion mounting within her that he had never seen in a woman's eyes. He watched it glisten and grow until it encompassed her mouth and nose and cheeks — he stepped back to see that her entire being radiated this strange emotion.

Placing her free hand around his neck, she pulled him close. "I love you, too."

She pressed her lips against his. An explosive force gripped him like lightning through his lips straight to his brain. He had enjoyed his share of women before but never had he experienced such passion in nothing more than a kiss. Even as he picked Lucy off the floor and climbed the stairs, even as he carried her into the apartment, part of his brain watched with sheer amazement. The only thought repeating — *So this is what the fuss about love is?*

When he put her onto the lumpy mattress in the back, she placed a hand on his chest. "I have to tell you something," she said, her brow getting that worried furrow he had seen on her before.

Another mark of love, perhaps, he thought. *I'm noticing little details about her.*

Sitting up, Lucy smiled bashfully. "I ... I'm not a virgin."

Though he knew it was the wrong reaction, he couldn't help himself. Duncan laughed. "It's okay. I didn't expect you to be."

"What? What kind of girl do you think I am?"

"No, no, don't get offended. I didn't mean anything like that. I never assumed anything about you. All I meant was that where I come from, being a virgin is not a big deal. I don't care. I want you. That's all."

She watched his face closely and then seemed to decide he told the truth. She smiled, rose to her feet, and waited until he looked at her in passionate need. She didn't have to wait long.

Slowly, she disrobed. It was quiet and sensual and utterly new to Duncan.

I'm the virgin, he realized. And for the first time since he was a teenager hiding in the backseat of Pappy's car, screwing a girl with too much curiosity and not enough sense, Duncan felt nervous. He knew how to take a woman, but what was expected of him here? This was unknown territory. This was more than taking what he needed for a night. In fact, as much as he wanted her, he discovered another desire.

Duncan gazed upon her body, his mind drifting from any sense of reality. All that existed was the bed, himself, and this work of art called Lucy.

He reached for her but she pushed his hand aside. "No fair," she said, her sweet smile as astonishing as her soft lips. "You've got all your clothes on."

"I should remedy that," he said.

And in moments, his skin pressed against hers. He felt her warmth and smelled her intoxicating skin. His hands caressed her shoulders, longing to cover her breasts, but shaking like that teenager. He worried over every action, afraid he would spoil what had become a beautiful, sensuous, truly erotic connection.

As he kissed her neck, Lucy let out a soft moan and that sound released his fear. His hands took command where his brain had second-guessed. Starting with her face, his fingers traced her body's curves. When he reached her breasts, her moans grew louder. His hands continued downward, and her reactions continued to mount. Each utterance from her excited him more.

She moved under him, pressing herself against him with fiery need. "Please, Duncan, don't tease me."

"Never."

Their rhythm launched into a fury. The instinctual animals within wrested control as they rose and fell, harder and faster. When she touched his sides, his bruised body mixed pain with his pleasure, his need overriding any desire to stop her hands. The room spun around them, both of them groaning with each thrust, both of them lost in each other.

Lucy gasped and her muscles tightened. She held onto Duncan, lifting herself off the bed as he continued to push deep inside her. With a long moan, she released, squeezing him as if she could meld into his bones. And she fell to the bed.

Duncan rolled onto his back, and after a moment, Lucy moved smoothly on top. They kissed and licked and laughed. She placed him back inside her but did not move. With her breathing heavy and a trickle of sweat running between her breasts, she smiled. "I want to stay like this forever, feeling you in me."

Neither spoke any more. They locked eyes and listened to their breathing. Lucy leaned down and kissed him gently. With deliberate motions, she rose and fell upon him, taking him once more away from the real world and into the world of her pleasure. Her determined look told him all. This part was for him, and he let all control pass from his mind.

Lucy set the pace. Lucy ran the show.

When he came, his body flushed with pleasurable numbness. He felt so incredible that a touch of sadness overwhelmed him. All the sexual experiences of his life were empty ghosts compared to this. Love made such a difference, and he wondered how many other aspects of his life would be fulfilled with a loving relationship.

Holding Lucy in his arms as she closed her eyes to sleep for a little, decided that she would have to accompany him no matter what. He could not leave her behind to face Nelson Walter. For that matter, he couldn't justify leaving her to face World War II or Korea or Vietnam or any of the horrors of the twentieth century still to come. Not that 2013 was a field of flowers and puppies, but at least they would face the twenty-first century's horrors together.

DUNCAN WOKE TO THE RICH AROMA of fresh coffee on the stove. He rolled to his back, the mattress forming new lumps beneath him. As he stretched in the beams of sunlight casting on the bed, he listened to Lucy setting the table. He would tell her this morning, he decided, tell her everything — exactly who he was, where and when he came from. She had to know so that when they found the Door, she would not hesitate to come with him. But more than that, he could no longer justify keeping secrets from her. He loved her, and that demanded a level of honesty entirely new to him. But he was willing to try.

When he stepped from behind the curtain, he saw the table set with coffee and fruit as well as the local paper. Wearing another summer dress that both covered her appropriately for the time and yet accentuated her lovely curves, Lucy walked over and kissed him. He scratched his chest and stretched again. "Good morning."

"Good morning. I've got a little breakfast for you."

"So I see."

"Get some clothes on so we can eat. I'm starving."

The idea of dressing for breakfast instead of eating in his underwear tickled Duncan, but he did as asked. While he slid on his pants, he asked, "Have you heard from Vincent yet?"

"Don't worry about him. He'll show up when he's ready. You've got to learn to let Vincent be Vincent. Trust me. If you start searching for him, he'll do everything he can to avoid being found. Why do you need to see him anyway?"

Duncan returned to the table, dressed and smiling, and he sipped his coffee. He could feel the worried tension pulsing off Lucy. She was smart. She had to know that whatever Duncan wanted with Vincent had to do with whatever he was being secretive about.

Well, Lucy, today your entire world is about to change.

He held her hands across the table and saw the concerned, torn expectation in her eyes. She wanted to know, but she also feared knowing. "You've been so patient with me, and I want to thank you for that. I've tried to protect you, even while you were yelling at me that you didn't want my protection."

"All I meant was—"

"You'll understand now. This secret of mine is the kind of thing that can change a person forever and I didn't want to burden you with that before. But after last night ... I ... I don't know even know how to say this. I don't want to scare you, but I can't stop thinking about you and me and ways we can stay together in the future, and yet I'm afraid if I tell you this, that you'll see me so differently that you won't want to give me a chance, but I know I have to tell you and yet—"

Lucy squeezed his hands before letting go. "I've never seen you ramble like this. Calm down. Look, I understand that you're nervous. Obviously, the thing you've kept inside all this time is big and important to you. I can't say how I'm going to react, but I promise you, I won't change the way I feel about you. I love you. I don't throw those words around willy-nilly."

"Willy-nilly? Do you want to go play hopscotch and get on the swings?"

"You're going to make fun of me?" Lucy teased. "Not a great way to endear me."

Raising a hand, still chuckling, Duncan said, "I'm sorry. Really, I am. I didn't mean to poke fun. I just ..."

A chill crossed Duncan's heart as he caught sight of the newspaper's front page.

"What's wrong?" Lucy asked.

He lifted the paper, reading the article twice before setting it back down. Lucy stared at him, frowning as she waited. He pointed to the black-and-white photograph in the two-column piece. It depicted a young man holding his bleeding head while police stood nearby.

"That's Morty's friend — Forrest. We met him yesterday."

"Forrest from Lady Lane's?"

"Not what you're thinking. We went to see Forrest and only Forrest. Morty thought he knew something about Verido."

"You told Morty about what we're doing?"

"No, no. It's not like that. I need to find Verido for myself."

"Why? Is this what you wanted to tell me? That you've been after Verido's trick this whole time?"

"No. Well, sort of. It's ..." Duncan trailed off into thought. From what he had seen, Forrest was a nice young guy who never bothered anybody. And with the doorman at Lady Lane's, not to mention Lady Lane herself, nobody would mess with him unless she allowed it. Or unless that person had enough power to scare a whore who knew an entire town's dirty secrets. Only one man fit that description. Nelson Walter.

But why? Was it meant to be a warning to Duncan? His way of saying, "I'm still watching you?" Duncan looked up at Lucy.

"What's going on? You look worried?"

"I need your help. I'm going to tell you everything. I swear I will. But it's a long, complicated story and I don't have time right now. You're going to have to trust me. The situation I'm in has become far more serious than I realized and some of what I've been trying to protect you from is about to come on to us. Come on real strong."

"Did somebody beat up Forrest because you talked with him? Why would they do that?" With a shake of her head, she put on a stern face. "Look, whatever you've gotten into, we can work through. You just need to tell me—"

"That's what I'm trying to do. And I will. I promise. But right now, I have to go."

"What? Where?"

"I need you to do something for me. I'm sorry to ask this. See, I was hoping Vincent would be back by now because I need a car. Is there anybody you know who can let us borrow one?"

"A car? You're asking the sister of a guy who steals cars for joyrides if she can get a car? Of course I can get a car."

"I don't want you stealing a car."

"I'm not Vincent. But I know where he goes to sell them. I know how to get a car cheap. Only problem is that I don't have nearly enough to buy one. Even a cheap one."

Duncan got to his feet to retrieve the rest of his clothes. "I'll pay for it. I've still got cash from the tableside gig."

"Enough for a car?"

"You'll have to do some heavy negotiating, but I don't think that'll be any trouble for you. If you need to hock my watch or anything of mine, let me know. Just set up the car and when I see you, I'll pay for it."

"Please tell me what's going on?"

He rushed over to her and kissed her with every ounce of emotion he felt. "I love you. Okay? Please, trust me. I'll be back by noon at the latest."

"Okay, I'll get the car. I'll be here at noon. You better be here, too. And you better explain all this."

"I will." He kissed her one more time. He headed for the door, paused, and turned back. "If I don't show up, it means things went really bad and you're in danger. Go find Morty, find Vincent, and get out of this town. Don't ever come back."

"What the hell did you do?"

"Promise me you'll do that. I don't show, you run as far from here as you can get."

She barely nodded, her fear and confusion building tears in her eyes. Duncan knew he had terrified her with his final words, but they had to be said. He planned to confront Nelson Walter, and he knew the kind of man Nelson Walter could be. He only hoped Walter would be too tired in the morning to bother with a golf club.

Chapter 22

Duncan chose to walk to The Walter Hotel, partly to stall, partly to build his courage, and partly to tap into the anger seething underneath. He hated when somebody's impatience screwed things up. A little time often made the difference between success and failure, but too often the people he had worked with wanted instant results and fast money without a sliver of complication. If Walter would have simply waited, Duncan could have found Verido, found the door, and found a solution that, at the least, made everyone think they got a good deal. Instead, he had to deal with a glorified thug who beat the crap out of a decent, young man that had had more than his share of brutality in his life.

By the time he reached the hotel lobby, Duncan's jaw set square and firm. He strode across the lobby floor, ignoring the cheery *Good Mornings* from the bellhops and desk managers. Narrowing his eyes on the private elevator to Walter's apartment, he passed by Freddie who dropped his morning paper in shock.

"Hey, Rose," he said, but Duncan kept on his course for the bank of elevators. The operator on the far end jumped up from his small stool, adjusted his cap and uniform, and attempted to look professional. Freddie called out again. "Rose? What're you doing?"

Freddie made a crucial mistake — he underestimated the level of anger a man could have when protecting someone he loved. Freddie placed a hand on Duncan's shoulder, no doubt expecting the typical reaction of fear and compliance that went along with that strong, thick hand. Instead, Duncan whirled around and kneed Freddie in the groin.

As Freddie doubled over, Duncan said, "Sorry about the cheap shot, but I don't think I could stop you any other way." To the elevator operator, he said, "You — take me to Mr. Walter."

The kid watched Freddie stumble against the wall, breathing hard and cupping his crotch.

Duncan snapped his fingers in front of the kid's wide eyes. "Hey. You take me to Mr. Walter now or you can be on the floor holding your balls, too."

With a vigorous nod, the kid stepped into the elevator. "Yes, sir. Mr. Walter's floor. Right away."

Stepping into the elevator, Duncan said, "Get some ice, Freddie."

The ride up slowed in Duncan's head. He heard every clink and clank from the machinery. He felt every vibration ripple up his legs. His head thumped with the bump in the elevator as they passed each floor.

Part of his mind screamed at him to stop, turn around, get Lucy, get the car, and just get. Go into hiding if necessary. Forget about Verido, the Door, Walter, everything.

But he had done too much hiding in his life. If he were honest with himself, that's all he had ever done — hiding from family, from responsibility, from accomplishing anything of value. Why else spend his nights screwing over fools and spend his days escaping the inevitable retaliations? It was a way to avoid the real world. It was easy for him because he didn't care about anybody. The closest to a loving relationship he had was with Pappy and that had drifted away with Pappy's sanity.

Except now love had captured him. The real thing. Now he cared. His behavior, the risks he took, the life he led, had real consequences now. Hiding would only destroy what he had begun with Lucy.

"Here you are, sir," the elevator operator said. As he slid open the gate, he lowered his head and in a quiet voice, added, "Please don't tell Mr. Walter I took you up."

"Don't worry. If he asks, I'll tell him I tossed you out of the elevator."

Duncan stepped into the hall. To his left, the office door stood ajar but no lights were on. To his right, he heard the clinking of silverware and inhaled the morning aroma of eggs, coffee, and toast.

He stormed down the hall, following the sounds and smells. The door at the end led into a well-furnished sitting room nearly as big as Vincent and Lucy's apartment. To his left was an archway and through there, Duncan saw Nelson Walter sitting at a table with his wife and son.

Walter wore dress pants and suspenders over a clean, white undershirt. The bit of hair he had stuck out and stubble darkened his face. His wife looked exhausted and his son looked pampered. They all stared up at him.

Walter froze with a forkful of egg halfway to his mouth. His face flashed outrage before pulling back into control. "Mr. Rose," he said, his voice calm, his eggs shaking from his clenched hand. "I didn't realize we had an appointment this early."

"We didn't." Duncan thrilled to hear his own voice calm and controlled.

Walter looked at his wife. Her eyes were stuck on the eggs. He lowered the fork slowly and wiped his mouth with a cloth napkin.

"I'm having breakfast with my family. This is a sacred time for me. That's why I don't schedule anything until later in the day. It's disrespectful to me and my family. But I can see you're upset about something and I consider you a valuable friend, one who deserves a little leeway. So why don't we go talk in my office?"

"I'd rather talk right here," Duncan said, knowing the only

thing keeping Walter at bay was the presence of his family. "Did you read the paper this morning?"

Walter indicated the paper at his elbow.

Duncan stabbed a finger toward the picture of Forrest. "Right there on the front page. A good friend of mine knew that guy who got beat up."

"It's a tragedy. I can see why you're so upset. Your friend has my sympathies. If there's anything I can do to help, you let me know."

"I'll do that. But there's a problem."

Shifting in his seat, his face reddening as he crossed his arms, he said, "What problem?"

"You asked me to find some information for you, and I visited this young man, Forrest, as part of that search. This assault happened on him shortly after."

"And you think that had something to do with you?"

"I think you know exactly what that had to do with. I want it to stop. I'm doing everything you asked. There's no reason to have other people messing up my work."

Walter's boy frowned. "What's he talking about, Pop?"

Walter shot to his feet, his chair falling over. In a low growl, he said, "That's enough. You work for me. You don't dictate the terms. Now I'm not saying what happened to that kid had anything to do with you. It didn't. He worked in a disreputable place serving disreputable people. Bad things happen in places like that. But if I had been involved, it would only be a form of insurance. After all, you're not very trustworthy, are you? One look at you tells me as much."

"I'm trying hard to do my part, but I can't when your—"

"Milly, take the boy out of here, now."

"Nobody's leaving here, yet," Duncan said but Milly clearly knew who to consider the real threat. She quickly gathered her son and scampered out of the room. Duncan's body tensed. Only a breakfast table stood between him and an enraged gorilla. "Look, you said that if I—"

"You ever come into my home again, and you won't walk out of here. As for Forrest, you better figure out your real position in all this fast or you won't live long enough to piss me off."

"You said if I got you Verido and the Door—"

Walter picked up a butter knife as if it were a dagger. "That's right. And instead, you're still playing boyfriend to that whore you've got wood for."

"I'll get what you want, but you've got to be patient."

Walter jabbed the knife into the table with such force, the dull blade dug into the wood and stuck. "Get this into your moronic head. The only reason you're alive here is because I think I need you to figure out how this door works. But if I find Verido myself and get the Door and figure out how it works myself, then I won't really need you anymore. And I certainly won't need Lucy or Vincent Day. So stop worrying about what I'm doing, stop wasting time in my home, and stop fucking the girl. Go get me my Door of Vanishing."

Duncan stared at the butter knife. "Yes, sir," he said because there was nothing more to say. He edged out of the room, not willing to turn his back on Walter, and when he reached the hall, he rushed to the elevator.

When the operator arrived, he glanced over Duncan and paled. "Guess it didn't go too well?"

"Shut up."

In the silent ride down, his mind tried to sort everything out. If Walter's men had beaten Forrest, then Walter most likely also got the name Claude Wilkinson. The only way to stay valuable to Walter, then, would be to get to Wilkinson first. Stay ahead of the information so he could find the Door first. Otherwise, he would end up dead. Worse, Lucy would end up dead, too.

CHAPTER 23

DUNCAN LEANED BACK AGAINST THE FORD'S headrest as Lucy drove towards Gettysburg. She had taken several excruciating hours to get the automobile — one of the "New" Fords, a 1930 Model A. The black two-door sat two, had an off-white cloth top, and a spare tire strapped to the passenger-side runnerboard. While waiting for Lucy, Duncan had paced her apartment, his imagination developing one horrid scenario after another of what had happened to her. After negotiating a deal on the car (involving a promise to have Vincent perform at a birthday party for the fence's kid), Lucy set about finding Vincent and Morty.

She caught Morty leaving his apartment, suitcase in hand. He had read the paper and figured that whatever Duncan had gotten tied up in was bleeding out onto others. "And I don't like blood," Morty said, and hoofed it toward the bus station.

She never found Vincent. Normally this would be fine, but under the circumstances, she worried that he might be unconscious in a hospital somewhere. Or worse.

When she finally showed up at the apartment and rattled off all that had happened, Duncan hugged her, kissed her, and turned her right back to the car. He had packed a bag for her and put what little food he found into a box.

"But I just got here," she said.

"Sorry, but—"

"And we can't leave without Vincent."

"This isn't a permanent thing. We need to get to Gettysburg—"

"Gettysburg? Why?"

Grabbing the keys from her, he ushered her downstairs. After one look at the massive size of the car, he returned the keys to her hand. In 2013, he had driven hatchbacks, compacts, and on a few occasions, sleek but small sports cars like a Porsche 911. This wasn't the time to learn how to handle a boat of a car.

Though the Model A was capable of hitting sixty-five miles per hour, there were no highways yet (that was Eisenhower's deal and he still had World War II to contend with before becoming President), so they never got above forty-five as they traversed the dirt roads and pothole-filled paved ones. Despite their slow progress, every minute brought them closer to Gettysburg and further from Nelson Walter. Duncan hardly felt relaxed, but he was able to close his eyes and feel the warm, summer air blow over him. He could let his mind float, even if only for a moment.

"We've got at least an hour until we get there," Lucy said. "I think it's time for you to live up to your promise."

"My promise?"

"I've been more than understanding, and I've shown you more trust than you probably deserve. But I can't go on with this until you tell me what's going on. You said you would, and we have the time, so out with it."

Duncan sat up and watched the tree-lined road ahead. Of all the balls he juggled in the air, this one required the most delicate touch. Should he fail, it would blow a hole through him that would cause the rest to come crashing down. He had to tell her as much as possible — because he loved her, for her safety, and because he didn't want to lie to her — but he couldn't tell her everything until she saw it with her own eyes. Otherwise, she would think he was insane and would feel betrayed by all that he had said previously. She might even turn the car to the nearest asylum.

"I'm waiting," she said without any playfulness.

Duncan raised his index finger to hold her for a moment longer. Then, after he collected his thoughts, he said, "This door we're going after — the Door of Vanishing — is more than you think. It's not just a trick. It's real."

"Don't play games with me. I want to know—"

"I'm telling you," he snapped. "It's real. Those people that disappeared — that wasn't a trick. They went into the Door and emerged somewhere else. Somewhere far away from here. So far that they'll never make it back. That door is real. I mean — real magic."

"How?"

"I don't know. But it's true. I'm proof of that."

"You?"

"That's my big secret. I'm not from here. I'm from far away, and I came through the Door. I didn't mean to do so; I didn't know what it was. I came here by accident. That's why I've been trying to find it. It's the only way I'll get home."

Lucy stayed quiet for two miles, and Duncan kept his eyes forward. He chilled at the idea of seeing her reaction. When she finally spoke, her words came out measured and soft, and she asked the question he dreaded. "Exactly where is 'far away'?"

"I can't tell you." He watched the bridge of trust between them crumble apart. "I want to. I do. But you have to believe me that if I tell you that, it will cause more harm than good."

"That doesn't make any sense."

"I know, but it's the best I can do."

She thought on this longer. "If these people, people like you, went through the door and never came back, what makes you think you'll get back to your home?"

"Because they didn't know what was happening. They thought they were going through a trick door and by the time they realized what had really happened, they were lost. Some of them might not even know yet that it was a real trick. Heck, some of them might have figured it all out quick, and they'd be looking for the Door to get back, but they haven't found it. I've been lucky finding you and Vincent. If I hadn't, I could have spent the rest of my life searching for the Door."

"Why don't you just go home another way? Take a train or a boat or something?"

"I can't explain that now."

"You know you sound like a lunatic."

Bile crept up Duncan's throat. "You don't believe me," he said, gazing out the window to hide his despair.

"I didn't say that. I'm just trying to grasp it all. There's been a lot of strange things told about Verido and the Door of Vanishing. I've even read that some people thought the Door held real magic. So, what you're saying isn't so insane."

"Then you believe me?"

Lucy shrugged. "I think that we've got to find the Door. Real magic or not, it's certainly got a lot of power associated with it."

"That's the reason Nelson Walter wants to find it. He knows it's real, too. And in the hands of a man like him, it could be disastrous."

"Nelson Walter? Is that who you've been worked up about?"

"He'll hurt anyone in his way. We've got to be careful."

Pulling into Gettysburg Gas and Repairs, Lucy said, "I don't know what to think of this." She parked the car and looked straight at Duncan, waiting until he met her eyes. "I guess I figured your big secret was going to be some crime you committed in the past or that you were married or something like that."

"I wish it was that simple."

While a station attendant came out and filled the car with gas, Lucy said, "My problem is that I've fallen in love with you. So, either I've fallen for an insane man or I've fallen into a mess of trouble that doesn't make much sense. But it doesn't really matter because that's the way love is."

"What are you saying?" Duncan asked because, though he thought he knew, he had to hear her directly.

"We're going to find the Door, and if it's real or not, we'll handle whatever happens. I'm by your side on all of this. I love you. That's what I'm saying."

Duncan leaned over and kissed her.

A knock on the car window interrupted them. With an embarrassed grin, Lucy rolled down the window to pay the attendant. "Excuse me, sir," she said, "maybe you can help us?"

"Sure, ma'am. What you need?"

"We're trying to find Claude Wilkinson. He once ran a—"

"Wilkinson's Wonders. Oh, yeah, anybody growing up around here knows about Claude. I haven't gone and seen his show since I was a kid. Don't think it's still running, to tell the truth. But he's got his little showroom place for anybody willing to go out that way."

Lucy flashed her cutest smile. "Terrific, because that's us. We're willing."

The attendant put his elbow on the door and gave out the directions to a small house on the edge of the other side of town. As they pulled back onto the road, Lucy glanced over at Duncan. "See? We're in this together."

Duncan watched Gettysburg pass before him without taking much in. Instead, his mind retread the same territory — what an incredible woman Lucy was and how lucky he was that she hadn't left him by the side of the road like a gibbering idiot.

When they reached the opposite end of town, they found the Wilkinson house without trouble. It would have been hard to miss considering the wide, colorful sign post in the front yard reading *The Wilkinson's Wonders Show*. Behind the sign stood an old brick two-story house with a brick porch that had to have been built before the Civil War. Wilkinson had kept it in good condition — the painted trim looked new, the windows were spotless, and even the gravel drive lacked a single weed.

Before they reached the porch, the screen door opened. Wilkinson came out with an enthusiasm to match his untamed, curly white hair. He had a slight hunch and walked with a cane but, for a man who appeared to be in his seventies, he acted spry and sounded fully alive.

"Welcome, welcome. Come inside and see the secrets behind the magic," he said, the old barker in him sneaking through his delivery.

"Hi. My name is Lucy and this is Duncan. We wanted to ask you—"

"About magic, no doubt. Nobody comes to see an old man like me about anything else. Come, come. I'll show you everything there is."

"How much is a ticket?" Duncan asked.

Wilkinson waved him off. "No, no. I don't charge. I've made my money off this stuff long ago. This is for the discerning magician and the novice enthusiast. This is a way to give back to the world of magic that served me so well. So come on in and see. I promise you won't be disappointed."

While they had important, pressing matters to deal with, a spark of curiosity struck Duncan. No matter that his history with magic had been one of card cheating, his original love came from Pappy and that was for the wondrous, astounding events magicians could create on stage. Craning his neck to peek beyond the door, Duncan licked his lips and walked inside.

The visible rooms in the house were chock full of old magic props — many were even old by 1934 standards. A small table with a blue felt cloth held numerous decks of cards — marked cards, Svengali decks, and other types of gaff decks. There were stacks of old issues of *The Sphinx: An Independent Magazine For Magicians*. Duncan could have spent hours on those magazines alone.

On another table, Duncan found letters and notes written by Johann Nepomuk Hofzinser, one of the great innovators of card magic. The Hofzinser pass, the slip force, the pinky count were but a few of the numerous sleights Hofzinser either created or perfected. And right there on the table, Duncan saw crinkled, brittle papers written in Hungarian with drawings that clearly demonstrated Hofziner's classic routine called "Think and Forget." The spectator would choose two cards, focus on one and forget about the other, and the magician would locate the focused card, then magically transform it into the forgotten card. Such a wonderful trick, and it lay before Duncan in its creator's handwriting.

"Look here," Wilkinson said, pulling Duncan and Lucy into what was once a dining room in the house. "This is a marvel."

To one side, Duncan saw a straightjacket with a signed photo of Houdini next to it. As he stepped towards it, Wilkinson said, "Not that. I want you to look here."

Duncan turned around.

"Holy shit." The words escaped his lips as he laid eyes on one the great illusions of the past, Robert Houdin's Marvelous Orange Tree. Houdin was a French magician considered to be the father of modern magic. The Tree was one of his most beautiful and elegant creations.

On a special side table, Houdin would have an egg, a lemon, and an orange. He would pick out a lady from the audience and borrow her handkerchief. He rolled the handkerchief smaller and smaller, telling the audience that he was placing it inside the egg. Once the handkerchief had disappeared, he picked up the egg, and of course, the audience expected him to crack it open, revealing the lady's handkerchief. Instead, he made the egg disappear into the lemon and then the lemon into the orange.

Up to this point, the trick was rather a simple matter of skillful sleight of hand. But then the incredible happened. An assistant rolled out a lovely pot holding a small orange tree. It was, in fact, a mechanical marvel of the 19th-century. Once wound up, the tree "blossomed" flowers and then sprouted oranges. Houdin would plucked the oranges, cut them open, and hand them out, proving they were real oranges. He continued until only one which was not real remained at the very top. The orange split into four sections and something white and fluffy could be seen. Then two mechanical butterflies rose from behind the tree to grab and spread open the lady's handkerchief.

Houdin died in 1871 making the tree that Wilkinson displayed an antique in its own right. "Does it work?" Duncan asked.

Wilkinson's mouth broke into a rotten-tooth smile that still managed to be endearing. "It most certainly does. Would you like to see it?"

"I'm sorry," Lucy said, "but we actually came here for some information."

Duncan could feel the little boy face he wore as he said, "This won't take long, and it's really amazing. This machine is nearly a hundred years old and it's a remarkable—"

"Okay. Run the machine. It'll go quicker that way."

Giddy, Duncan nodded to Wilkinson who turned the crank in the back of the tree. "I won't slow things down with a demonstration of the performance," Wilkinson said, though the disappointment he showed said far more.

As the tree cycled through, slowly pushing out the orange blossoms and then pulling back leaves to reveal oranges, Duncan peeked at Lucy. Bless her, she watched it with every bit of excitement he felt. *Of course, she did,* he admonished himself. She had spent a lifetime learning tricks from Vincent and several years researching magic for Vincent's book. She knew exactly who Robert Houdin was, and as much as she was right to keep them focused on the Door, Duncan could tell she enjoyed every bit of this moment.

While the tree sprouted the last orange and split it open, Duncan squeezed Lucy's hand. "Thank you," he said to Wilkinson. "That was wonderful. Unbelievable."

"But you didn't come here to see Houdin's tree, did you?"

"We were hoping you could help us locate a specific trick, one by a magician who traveled with you for some time. It was called the Door of Vanishing."

"Ahhh," Wilkinson said, touching the tip of his nose with his index finger. "That is a part of my life that I'd sooner forget but I'm afraid I never will."

"Then you remember The Amazing Verido?" Lucy asked.

"A strange man. Nervous all the time. Dark and mysterious. It played great on the stage and when the crowds saw him slinking around before the show, pacing and muttering to himself, oh my, the intrigue he built. I couldn't have bought that kind of interest. I never really thought too much of him as a magician to tell you the truth. Not until he developed the Door. Before that he would do some card tricks and a few bigger illusions but nothing very exciting. People liked him enough and they left happy but I wanted the kind of show that would spread word from town to town. I wanted it to be that when Wilkinson's Wonders arrived in a town, the folks already knew we would put on an incredible show. I wanted them to be clamoring to see what we had. And, frankly, Verido was going to be fired if he didn't come up with something good."

"But he did."

"Yes, yes, little lady, he sure did. We had taken two weeks off to let everyone visit family and for me to line up more shows and such. I sat down with him before he left and told him the bad news. I never liked threatening someone's job, but any old magician could do what he was doing. I told him I needed somebody that got people talking, and he promised that when he returned, he'd have something that would put Wilkinson's Wonders on the lips of every kid in every town. I didn't think anything of it. I've heard all kinds of boasting before, and honestly, I suspected I'd never see him again. I remember getting ready to start looking for a new magician when he showed up a few days before the rest of my people. And he had the Door of Vanishing with him. He wouldn't let anybody look at it, kept it from prying eyes all the time. Of course, we managed to get a look anyway, and as far as anybody could tell, it was just a door with a bunch of 'magical' writing on it."

Duncan asked, "Where did he get it?"

Wilkinson raised his eyebrows. "He's a magician. He'd never tell me that. Anyway, the show took off and he built a small name for himself. I had dreams of the trick hitting it to worldwide proportions — maybe even put us in for a licensing deal so the money would keep rolling in. I even started worrying I'd need a new magician because pretty soon he'd be leaving me for a bigger stage. But then one night, he sent somebody through the Door and they didn't come back. He covered it up well for the performance, and though the audience was confused, they still ate it up. All except the wife of the man who disappeared. After the show, I asked him why he changed the script, and he was whiter than a ghost. Terrified. He told me something went wrong and we better leave town before they turned the cops on us. It happened twice more. After that there was no hiding that something bad was happening. When the police showed up, though, Verido had packed up and disappeared himself. They searched for weeks but nobody ever found him."

Lucy said, "We're trying to find him. We want to know more about the Door trick."

"He won't tell you a thing."

"Then you know where he is?"

Wilkinson shook his curly head. "Haven't seen him in ages. He showed up once, a few years after his escape, and we chatted about nothing in particular. Haven't seen him since. I merely meant that if you do find him, he won't talk. He took his magician's oaths very seriously."

Pouring on her sweetest voice, Lucy said, "You wouldn't, by any chance, be able to tell us his real name? That might help us in our search."

"It won't help you, but if it makes your day, his name was Dominic Rosini. He's not a stupid man though. He would certainly be living under a different name now."

"Probably," Duncan said, "but it's a big help. Thank you."

"Yes, thank you," Lucy said, and taking Duncan's arm, the two headed for the door.

Wilkinson cleared his throat. "Wait a minute. Don't go yet."

"I'm sorry, but we've still got a lot of work to do."

"But you haven't seen the Door yet."

Duncan's stomach lurched. "You have the Door?"

"I have one of them. He had several he rotated, and when he left, this one stayed behind. It's in the basement." Without waiting for an answer, Wilkinson shuffled down a hall and into a kitchen with Lucy and Duncan close behind. He lifted the latch on a weathered wooden door and flicked on a small bulb. "This way," he said, climbing down a wobbling staircase, his white hair reflecting the dim light like a beacon in the fog.

When Duncan reached the bottom, he coughed hard and wondered how far back in time radon began contaminating basements. Dust caked the air thick enough to see. The basement housed all the items not on display — hundreds of items. Old posters and older costumes, moldy boxes of cards and torn photographs, warped ledgers and stained receipts bearing the names of every city, town, and village Wilkinson had traveled through. In the back, covered in dust and surrounded by faded crystal balls and fortune telling boxes, the Door of Vanishing lay flat across two card tables. And in two pieces.

A diagonal slice cut from right to left starting near the highest hinge and ending right under the doorknob. It was a rough cut as if made by a dull saw and jagged with fury, going off the intended path several times. Duncan ran his fingers across the rough cut, and he nearly burst into tears.

Seeing the door, feeling the wood, looking at the writing scrawled across the finish — it transported him back to Pappy's apartment. He saw Pappy's door leaning against the wall and heard the old man warning him to never, under any circumstances, mess with that door. He smelled the stale air of a man so old that his demise hung over him like a shadow in reverse. Pappy knew. Maybe not every detail, but he had to have known about Verido and the Door of Vanishing trick. He had to have known that anybody who went through disappeared.

"He knew," Duncan whispered. Until that moment, part of him deep inside where he never looked had lived in denial. Living in 1934 was real on the surface, yet in his core, he ignored reality. He lived the last few days like a movie or a dream, but standing in this basement, hearing his words die in the thick air, the last part of him clinging to some false fantasy loosened and fell.

"I've tried to figure that thing out for years," Wilkinson said.

"Never got anywhere with it. When Rosini sawed it in two, I think he must have removed some secret mechanism is all I can figure."

Lucy stroked Duncan's back. "May we take a closer look at for a while?"

"Be my guest. I'll be upstairs — got to reset the orange tree. If you need anything, give a holler. And if you figure it out, please let an old man in on the secret. I'd love to go to my grave with that little chestnut in my brain."

After Wilkinson clumped up the stairs, Lucy turned to Duncan. "You okay?"

Duncan's eyes burned. "It's strange. I didn't think it would hit me like this, seeing the door."

"Anything I can do?"

Duncan stepped in close and kissed her. "Stay with me."

"I'm right here with you." She pulled a pencil from her purse. "How about I sketch this door so we have something to refer to later?"

"Excellent idea," he said, but he sounded dismayed.

Lucy flipped one of the old posters over and began drawing a detail of the door. Meanwhile, Duncan brought his face close to the wood, inspecting every inch of it. He paid particular attention to the sawn area, looking for any sign of a hidden compartment or the markings of where a mechanism had once been.

From Wilkinson's story, Duncan surmised that The Amazing Verido, aka Dominic Rosini, had built several fake doors perhaps as decoys to thwart prying eyes. Such a secretive magician would undoubtedly go to great lengths to protect his trade. In fact, the door Duncan looked at may never have been anything but a decoy — the sawing in half an effective misdirection designed to force those who kept the door into wasting countless hours trying to figure out a trick that didn't exist.

But Duncan, of course, did not seek a solution to a magic trick. He wanted to know how to use the door — the real door. And while the door in Wilkinson's basement would never get

Duncan to 2013, let alone the other side of the room, it did prove they were heading in the right direction.

"We've got a name now," Duncan said.

"And this door." Lucy showed off her quick sketch — wonderful.

"We're getting closer."

Banging came from above. Somebody pounding the frame of the screen door. Wilkinson mumbled something along the lines of *Be patient* which followed rapidly by a deep, harsh voice — a voice Duncan knew too well after only a few days. Nelson Walter.

Chapter 24

Duncan put a finger to his lips, and Lucy stayed quiet. He moved cautiously to the bottom of the stairs in order to hear better, but all the voices came through muffled. Though the thumping of his pulse filled his ears, he picked out Wilkinson's tone and had identified Nelson Walter which left one other heavy voice. It had to be Freddie.

The deep voices raised and Wilkinson's grew meek. Duncan scanned the basement for anything that might spark an idea of how to help, but nothing came to mind. Besides, he couldn't dare reveal his presence. If he did, Walter would check out the basement, find the door, and be done with Duncan in a dead and buried out back sort of way. If he were lucky, Lucy would be collateral damage, scarred physically and mentally forever. If unlucky, Lucy would share a shallow grave with him.

Cold silence stilled the air. Then glass shattered, and Duncan heard the distinct sound of an old man being punched in the gut. Lucy's eyes widened as the punches continued. With each blow, Walter's voice asked the same question in one word, spoken loud enough to be heard clearly even in the basement.

"Verido?"

Punch.

"Verido?"

Punch.

"Verido?"

Lucy brought her mouth close to Duncan's ear. "What are we going to do?"

Feeling every bit the coward, he shook his head. "That's Nelson Walter up there. If we go up, we'll be killed."

"Over an old magician?"

"Walter believes this door is real magic just like me."

Lucy's eyes drifted to the door when Wilkinson finally cried out for mercy. He spoke for a moment, soft and unclear. But it was clear enough to satisfy Walter.

A final punch sent Wilkinson crashing through furniture. Two sets of footsteps strolled out of the house. Wilkinson did not stir.

"I think they killed him," Lucy said, making to go upstairs.

Duncan put a hand on her arm. "Wait."

"But that old man—"

"Wait." Duncan listened close for another minute, all the time gripping Lucy's arm. Finally, he heard Walter's car turn over and, a moment later, the sound of gravel under wheels. "Now, they're gone." He set her free.

They flew up the stairs and into the showroom. Wilkinson lay in the corner amongst toppled books and magazines. Bruises mottled his face and blood streamed from a gash in his forehead.

"Get some towels or something for that wound," Duncan said, and Lucy rushed to the kitchen.

"D-Don't worry," Wilkinson struggled to say. "I—"

"Shh." Lucy pressed a white towel against Wilkinson's head.

"You what?" Duncan asked.

Lucy scowled. "He's been beaten to a pulp. Let him be."

"Sorry. Would you get him some water, please?" Duncan took over on the towel and waited until Lucy left the room. Then he spun back on Wilkinson. "What were you trying to say?"

"V-Verido."

Duncan heard Lucy opening and closing cupboard doors.

"What about him?"

"Like you, they wanted his real name, and ..."

Duncan heard water filling in a glass. "And what? What did you say to them?"

Wilkinson's head drooped back.

For the longest second of his life, Duncan was sure the old man had died. He thought he smelled Death. But then he saw the old man's chest rise, and he heard a gurgling in the old man's throat. Lucy returned with the water, and as she leaned the glass to Wilkinson's mouth, Duncan noticed blood near his waist.

"I think he's broken some ribs," Duncan said.

"We need to call the police. We need help."

"Absolutely not. The kind of guy Walter is, he probably owns half the police in Pennsylvania."

"Then we'll have to hope for the other half to answer our call."

"You don't understand. We cannot have the police involved. You'll be in too much danger."

"Me? Why would the police be after me?" She took one look at Duncan and her jaw set in anger. "This is another damn secret, isn't it? Tell me why the police will be after me."

Duncan paced the room, wrapping his arms around his head as if this could hold back his words. "Not the police. Walter. He threatened to harm you. To make me do what he wanted, he threatened your life. He'll do it, too. You'll end up worse than this guy."

Wilkinson coughed and blood spurted out his mouth.

"That doesn't make sense. Walter doesn't even know me."

"He knows everyone and everything in Reedsburg. He's had his eye on you and Vincent for a long time. He wants the Door, and you two were the only ones pursuing magic deeply enough to find it."

Lucy frowned. "Until you came along."

"I swear I didn't know what he was really after. When he hired me to join the magic club, I thought he wanted to swipe a few of Vincent's card tricks, maybe write a book of his own. I never knew—"

"You've been working for him?"

"He forced me. He would've killed me, if I didn't help."

"You see what happens with all these secrets? You see?"

"I'm sorry."

"No more. This is over."

"Lucy, don't say that."

She stood, her face red with fury even as her eyes welled up. "I could have taken a lot from you. I have already. I even was willing to follow you down this crazy path. But it seems we keep coming back to this same part of you. These secrets upon secrets."

"Please, let me—"

"I don't care. You go do whatever your secrets require you to do. I won't go any further. I won't go to the police, so don't worry. But you help me get this man into the car. He's going to die if we don't get him to a hospital, at least."

Duncan tried to speak to her as he assisted Wilkinson to the car, but Lucy refused to engage him. Her stern face cut apart all of his pleading. He rested Wilkinson across the back seat, and then opened the passenger side door.

"I forgot my purse," Lucy said. "It's in the kitchen."

Duncan jogged into the house and made his way back to the kitchen. The counter was bare. "Lucy, wait!" he called out, but she had already driven away.

CHAPTER 25

Duncan stared at the empty driveway like a dog waiting for his owner to return. She had to come back. She wouldn't just leave him.

Except that he hurt her. Time and again, he built up her trust and then smashed it apart with his secrets.

Except he couldn't tell her the truth. He had tried to give her as much as made any semblance of sense. More than that and she would doubt his sanity beyond the playful way she had already questioned him.

Except all his holding back had resulted in him standing alone in Gettysburg.

Duncan rubbed the back of his neck. He looked at the gravel pebbles, and a swift kick sent a smattering of them across the grass. His heart felt like those little rocks strewn out by Lucy's kick.

He lost track of time. Ten, maybe fifteen minutes passed by and he remained standing on the gravel drive. Slowly, his brain poked through the thick gauze of heartache that dulled him.

He remembered that he came from 2013 and had fallen into 1934 because of one thing — the Door. He remembered what had tangled him in these relationships in an effort to find his way home — the Door. He remembered why he had pursued

Verido all the way to Gettysburg — the Door.

Lucy had been a mistake. No matter what he felt for her, and he suspected he would continue to feel a great deal for a long time, they were worse than star-crossed lovers. They were time-crossed lovers. The longer he spent indulging his desires for her, the more damage he created for the world and for her. Already he had done so much to alter Time that perhaps he wouldn't want to see what the world was like in the future. Perhaps he had destroyed everything worthwhile about going home.

"Doesn't matter," he muttered. Nothing had changed regarding Nelson Walter. Lucy or no Lucy, Duncan still had to protect her. Love was like that.

Duncan gazed down the still road. "Goodbye, Lucy."

Walking back into the house with a firm, steady stride, Duncan headed straight for the phone sitting on a small table underneath the stairs. He had one piece of information, and he had to make use of it before Walter did the same.

With the receiver held to his ear with one hand, and the mouthpiece held with the other, Duncan tapped for the operator.

"How may I help you?" a voice said on the other end of the line.

"I'm trying to contact Dominic Rosini."

"Is this a local call?"

"I think so. I don't really know."

"One moment please."

While he waited, Duncan wished once more for a computer. In the short time he waited, he could have easily googled Rosini, found several addresses and phone numbers scattered across the country, located numerous photos of Verido related materials, seen an aerial view and a street view of each address, and been on his way to hunting down the correct home. Instead, he paced the worn carpet and ignored the bloody glass in the corner.

"I'm sorry, sir," the voice returned. "There's no Dominic Rosini in Gettysburg. There are several D. Rosinis in

Harrisburg. Would you like one of them?"

"No, thank you." Duncan hung up. There were probably several more D. Rosinis in Pittsburgh and even more in Philadelphia and tons in all of the United States, let alone the world. He needed something to specify which Rosini he sought before he could get any help from the phone company. He needed another clue.

But I've got one. Running through to the kitchen and down the stairs, Duncan reached the back of the basement. The Door. That was the other clue he had. Better still, it was something Walter did not have.

Blowing off dust, Duncan searched the Door starting in the top right corner and working his way down and across until he hit the bottom left corner. He moved in a slow, deliberate pace, investigating every notch, every mark, every bump and bruise in the wood. He paid close attention to the hardware — an art deco, black metal plate with a glass knob. The plate had been stamped 1928 but wear had obscured the city name.

That was the closest he came to finding anything regarding a city, and it meant nothing. Rosini could have bought the hardware anywhere in the country. The knob looked like any other he had seen in the last few days.

Wait. Not exactly like any other knob. The Door lay flat on the table. Flat. That meant the knob on the opposite side had been removed, otherwise the Door would be propped up at a slight angle.

Carefully, Duncan ran his fingers along the edges of the door. He didn't feel anything odd. He looked over it and saw no sign of anything wrong. Wilkinson never struck Duncan as the kind that would have booby trapped a door, but from what he heard about Rosini, a little caution seemed prudent.

"Here goes nothing," he said to the room and lifted the bottom half of the door first. Disrupted dust plumed around him, and he had to put the door back before he dropped it. Rubbing his stinging eyes, he coughed and hacked, spitting up dust and mucus. Each time he inhaled, his lungs filled with more dust and the hacking continued.

He had to tramp upstairs for fresh air. After a few minutes passed, he regained control but his eyes itched and he had the constant sensation that another coughing fit would erupt with every breath. He wanted to wait a little longer, but he knew that Walter would not be wasting any time in this search.

Covering his mouth in the neck of his shirt, Duncan hurried downstairs and waved away some of the dust fog. Once in the back, he turned the same half of door over. He moved it slower this time, trying to keep the dust plumes to a minimum. When he finished, he turned to top half over. He still coughed but the shirt helped.

As the dust found new places to light upon, Duncan spied a yellowed envelope stuck in the top of the knobless hardware. He grabbed the envelope and hurried back upstairs. In the clear air of the kitchen, he saw the envelope had been addressed to Wilkinson in a neat but shaky handwriting.

Duncan removed the letter inside and read:

Dear Claude,

I'm sorry to have left you and my colleagues in such an abrupt manner. It had never been my plan and while I know I am breeching the contract with you which I signed, I pray you can forgive this transgression. No harm to you or the Wonders Show, financial or otherwise, was ever intended. But events have transpired, which you will undoubtedly learn of, that require my exit from a life of performance. No matter what some may charge, I ask that you have faith in me, your loyal servant of the stage. I am no monster and my mind is as cogent and sane as yours. I have never harmed another with my show and I never will. I care too much about my art to do so.

Unfortunately, my sudden departure has also put a strain on my means. If you can find it in your heart to send me the funds for the final week of performances I fulfilled, I would be eternally grateful. I need to rebuild and those monies will be crucial to my survival.

Please consider this request as coming from a man that has always considered you, and hopes to continue considering you, a friend.

*Always my best to you,
Rufus Clubb*

Duncan re-read the letter. *Who the heck was Rufus Clubb?* He wracked his brain for the name, going over all the history of magic Pappy had instilled in him, but he could not find the name. He thought about those who wrote for *The Sphinx, Jinx,* or other magic magazines, names like Mulholland, Brush, and Annemann. But those didn't seem to have anything to do with this nor could Duncan recall any name ever being associated with The Wilkinson's Wonders Show. He'd never even heard of Wilkinson's show before all of this.

The letter had to be from Rosini. Not only had Duncan found the letter clinging to Rosini's Door of Vanishing, but the content of the letter could be easily referring to the incidents of disappearing audience members who never returned. The name Rufus Clubb had to be a false name, merely a simplistic diversion.

Duncan checked the envelope. Sure enough, he found a return address for a home in Lancaster, Pennsylvania. Since the letter never specified an address, Duncan felt confident the return address was authentic. Why give a false address if the goal was to be mailed money?

Lancaster would take an hour, maybe two hours, to reach by car. He could be there by early evening if he got moving soon.

But Lucy took the car.

Duncan stepped outside and followed the driveway around back. A large shed with peeling green paint stood about twenty feet off the back corner of the house. Locked. Through a dirty window, he peered into the shed. A car that looked old even compared to the ones he saw daily sat inside.

He hurried back to the house and searched the kitchen for keys. Nothing. He checked around the showroom, focusing hard on the area Wilkinson had collapsed upon. Nothing. He went upstairs and checked the bedrooms. Bingo. In the bedside table, a ring of about ten keys.

Back outside, he found the shed key on the fourth try. The car revved up on the seventh.

As he sat in the shed, letting the engine warm while he familiarized himself with the machine, a feeling of confidence overcame him. More than that, though, he had the secure sense that this was right. That this was the path he should be taking. He had been in 1934 far too long.

Lucy would never have encountered the treacherous world of Nelson Walter had she not met Duncan. At least, not in the same way. Even if Vincent had become mixed up with Walter, Lucy would have simply been a side issue instead of main threat to Walter's plans.

This was for the best. He couldn't provide her the full truth that she sought. Even if he brought her to the future, he could not see himself confessing to the lowlife world he had inhabited before. What would she think of people like Pancake? What would she think about how he had used Pancake?

This made more sense. They had shared in a touch of something special, and he knew many people who would never get a glimpse of that something. To demand more would be arrogant and greedy. He would have to hold on to Lucy in his memory for all its deep, endless value. Because there would be no more.

It was time to drive to Lancaster. It was time to find Rosini. It was time to get the Door and go home.

PART IV
1934

Starting on your left and moving right,
deal the five face down cards into a row.

Think of a number *between* one and five.
This is your secret number.

Count that many cards from left to right.

Turn over the card at your secret number face up.
Beginning on this face up card, count again,
moving to the right.

If you reach the end,
simply loop back to the left side and continue.

Repeat until four cards are face up and one is face down.

CHAPTER 26

THE DRIVE TO LANCASTER TOOK LONGER than Duncan had expected. Had he known how to drive in 1934, he would have made it with time to spare. But sitting behind the wheel of a massive body of metal that lacked all the aerodynamic and ergonomic designs of the modern day proved as difficult as he feared. Turning the wheel became a full workout since power-steering had yet to be invented. And without the aid of rack-and-pinion steering, Duncan had to turn the wheel and turn the wheel and turn the wheel just to get the darn thing out of the driveway. However, after a little time, he adjusted, and since much of the road to Lancaster passed through open farmland, he encountered few obstacles (such as other cars) to deal with. He hit the worst traffic in York and consequently stalled the car twice, but eventually he pulled through.

Though Lancaster dated back to the Revolutionary War (and beyond), the city was still rather small in 1934. None of the sprawl that would eventually eat up all the precious farmland and push out many of the Amish had yet to occur. As a result, Duncan found the address well before he reached where the city stood.

He pulled up the drive, and what he saw in the yellow headlights sucker-punched his gut — a dilapidated farmhouse with a wide hole in the roof. The rest of the roof retained shingles sporadically while one side of the house appeared to lean over as if daring to collapse. The pasture fencing looked rusted and several posts lay askew or were missing entirely. Weeds encroached on all sides.

Duncan walked onto the covered porch, his steps forcing the wood to whine and groan. A breeze picked up as the sky darkened. Nailed to the front door, a piece of paper fluttered — *Notice of Foreclosure.*

Duncan ripped the paper from the door. Angling it to catch what he could of the car's headlights, he read the formal, official detail of a mortgage that had gone unpaid for over a year. A year. Rosini had abandoned this address long ago. He could be anywhere.

It's over. I've reached the end.

The wind grabbed the paper and flew it into the distance. Duncan watched it go, its flapping noise mocking him, and his heart sank. This address had been his last lead. He had nothing else. Not even Lucy. He had ruined his relationship with the only woman he ever understood the word *Love* and had gained nothing for it.

"It's not fair." He pressed his forehead against the front door.

With a fist, he thumped the door repeatedly. Each time, the strike grew stronger. He rolled his head back and forth, his frustration mounting a greater assault through his fist. Then he kicked the foot of the door.

"It's not fair," he said louder. He whirled around, stomped to the edge of the porch and screamed out, "It's not fair!"

Red faced, he turned around and thrust-kicked the door as hard as he could manage. The old door splintered. Duncan kicked it again, aiming for the lock. A third kick slammed the door open, shredding the framework in the process.

Grunting, he trudged into the home. Anything he thought he could destroy, he attempted to do so. He scoured every room for any discarded items to unleash his frustrations upon. Most of the place lay barren, but he found enough — the stair's handrail, a forgotten chair, a bathroom mirror. Each one took the brunt of his rage until it had been strewn across the floor in numerous pieces.

When he reached the front door again, he stood in the entranceway, huffing for air, staring at nothing. His mind blanked. No planning. No recounting his steps. Nothing. His thoughts became as empty as he felt inside.

He might have remained standing there into the night if not for a simple, basic need. His stomach growled. At first, he ignored his hunger, but the growling continued and soon he felt sharp pangs. After an hour passed, his shoulders drooped and he slipped back into the car like a criminal slinking off under cover of dark. Nobody witnessed his outburst nor his relenting to hunger, but he felt judgmental eyes upon him nonetheless.

He drove in a haze, heading toward Lancaster City but not really paying close attention to anything around him. By the time he stopped at a roadside diner, darkness had taken over the sky and his heart.

"Sit where ya want," a pencil-thin waitress with a brunette bob said in a voice as tired and beaten as Duncan felt.

He settled in a booth near the back of the narrow diner and watched the waitress at work. She looked every bit of a woman in the '30s. He could write her history, it read so clearly on her face. A free spirit type of gal who spent the last part of the 1920's in a flapper dress, dancing and drinking through the speakeasies, always on the arm of a well-dressed guy, having a blast every night. Until the stock market crashed. The married men who paid her way no longer could afford a mistress. Broke and getting older, she lost the charm that paved her road on the party circuit. She probably came back to the Pennsylvania farmland because her parents lived around here. Except they didn't want anything to do with her. She had shamed them, perhaps insulted them when she left, maybe even said something foolish about never having to see them again. So, now she was stuck in this diner, wondering if this was all her life would amount to.

"You want a coffee?" she asked as she poured him a cup.

"Thanks. Can I get some eggs? Overeasy?"

"Honey, you can get anything Jackie can make. You want toast with that?"

"Please."

"Coming up." A bell jingled as new customers walked in. The waitress craned her neck and called out, "Sit where ya want. I'll be right there."

After she left, Duncan took off his fedora and placed it on the table. He looked at its brim and the band running around the base. He might be wearing this for the rest of his life. What he wouldn't give for a pair of jeans, a plain t-shirt, and some beat-up sneakers. Comfortable clothing for a comfortable world.

But that world was gone forever. Not only because he couldn't get back but because he had changed things. He had messed with the past, so what was the point in getting back anyway? Before he would have had Lucy by his side to face whatever the new future brought. But now ...

Strange how he never felt lonely in his old life. Without Lucy, though, it all seemed empty. Like some clever magic trick, she slipped away without him ever getting a grasp on what had happened until it was too late. Yet another marker to remind him that he had fallen in love — the real thing — and had lost that love to his stupid situation. How else to explain this dark loneliness plaguing him?

At length, his food arrived but he found his appetite had waned. He tucked into it anyway, more to waste the time than anything else. A few conversations murmured around him but most of his meal passed to the music of forks and knives clicking against plates. The waitress cleared his plate and refilled his coffee. He knew he should get out of there. Drive off and hole up somewhere that would limit his contact with the world. Maybe he could hire a private detective to find Rosini.

That idea struck him as pretty good. A detective would know how to find somebody in this era far better than Duncan, and a detective could do so without causing as many ripples in time. Only one problem — a peek into Duncan's wallet confirmed that he had about ten dollars left. If he hired anybody, he would have to find some money soon. Of course, he could always play cards for the cash. Yet part of him balked at the idea as if he had a tiny Lucy on his shoulder, whispering in his ear, telling him to become a better man.

Jeez. I'm starting to think like a 1930s movie.

As he sipped his coffee, a sporty car zoomed by, tearing up the road even by Duncan's standards. A few feet beyond the diner, the driver slammed on the breaks, burning the tires into the road with a high screech. The few diners, the waitress, Jackie, and Duncan all stared at the small red break lights. The car idled, exhaust clouding the lights. Then the car backed up and turned into the parking area of the diner.

Everybody resumed eating or cooking or waitressing. Except Duncan. He watched as Nelson Walter stepped out of the car and lugged his bulk toward the diner.

A hush like a nighttime snowfall blanketed the room. Walter had to move sideways down the aisle yet none of the patrons dared to say a word as he brushed by them. When he reached Duncan, sweat dappled his face. He slid in on the opposite side and dabbed his forehead with a napkin.

"What can I get ya?" the waitress asked.

Walter shook his head, and she walked away. He raised his index finger and pointed it straight at Duncan. Once Duncan focused entirely on the finger, Walter turned his finger toward the car, still idling.

Duncan looked closer, a bad twist forming in his gut. He saw Freddie outside, leaning against the car's long hood. Two figures huddled in the back seat. At first, Duncan couldn't make them out. He squinted and inched closer to the diner window. Then he knew how awful the world could be. He shouldn't have been surprised, but he was. In the back seat — Lucy and Vincent.

He faced Walter, whose sadistic smile chilled his skin.

Walter pulled out a deck of cards and set it on the table. "Time for me to show you a trick."

Chapter 27

Duncan placed his elbows on the booth table and pressed his mouth against his laced fingers. To most, he looked thoughtful. To some, he might even have looked threatening. In truth, he wanted to hide the fact that he had almost thrown up his eggs.

"Why are you all the way out here?" Walter asked. "We spent a long time looking for you and ended up in the middle nowhere. All I can think is that you and your lady were planning on getting away from me. You split up to make it more difficult to follow you, and then maybe you're heading for the train station. Lancaster's got a good one. You can head off most anywhere. Was that your plan before I got your girl into my car?"

"I've been looking for Verido and the Door, just like you asked."

Walter picked up the cards and shuffled them. "I learned a long time ago that a magician's trade said a lot about life. I mean this sincerely. Think about it. Life and magic. It's all about getting everybody else to see each moment the way you want it to be seen. A person skilled at life, like a skilled magician, can shape a moment, an experience, to be whatever he wants it to be. Doctors can convince a patient he's sick when everything is fine. Lawyers can take a guy caught in the act of a crime and convince a jury the guy's innocent. Politicians — well, reshaping reality is their stock and trade, ain't it? It's controlled perspective. There are people, for example, who think of me as the most magnanimous, kind, and giving man they know. Others see me as a prosperous, intelligent business man."

"And then there's those of us who know you."

Walter winked as if Duncan's comment were an old joke between friends. "I admit my methods can be harsh. But it's a harsh world. With the Door, with me in charge of the only organized family, well then, the world will be a little less harsh. Maybe you and your gal could settle down and forget all about those of us who have to make the tough calls."

"Is that what these threats are? Some tough calls?"

"You're not listening. Magic, Life — it's the same thing. A magician chooses what reality spectators will see. That's exactly what everybody tries to do in life. Some of us are more capable than others, but in the end, we all try. And in doing so, we tell our life's story."

Duncan wanted to say more, but he merely shook his head. The cigar smell drenching Walter sickened Duncan's already sour stomach.

"Here's a story for you," Walter said as he squared the deck. With a flourish and a snap of the cards, he cut directly to the Queen of Hearts. "There once was a girl named Lucy. A sweet, lovely girl who wants to please the men in her life. She's also got spunk, which is probably what attracts a guy like you. And that drives her to think she's your equal. Like the queen, she won't be happy merely serving, but she must also share the rule."

He flipped the deck over, pulled the Queen from the bottom and turned it face up on the top of the deck. Then with one quick cut, a face up card popped out of the middle of the face down deck. The Joker stared at Max with its mischievous, daring grin.

"This is Vincent," Walter continued. "Brother to the Queen,

and a wild card at that." He shored up the deck and fanned the Queen and Joker on the table. "These two are fine on their own. They struggle to make their life work, but they manage. The Joker gets into trouble and the Queen bails him out. Partly because he's family. Partly because he has a gift. See, the Joker has his passion and talent for cards, and they both pray that this will lead them to a life of riches. It's that reality they try to create that leads him to this small town in Pennsylvania."

Walter performed a series of cuts and shuffles, dropping bits of the deck into a small pile until he was left with one card. "This is where I come in." He revealed the King of Clubs. "Not the most powerful King in the deck, but a King nonetheless. Now if this King never came into contact with the Joker, if the Joker never sought Verido, if the Queen wasn't so damn smart, and most of all, if you — a nothing Two of Clubs — hadn't come into the area, then none of this would be happening. But those things did happen."

He placed the King on the top of the deck and held it facing Duncan. "So now we have a battle of magicians. Lowly Two of Clubs, wild Joker, and a King all trying to shape how the others see things. You want the Door to impress your Queen. Joker wants the Door to impress the world. And I want it," he said, rubbing his hand over the King until it disappeared, "so that I can use its power to make a better world for every damn one of us." He spread the deck across the table. Sitting in the middle of all those face down cards was one card face up — the King of Clubs.

"The problem here," he went on, "is that you keep getting into the mix of things." He laid his hand flat over the Queen and Joker. Spreading his fingers apart in a fast motion, he revealed a third card, face down, nestled between the Queen and Joker. "Meddling like you do can be good for you at times. It certainly brought you close to these two people. But it can also be dangerous. For you, and for them." He turned the card over. The Ace of Spades.

Duncan's eyes widened. The Ace of Spades was also known as the Death card. He sat back and folded his arms across his chest. Another move that put on a brave face despite the horror he felt churning inside. "Why don't you stop toying with me?"

"I need you to figure out the Door. I could do it myself, perhaps, but I've learned that some people are better suited for certain tasks. It'll be easier, faster, and less messy to have you handle this end of things."

"Sorry, but it's over. I can't find Verido which means I can't find the Door which means I haven't got anything to figure out."

"You'll keep trying." He tapped the Ace of Spades. "I'm confident of that. I don't trust you about anything except your Queen of Hearts. You'll keep at this for her sake. I have no doubt."

"I haven't a single lead. This farmhouse here was my last chance. I don't know what name he's using, I don't know what he looks like, I don't know if he's even around here anymore."

Walter picked up a card from the deck and placed it face down in front of Duncan. "That's what Uncle Nelson is for. Freddie and I paid a visit to an old employer of Verido. He told us the name the man is using now, and I've written it on this card for you." He grabbed Duncan's wrist. "You try and screw me over, I'll play that Ace of Spades."

"I'm well aware."

"And you, Duncan Rose, will play the patsy."

"How could it be any other way?"

Walter scooted out of the booth. "Your Uncle Nelson has one more gift for you. I figure you could always use some help, and the way you're whining and complaining, I know I'm right. So I'm loaning you the assistance of my most trusted man, Freddie. Consider him my surrogate while I spend time watching over your Queen and Joker."

Duncan looked at the card in front of him while Walter side-stepped his way out of the diner. Walter acted like this would change everything. Except Duncan not only knew the name but he also knew it led to a dead end.

He tried to muster the strength to turn the card over, but he sat there. Not only had he lost his chance for finding the Door, but now Lucy and Vincent were doomed to an awful death. The weight of it all pressed him low into his seat.

Glancing outside, Duncan watched as Walter gave Freddie some final instructions. He wanted to avert his eyes, but he couldn't stop himself from peering into the car. Lucy's eyes were wet and her mouth quivered as she darted from looking at her hands while Vincent spoke to pressing against the car window, searching for a sign of help. Vincent looked perturbed, but even at that distance, Duncan could tell it was an act. Walter had probably picked him up the other day, so while his initial fears had mellowed by now, he still knew they were in big trouble. Though neither of them appeared to notice Duncan, he felt their eyes upon him, pleading with him to find a way to save them.

He looked back at the table, his fingertips nudging the card. He knew the name written on it and yet as long as the card remained face down, it wasn't real. When he turned it over, when he saw *Dominic Rosini* scrawled across the card, all chances of saving Lucy and Vincent would vanish like a magic trick gone awry.

Walter got in the car and drove off. Duncan eyed the empty spot and tried to blot out the horrible images his mind conjured of what Walter would do to Lucy.

"What do ya want, big guy?" the waitress asked Freddie as he entered.

Duncan flicked the edge of the card. He heard Freddie ask for a menu and a coffee. That burly man's voice grated into Duncan and his imagination unleashed. He saw Freddie's eager hands on Lucy, his slobbering lips on Lucy, his overpowering weight pressing on Lucy. He saw Walter holding a gun to Vincent's head, forcing him to watch.

I can't let that happen. I have to save them both.

Duncan flipped the card. He stared at the Jack of Diamonds and the name written across the top — *Carl Wolfe*. It's wrong — Wilkinson had given the wrong name. And that meant Walter really needed Duncan for the moment.

Freddie settled into the same spot Walter had used. "What are you grinning about?"

"Nothing," Duncan said, trying to clear his face. He had a sliver of leverage. Blowing it with a bad poker face would be unforgivable.

"Right." Freddie buried his head in his menu.

Duncan stared at the card, the false name, and tried to think of what to do. The fact that the real name led to an empty farmhouse had not changed. Had he lived in the era longer, he would know how to find a man without a computer. But he was a child of the Information Age, not the Jazz Age.

Freddie peeked at Duncan's empty plate. "What did you eat?"

"Eggs. Why?"

"Were they any good?"

"I suppose."

"Yeah, I don't know." He returned to the menu.

Duncan wracked his mind for a simple solution. Despite this change, he was still in tremendous trouble. The false name gave him a slight advantage, but he would have to stay ahead of Walter and Freddie if he wanted to keep that advantage alive. That would be hard with Freddie "assisting" him. Yet even a sliver of leverage could grow into something bigger, something better.

Chapter 28

Freddie ordered the eggs after all.

Duncan observed him eating — not a particularly pleasant sight; Freddie tended to let his food hang half-out of his mouth before slurping it in. Despite the grotesque scene, Duncan continued to watch, searching for tells that would help. Not gambling tells, but tells that would clue him in to how to control the situation.

"So," Duncan said as Freddie shoveled in another mouthful of scrambled eggs, this time dipped in ketchup, "you've been demoted to babysitter."

Freddie glanced up. "Takes more than a babysitter to do my job."

"Oh, that's right. You're also Walter's thug."

"You trying to tick me off?"

"No, no. But let's be honest, that's why you're here, right? I mean, if I screw up, you're going to hurt me, right?"

"Shut up."

"Isn't that what you do? Isn't that why a man like Walter hires you?"

"Let me tell you something." Freddie pointed his thick finger at Duncan. "A man like Nelson Walter is special. Not just anybody can be him. Why do you think there's only one

President or one King in a country? It's because only a special kind of man can do that job. You gotta be smarter than everybody and have the strength to make everybody follow you. You gotta be able to see ahead, know what others are gonna do. Be a real, um, what do you call it? A real strategy man. And, yeah, sometimes you have to use force. That's what I'm good at. I ain't saying I like it or agree with it always, but it's the way it is."

"Does that include the little back room and the golf club?"

"See, that's why Mr. Walter is the King and you're just a peasant. You don't know the hard things a real man's got to do to keep everyone in line. You don't have the guts to do what's needed."

"Still means you're just my babysitter. At least for now."

"You watch your mouth."

"Maybe I'm wrong. Maybe you can beat me up whenever you want. Then again, I'd imagine your boss wouldn't like me getting hurt anymore. Not right now. After I find the Door for him, sure. He'll throw me to you like a bone to dog."

"I ain't no dog."

"Of course not. You're an independent kind of man. Loyalty is nothing to you."

Freddie plunked down his fork. "Hey, I been nothing but loyal to Mr. Walter, and I'll be nothing but loyal to him. You think you're going to talk me into betraying him, you're out of your head."

"All I was saying was—"

"You want to help your girlfriend, then you listen to me — do what Mr. Walter told you to do. Find the Door." Freddie gave one sharp nod as if that made his point, picked up his fork, and returned to his meal.

Easier said.

Tapping his chin with the bottom of a spoon, Duncan regrouped. He knew Verido's real name, Dominic Rosini, and he knew that Nelson Walter had the wrong name. He knew that Verido faked a letter to Wilkinson asking for money and signed it Rufus Clubb, and that letter led to an abandoned farmhouse.

A thought struck Duncan and he used all his card cheating skills to look as frightened and unsure as he had been looking since Freddie arrived. He couldn't let on that he knew something far more important than all the rest — he knew magicians. If he wanted to find Verido, he had to start thinking like the man. Instead of a skilled magician from the twenty-first century, he had to think like an old-time magician, one who thrived on the image of mystery, the occult, and the idea that he alone had knowledge of secrets to powers that others only dreamed of.

If Duncan had been that kind of magician and wanted to disappear from the law and the world, how would he do it? A lot of early tricks were based on basic mathematic principles, except the majority of those tricks were the small, up close variety. Erasing a person from the world was a much larger trick and it most readily fit in the category of an illusion.

Big stage illusions relied heavily on all kinds of misdirection — diversions of one kind or another designed to draw the audiences' eyes away from where the trick really took place. So what kind of misdirection would Rosini require? For starters, he would have a false identity that he could utilize when contacting others. One like Rufus Clubb, for example.

Duncan thought over the note Wilkinson had kept hidden in the Door. Wilkinson said that he hadn't spoken to Rosini in years, so why would Rosini make contact suddenly? As Clubb, he had reached out to a man he knew could have been angry at being abandoned, could have turned him in to the police, or could even have concocted a lie to loose tough guys like Nelson Walter on him. What was so important as to risk an already successful escape?

The answer came in a flash — money.

The note had explicitly asked for it and in the hard times of The Great Depression, Rosini may have been in a financial situation so desperate that he saw no other choice. But he had a major problem. The law wanted him in connection to the disappearances during his stage show, and since nobody had turned up, those disappearances were starting to look like murder.

"He never meant to get the money himself," Duncan blurted out.

"Huh?" Freddie said.

Using a false name helped, but that didn't mean he could trust Wilkinson with the rest. The address may actually have belonged to Rufus Clubb, if there ever had been a man with that name, but that was all part of the illusion. If Dominic Rosini wanted to vanish and stay vanished, he needed for Wilkinson to think the money had been sent to the right address. That way, if the police questioned him, Wilkinson could only tell them where he mailed the money to.

Think, think, think.

Stage illusions were not Duncan's forte, but he understood the basic principles. And the most basic part of a stage act, especially one in the 30s, would be having a beautiful assistant — eye candy being one of the best misdirection techniques. So, Rosini required an accomplice. But how would that person get the money from the farmhouse without the police knowing, if they were watching, or the real Clubb, if he existed?

The ideas that came to Duncan all utilized modern surveillance — mini-cameras with a direct feed to a smartphone or a laptop, or even something as simple as night vision goggles. How would a man in the 1930s, one who was a criminal (at least, technically), solve this problem? As Freddie slurped his coffee, Duncan smiled.

"Let me ask you something." Duncan waited for Freddie to set his coffee down. "If you wanted money mailed to a false address so you could get it without anybody knowing, and it was possible that the cops were watching the address you gave, how would you get the money?"

Freddie gestured to the waitress for the check. "I don't talk with you. Understand? Just find the Door so I can go home."

"This is about the Door."

"How's this about the Door?"

"Look, I'm trying to do what your boss wants me to do, and

he said you were here to help me. You don't help me, I can't do what he wants. That means we both fail him. You want to be responsible for screwing this whole thing up?"

As Freddie dug out his wallet, he scrunched his face at Duncan. "You say you want money sent to an address for a pick up?"

"Yeah, but nobody can know. Whoever lives at the address doesn't know. Even the guy sending the money doesn't know what's going on exactly, though he might know more of it than anybody else."

"Doesn't really matter. The only way you'll succeed is to have some help."

"I figured that much."

"If you're so damn smart, then stop asking me."

"But how do you use this person? Won't he be caught the moment he starts checking the mailbox of a stranger?"

"Which is why only a stupid person would do that. No, if you want to do something like this, you got to have a guy on the inside."

"Like a cop?"

"If you can get the cop watching the house, that'd make it simple. But cops out here aren't as easy to bend as those in a big city, and those that are already on the take belong to somebody else. You don't get a cop on your side for one job. It's a career move for them. Changes their entire lives. So, unless you're putting them on your payroll, that wouldn't work."

"Then what?"

"I'd find someone who works for the Post Office to help you out. Have him be looking for the false address with a specific return address, then he intercepts the letter and the police can sit on the house all they want."

"Because the letter never gets delivered." A great illusion. "That's how he did it."

"Did what?"

Duncan shot out of the booth. "Come on."

"Hey, I'm not done eating." Freddie hurried to catch up.

"What's going on?"
"We're going to the Post Office."

Chapter 29

Freddie did the driving. At least some good came from having him around — Duncan had no desire to get behind the wheel in the near future. But Duncan's good luck was short-lived. When they reached the square, brick building with a painted sign that read *US Post Office — Lancaster*, they found the doors locked and the lights off.

"What did you expect? It's four in the morning," Freddie grumbled. "I knew I could've finished my food."

"I thought they worked all night."

"Maybe in Chicago or New York, but out here, they'll start around five, maybe five-thirty, if Johnny and the boys drank too much."

"And Johnny runs the route?"

"No. But he'll help us. Now, I'm still hungry and I'm tired. We got at least an hour until anybody shows. So shut up and close your eyes." Freddie slouched down and tipped his hat over his face.

An hour. A long time to wait. An eternity. Duncan's instincts fired up. No need to waste this time. He had no solid idea of what lay ahead, but after years of card games, he knew how to plant a seed for later use.

"How'd you end up in this racket anyway?" he said.

"Go to sleep," Freddie said from beneath his hat.

"I'm serious. A guy like you could be doing a lot better than being Nelson Walter's monkey."

Freddie whipped his hat off. "I am my own man. You understand that? I chose to work for Mr. Walter and I can leave whenever I damn well wish. I'm no monkey."

"Then why do it? I don't mean the illegal stuff. I get that. Heck, I haven't worked on honest day in my life either. But Nelson Walter? You shouldn't be stuck in the middle of Bumpkinville, Pennsylvania. A guy as tough and smart as you should be connected in Chicago. That's where I see you."

"Yeah, well, life don't work out the way you want it, and it ain't worked out for Mr. Walter either. But I don't betray people who been good to me just because times get bad."

"Loyalty is an admirable thing. Provided the man you're loyal to deserves it."

Freddie squinted as if Duncan's words had soured his mouth. "You tell me. My pop lost a lot in the Crash but not everything. We could've made it. Instead he kicks my ma and me to the curb. Probably wanted to get rid of us since I was born, and now he had his excuse. My ma tried to get a job but that was a joke. It wasn't long until she became a whore and ditched me, too. Hell, I was sixteen, so why not? What did she need me hanging around for? I lived in the streets for a week or so. Then Mr. Walter found me and took me in. He took care of me, he provided for me, and he never once thought about tossing me away. So, you tell me. Who should I be loyal to?"

"I understand. I do. And when it comes to doing the things you've done to me, I don't begrudge you one bit. But what about women and children? I mean, do you really think you should be loyal to a guy who's roughing up Lucy just to get to me?"

"Nobody's roughing her up. You got my word on that. Vincent's another story, but she'll be fine."

"If I don't come through, he's going to take her into that back room. You know it."

"I won't let that happen."

"You won't have a choice."

"Listen, Mr. Walter can go overboard sometimes, I know. But that doesn't mean he ain't worth everything I do for him. He's lived a hard life, too. He knows how important it is to have people around you that you can trust. You know, you're playing this all wrong. Mr. Walter isn't just using you. He likes you. Likes the way you do those card tricks. I think he'd much rather you went along with us, became part of the group. And I don't think it's too late, neither. You do what he says, and you'll see. He'll reward you fine."

"Come on. You don't believe that. Not for me. Once he has the Door, he'll kill me — or he'll ask you to do it. And then he'll have you kill Vincent and then Lucy."

Freddie's hand snapped out and yanked on Duncan's tie. He curled his fist around it and shoved Duncan back against the car door. "You don't know nothing about this. And you don't know Mr. Walter. He ain't a backstabbing creep, and he don't kill women and children. You don't want to be in his good graces, that's your problem. But I'm telling you, so listen close — you do what he says and you and the girl and that fuck Vincent will all get out of this fine. You screw it up, and you'll find out just how hard a life I've lived."

With a flick of his hand, he released Duncan and settled back in his seat, once more laying his hat over his face. Though Duncan had not intended to rile Freddie so much, he liked the result. Whether or not he would be able to capitalize on it later remained to be seen but that was the way these things worked. If he kept hitting Freddie's sore points, it would keep the thug off-balance, keep him thinking with his emotions instead of his brain. That was often the best set up to cheat a mark.

For now, he had to let Freddie stew. Duncan checked his watch — not much time had passed. If he could manage it, sleep seemed the best thing to do. Down the road, he might not have the luxury. Though he closed his eyes, his mind refused to quiet, and he spent the next hour running one scenario after another like a parade of movie screens, each playing out different versions of the same story. Few of them ended well.

By the time the morning sun edged passed the roof of the post office, Freddie had been snoring like a rhino for a half-hour. Duncan poked him in the side three times before he woke. Snorting and startled, Freddie sat up, banging his knee on the steering wheel.

Squinting, he peered out at the dawn. He glanced around the parking area, pausing at the three cars that had slipped in while he had slept. "Follow me and don't say anything until we find the right man."

One step into the post office and Duncan knew that Freddie had muscled these guys before. They all ceased working and stared at Freddie like dogs that feared punishment would be dealt out soon. Freddie put out his hand to keep Duncan back.

He strolled deeper into the waiting room, a black-and-white tiled area with a long wood bench running the wall opposite a chest-high wooden counter. Freddie pushed open the door to the right of the counter and walked into the mail processing area. From the waiting room, Duncan watched through the opening above the counter.

As Freddie passed by clerks wearing visors on their balding heads and suspenders over their boney shoulders, Duncan witnessed the relief each clerk felt not to be the point of this disruption. Until Freddie stopped and the clerk before him shook hard enough to rattle the envelopes in his hand. Freddie leaned close to the clerk's ear and mumbled something. The clerk, shivering through each motion, reached across his desk, picked up a pencil, and scribbled on a piece of paper. Freddie snatched it away, read it, and then looked back at Duncan. Motioning with his head, Freddie whistled loudly. "Back here."

Duncan hurried through the door, navigating his way amongst the maze of desks and mail, making sure to avoid eye contact with the clerks, and reached Freddie in seconds. "What is it?"

Freddie handed the paper over. "Name of the letter carrier with your farmhouse in the route."

Duncan read: CLARENCE HOLSTEN. "Is Mr. Holsten

here yet?"

They looked at the clerk who nodded vigorously before pointing a quivering finger to the back.

As they weaved their way toward the back, the bustle of activity re-ignited behind them. Only one man worked in the back, taking stacks of envelopes and placing them in his own bag. The man was young, rather dumpy, and wore his slicked hair parted straight down the middle. He looked like a caricature of a man in a barbershop quartet.

"You Holsten?" Freddie barked.

The fellow dropped his envelopes into a disorganized slop on the floor. "Sheesh, you want to kill me? Don't scare a guy like that," he said in a whiny voice before bending down to pick up the envelopes.

"I'm gonna do a lot worse than scare you if you don't tell us what we want to know."

"W-What?"

Freddie shoved Holsten to the floor. "You were paid by a guy to watch for mail addressed to Rufus Clubb coming from Gettysburg. We want to know where that mail went."

"I don't know what you're talking abo—"

Freddie's fist popped Holsten in the mouth hard enough to knock the chubby man over. "You do know and you'll tell us, or I'm going to get angry."

As Freddie pressed upon Holsten further, Duncan had to admit that a guy like Freddie could be useful. Not that he wanted to consider what such ideas said about him in relation to Nelson Walter, but he recognized that without Freddie, he would probably still be in the waiting area attempting to charm whoever dealt with the public.

"Y-You shouldn't be here. I-I'll call for the police if you don't go."

Freddie grabbed the man by his suspenders and hauled him to his feet. Then, shoving his nose right against Holsten's, Freddie said, "I understand your problem. You're being paid well for this. Postman's wage won't keep a guy like you fat. You eat well and that costs money. But none of that should matter to you right now. See, if you don't start talking, I'm going to break your legs."

"No. Please don't. No, no, no." Tears dampened Holsten's face.

Duncan stepped forward. This, he decided, was what separated him from Walter. Nelson Walter would continue to sit back and watch this poor fellow be beaten for information. But Duncan couldn't do it. He tapped Freddie on the shoulder and gestured for the thug to back off.

"Sorry about him," Duncan said, watching Holsten's wild eyes settle into nervous curiosity.

"Who are you?"

"Doesn't matter. You need to be concerned with your situation, not who you're talking to." It hit Duncan that he had just set up Holsten with a good cop/bad cop routine. Though not his intention, Duncan decided to play it out for whatever it might be worth. He peeked over his shoulder as if concerned Freddie might jump in at any moment. "I don't know how long he'll listen to me, so don't waste this time."

"Look, pal, I'm not trying to do nothing except deliver the mail."

"Now, Clarence, don't start lying. You and I both know that you took money on the side to intercept some specific letters. We're not cops. We're not here to cause you trouble. But we need to know where those letters went and who they went to. Give us that and we'll be on our way."

"But—"

"Keep lying to me and I'll let Freddie do what he wants with you."

Clarence glanced around the room. Duncan could not tell if this was a search for escape or a search for privacy, but after his scan, Clarence lowered his head. "I'll admit that I took some money to get the Rufus Clubb letter but I won't be telling you no more. That guy can do things I never seen anybody do, and I don't want to be on his wrong side."

"You know whose wrong side you'll be in if you don't tell us, right?"

Clarence looked to Freddie and nodded on the verge of tears.

Duncan said, "You're telling me you'd rather let Freddie here beat you into mash, you'd rather piss off Nelson Walter, than cross some old magician?"

"Look, I need this job and I need his money. Okay? Nelson Walter's not going to kill me over a damn letter."

"You think this magician will?"

"I think this magician knows way too much about me to be normal."

Duncan pulled back a moment. He had no doubt that Freddie would work the guy over and get some kind of information from him — probably wouldn't be the right information, though. They would waste hours and by the time they came back, Clarence would be in another state. But Clarence feared magic in a clear and profound way. Anyone who would rather face Nelson Walter than a magician seriously believed in magic. Duncan could use that to his advantage, but it meant more than a card trick or two. He would have to rely on a psychological force which did not always pan out.

Lowering his voice and giving a furtive glance toward Freddie, Duncan said, "Clarence, you've got a real problem. I'm looking for this man *because* he's a magician. And that's because I'm a magician, too."

Clarence's eyes narrowed. "You're no magician. If you were, you wouldn't need that muscle."

"He doesn't know," Duncan whispered, "and I'd like to keep it that way."

"You're lying, and I've got mail to deliver."

"Think of a number between one and ten," Duncan said, splaying his fingertips near Clarence's head. "Got it? You thought of the number seven."

The shock on Clarence's face was enough. Duncan got it right. Though the odds were in his favor — eight out of ten times a person will pick seven as the number — he didn't like risking Lucy's life on the odds. For that matter, if this gambit failed, there would be no other immediate solution except for

Freddie, and Duncan did not want to become that kind of person.

"How'd you do that?" Clarence said, a new kind of tremor in his voice.

"I told you. I have real magic in me. How about this — think of card. Any card. Picture all the colors, big and bold in your mind." Again, Duncan splayed his fingers in an absurd show of mind-reading. "You've picked a Heart — King or the Queen — you're a bit fuzzy." Mentioning colors excludes black, and the words *big and bold* pushed people toward face cards. Odds favor the King or Queen of Hearts out of all in a deck.

"I picked the Queen."

Now that he had primed Clarence, Duncan had to sell the final threat. "Let's be clear on this. If I have to do so, I can pull the information I want straight out of your head. But if I do that, especially if you resist, there will be damage done. Even the little demonstration I just did has left its mark."

"You've damaged my brain."

"Quick, tell me what you thought while getting dressed this morning."

"Um, um."

"See that. Most people can answer within a second or two of thought, but you're struggling." Duncan had no idea if that statistic was true, but he figured Clarence didn't know either. "I'm asking you one last time to help me out. Refuse again, and I'm going to reach into your mind and grab what I need, no matter what it does to you. It's a risk you take. But then again, if you're brain gets screwed up, you can probably clean used bedsheets over at a whorehouse. I know one in Reedsburg that'll hire you. You ever hear of Lady Lane's?"

"Okay, okay," Clarence said, his hands covering his head to protect his brain.

"Write it down."

Clarence scribbled the address as fast as he could manage and thrust the paper at Duncan. "Now, go. Please. Don't ever come back."

"I want the name, too. Who did you send the envelope to at this address?"

"Fine, okay, give me that." Clarence snatched back the paper.

On it, Clarence wrote: DOMINIC ROSE.

CHAPTER 30

As Freddie drove the car across town, heading for the farmland between Lancaster and Philadelphia, Duncan tried not to betray the flipping, twisting, rattling of his mind.

Was Dominic Rose a relative? If so, then based on age, Dominic could actually be Pappy. That would explain a lot of things, chief among them — how Pappy ended up with the Door in the first place. It would explain why Pappy never discussed his past other than magic. It would explain why he taught Duncan all that he did. All because he knew that someday Duncan would come back in time to meet him, that Duncan would need all the skills he possessed.

Unless this was the first iteration of these events. In which case, Pappy would have had no clue that this would happen and it had all been coincidence. Except Duncan didn't believe in coincidences. Things that looked like coincidences were planned — not in the "everything happens for a reason" sort of way but rather in the "people are always trying to screw you" sort of way. And the man most trying to screw with Duncan at the moment was Nelson Walter.

If Dominic turned out to be Pappy, then what would Duncan's actions do to the future? He had done a good job of curbing these thoughts, dismissing these concerns, but he could not escape them any longer. In a short time, they would reach the Rose farm, and Duncan would have to make hard decisions. If, indeed, time travel went along with the butterfly effect. But maybe it didn't. Maybe the actions of someone as insignificant to the whole universe as Duncan would have minimal effect on the outcomes of the future. There was no way to be certain.

That did little to assuage his concerns. After all, he was leading Walter's man straight to the Door. If Duncan's presence in 1934 had already set history askew, he could barely conceive of what would happen when Walter started disposing of people through the Door. What had been considered murders before would now become unresolved missing person cases. People who would have buried their loved ones and learned to move on, would suffer an endless life of hoping for a reunion that would never arrive.

Duncan's thoughts settled one thing firmly in his mind — he had to limit Freddie's access to Dominic Rose. He had to keep Freddie feeling as if the man were in control but at the same time wrest that control away. Easy enough when playing cards, but Duncan suspected this game would be much more difficult to play.

As the car turned onto a dirt drive leading toward a white farmhouse a few acres back, Duncan felt woefully unprepared.

Chapter 31

Freddie shut off the engine, reached into his coat, and produced a snub-nose .38 Special. He opened the handgun and checked that it was fully loaded. Without looking up, he smirked. "Don't ask about the cop I took this from."

"Wait a second. We don't need guns here."

"This is the place, right? Then I got my orders."

Duncan peered out at the farmhouse, his mind whirring through angles and outcomes. "You go in there with your gun and you'll never see the Door, and Walter will be pissed off."

"Shut up. I know how to do this kind of thing."

"Then think for a second — this magician has gone to a lot of trouble to stay hidden. He's already scared of the police. He sees you coming with a gun and he'll vanish before you can get your finger on the trigger."

"He ain't Houdini."

"That's right. He's better. You ever hear of Houdini pulling off this Door of Vanishing trick? Besides, he's been hard enough to find once, we don't want him disappearing again. We'll never find him."

Freddie weighed it out, rocking his head from shoulder to shoulder as he thought. At length, he holstered his weapon. "Fine. I'll go in without showing the gun."

"He'll see it. Magicians like him train to observe little details. The slightest bulge in your coat will tip him off. And frankly, even without the gun, a big guy like you is going to make him nervous."

"Then what the hell do you suggest?"

"Let me go in by myself. I'm a fellow magician. I understand how he thinks, how to approach him, how to talk his language."

Crossing his arms as he strained his brain, Freddie said, "I don't know. Mr. Walter wouldn't like that."

With an incredulous look, Duncan said, "You really afraid I'm going to run? Look around you. Nothing but farmland. Where am I going to go? Besides, I've been wanting to meet this guy as much as Walter. Trust me, there's nothing to worry about here. Just wait a little bit so I can get him calm and open to meeting you. Then you can join us, and all will be fine. It'll be a lot better than scaring him off and never finding the Door."

"Okay," Freddie snapped. "Just shut up already. You yap like an old lady. Just get going. Don't take too long. I ain't staying back forever."

"Give me ten, fifteen minutes. That's all."

Duncan didn't wait around for a reply. Despite the heat, he buttoned up his coat, donned his hat, and moved at a brisk pace toward the front door. Like the house itself, the yard had been well maintained and free of clutter. The sweet farm aromas of earth and manure blended in the morning air.

When he neared the porch steps, he heard the steady clap of an ax chopping wood. He made a quick left and walked around the house. Turning the corner, he saw a boy in overalls no more than twelve chopping wood atop a tree stump. Behind the boy, Duncan saw a large chicken coop and run, and an endless field with a dark red barn in the distance. As the boy reached over for another piece to split, he spied Duncan and stopped.

"Hi, there," Duncan said. "Your father home?"

The boy stared, not moving or saying a word. Finally, he

appeared to have made a decision. He buried the ax into the tree stump and yelled out, "Pa! Fella here to see ya."

A man stepped out from behind the chicken coop. He carried a shallow metal bucket filled with eggs. Wearing denim overalls and a straw hat, the man looked every bit the farmer except for one thing. His hands. As he set the bucket down, wiped his hands on a handkerchief, and approached with an offered hand and a wary nod, Duncan noticed how gracefully the man moved. Hand motions that smooth only came about from endless hours of practice. Duncan had no doubt — this was Dominic Rose, an accomplished magician.

"You're a hard man to find," Duncan opened, flashing his best smile.

Dominic looked around the farm. "I been here all along."

Duncan smiled and nodded. "I suppose so." He searched Dominic's face for any resemblance to Pappy but saw none. Yet the man did look familiar. A strong, cold glare in the eyes that reminded Duncan of every disappointed look his father ever gave.

"You want something, Mister, or you just going to stand there all day?" Dominic asked.

With Freddie counting the minutes out front, Duncan had to jump straight into things. But the boy may not know anything, and a man trying to keep a secret from his boy could be difficult to work with. "We need to talk."

"So talk."

"I'm not sure this is something you want your son to hear. It's about magic."

Dominic shook his head and turned away. "You can leave now, Mister. I don't talk with newspaper people. I don't know anything about magic or magicians or anything like that. You people keep mistaking me for someone else and I've had it with you. You leave now, or I'll get the police to make you leave."

"You won't call the police." Duncan raised his voice to be heard as Dominic retrieved the bucket of eggs. "We both know it. And I'm not a reporter. So why don't you talk with me. I promise you'll be glad you did."

"If you ain't a reporter, then you're a nut. And I don't need nuts around here either."

Dominic made every indication that he would return to his farm work and ignore Duncan. Ten minutes later, Freddie would arrive and the trouble would start. "Sir, please listen to me."

"You get off my farm."

"My name is Duncan Rose. I came here through the Door of Vanishing."

Dominic's face paled and he dropped the bucket. It knocked over, and cracked eggs oozed onto the ground.

Chapter 32

Dominic sent his son to milk the cows. As he watched the boy walk off, his paled skin slowly regained some color. "Come on inside," he said without looking at Duncan.

The farmhouse had a low ceiling and wood floors. Practical, wooden furniture with little in the way of decoration fueled Duncan's suspicion that no woman lived here. Still, the place felt cozy and he couldn't help but note that in 2013, people would pay millions for an old home on a large farm like this.

"You want a beer?" Dominic asked.

"Little early."

"Not after what you said." Dominic entered the kitchen and indicated a chair for Duncan to sit on. From a white cabinet with a cylindrical apparatus on top, he pulled out a brown bottle and poured half his beer into a glass.

Duncan's surprise and curiosity took over for a second. "Is that a refrigerator?"

"Yup. Bought it a year ago. I hate iceboxes." Dominic drank the glass down, then decided to drink the rest straight from the bottle. "So, Mr. Rose, where are you from ... and when?"

Duncan opened his mouth to answer but hesitated.

Dominic nodded. "Worried about messing up Time? Don't. You can't. I don't know as much as you might think about all this. I kind of stumbled upon it. But I do know that people have gone through the Doors for a long time. You aren't the first. Which means that Time is constantly in flux. People are forever changing the timeline that we once knew. But the universe is still here. We still wake each morning and live our lives as we always have. It is what it is and somehow it works."

"But what about all the paradox stuff? Killing your grandfather and all that? After all, we might be related."

"Why the hell would you want to kill your grandfather?"

"I don't. But if I did it by accident then I would never be born, so I couldn't go back in time and accidentally kill him, so I would be born, but then I would go back in time — get it? It's an endless loop."

Dominic gulped down most of his beer. "I don't know about that kind of thing. But think about this — the Door is ancient, so somehow the universe can deal with these things. If it couldn't, we'd have vanished long ago. I sure hope so, anyway. I pray it's true every night. Because I messed up."

"What happened?"

"That damn Door is what happened. I gambled my life on it. It gave me everything and then took it away fast. See, when I was young, I struggled hard. I didn't want to farm like my daddy and I didn't want to be a miner or anything else like that. I never liked hard labor. Didn't see the point in breaking my back for a few bits."

He finished his beer, reached over to the refrigerator, and pulled out another. "Gentleman came along one summer and taught me a few magic tricks. What can I say? The bug had bit. I loved fooling the audience, but more than that, I loved simply performing. Getting on stage, getting their eyes on me, getting that recognition. If you've ever had it, you know what I mean. It's something you taste and then you want more and more. There's no stopping it.

"So I left home and started going around the country performing wherever I could. Speakeasies ate it up and everyone was so drunk I didn't have to be all that good. County fairs were big business to me, too. That's when I met Laura.

She had worked with a few stage magicians before and knew more than I did. She became my assistant and we joined up with one traveling show after another until we had a good set worked out. I became The Amazing Verido and we settled in with The Wilkinson's Wonders Show. We weren't anything all that special, but we put on an entertaining show and made a living. That's when I found the Door.

"We had finished a long weekend run in some Kansas town. They were tearing down the tents and packing up the show to move on that night when I decided to see if I could find a girl for a few hours. I don't want you to think I did that often, but I'm like any other man. And there's something about being on stage that got girls interested in doing more than they ever thought they'd do.

"Anyway, I didn't find any girls hanging around the tents where they normally waited to meet us. But there was a man. I'll never forget him. He had sharp, angular features and thick, black hair. His face was so narrow and pointy — he could've played one of them vampires in the pictures. Downright frightening. He told me he had a magic trick unlike any other in existence. He told me that if I performed his trick, I'd become the most famous magician ever to walk the stage.

"I don't think I was really enticed by all of that. Not much, anyway. But I had the sense that Wilkinson was gearing up to fire me, and I did get curious. Figured what harm would come from taking a look at this trick?

"I'm sure you've guessed some of this. He showed me the Door. And he walked through it. Disappeared. Never saw him again, of course. Now, I don't know why he did this. Maybe he was a relative, too, like you, and he knew I needed the Door for some Time-related thing. Or maybe he was just crazy. I'd think traveling through Time would scramble a man's brain. All I know is that I stood there looking at this door for a long time until I finally decided to take it and make it work for me."

Duncan drummed his fingers on the table as he thought. "You never went through the Door yourself?"

"Thought about it a thousand times, but the way that man

looked, the way he acted — haunted like he'd seen a lustful horror, something he knew he should never see again, and wanted nothing more than to go back. I'd seen that look on men who took to the bottle. I figured I didn't want a part of those sorts of things through there."

"But you sent others through it."

"I did. At first, I sent trouble-makers through. See, I built a door illusion that we worked into the show. It was nothing more than a real door on a frame and the frame was on a platform that could be rolled out. I'd set the door sideways and walk through it to show it was an ordinary door. Then Laura would come out, we'd turn the door to face the audience and she'd go through. I'd close the door and she'd curl up through a trap. The base looked like a narrow platform, too small for a person to fit in, but that was an illusion of the stage. From an audience perspective, it looked small, but it could fit Laura just fine. Set off a couple flashpots so we got some smoke in the air and when I open the door, she's gone."

Dominic reached into the refrigerator for a third beer and drank much of it before speaking again. "One night, Wilkinson comes to me like he'd seen the Devil. Some men were trying to rough him up, threatening to kill him, that kind of thing. I don't know why. I didn't want to know. But I got the clear message that if he didn't get out of this jam, he might not make it to see the next day, and even if he did, no matter what, the show would be over. I'd have to start from scratch, looking for a new place to work. I didn't have anything saved, squandered it all on foolishness. Worst thing was that when I had signed on with Wilkinson, I didn't know nothing about contracts. Turned out, the name The Amazing Verido belonged to Wilkinson, so starting over meant I'd be building a new name, too. I wasn't going to do that.

"I told Wilkinson to give these men free tickets to my show, and I promised him, it would all be fine. After Laura and I performed the Door of Vanishing trick, I stepped forward and rattled on for a moment to distract the audience. Laura wheeled the fake door behind a set piece and switched it for the real

Door, which I had mounted on a rolling platform as well. She didn't know what it was. Then I called for volunteers and picked out the men that were after Wilkinson. They walked through the Door without a second thought." He drank.

"And that ended your problem."

Dominic nodded but he didn't seem to see Duncan anymore. He spoke with a bitter tongue as he told the rest of his story. Duncan watched the magician disappear into memories as dark and mysterious as any performance he ever gave.

Dominic began drinking after that show. He had sent those men to a fate unknown. While he felt justified, the horror at his own darkness formed a fist inside him — a fist that pounded and pounded at his chest, trying to burst free, to spread its terrible poison throughout his soul. Only the oblivion of alcohol quieted it down.

As the show traveled on, as time passed, Dominic grew adept at performing his show while intoxicated. Sooner still, he became adept at performing his life while intoxicated. He continued to go out on stage, but he found no joy in the wowed audience, and he stopped performing the Door of Vanishing altogether. More often than he dared to admit, he spent his nights wallowing in tears, unable to drink away the faces of those men.

"I'm not a killer," he told Duncan. "I can't be one. Look at what it did."

Then came that final show. They were in some little Pennsylvania town — even when sober, the towns all blurred together — and he had been having a particularly rough patch with those ghostly faces haunting him every night. Awake and in his dreams, he saw their eager expressions as they laughed and stepped through into the darkness. That morning, Wilkinson came to him and asked that the Door of Vanishing trick be included in the show.

"It's a real draw," he said. "And we're hurting. We announce that you're going to do the Door of Vanishing trick, and we'll have nothing but full attendance. We'll clean up."

"I can't do that trick anymore."

"If we don't make some serious money, I'll have to start letting people go. You want me tell your friends they'll be losing their jobs because you're too sauced to do your job?"

Dominic tried to argue more but Wilkinson demanded the trick be included. If the trick wasn't performed, The Amazing Verido would be finished, and Wilkinson would make sure nobody hired Dominic again. But there was no need for that final threat — nobody would hire a drunk like him anyway. This was all he had left.

He agreed to perform the trick. While Wilkinson went all over town publicizing the inclusion of the Door, Dominic felt the ghosts surround him with their bone-white fingers, clawing at him, wanting to pull him through the Door and into the Hell they suffered. Though the sun had barely risen, Dominic guzzled a fifth of vodka.

It had been long enough since the last performance of the Door of Vanishing that he knew he should rehearse the whole thing a few times with his assistant, but the mere thought of seeing the Door sent him from one bar to the next. The day slipped away, and he continued to drink. Nobody recognized him in the bars, and at one point, he saw his reflection and did not recognize himself. He had lost so much weight, and his eyes — he had the very same look as the man who had handed him the Door to begin with.

When he finally stumbled backstage, Wilkinson was fuming. He was late. If not for the need to get Dominic dressed and ready for the stage, Wilkinson probably would have fired him right on the spot.

"I wish he had," Dominic said. "I wish he had thrown me out and kept that lousy, cursed thing."

But the audience stirred and rumbled, and Wilkinson knew he had no real choice. If he didn't send The Amazing Verido on stage, if the audience didn't get to witness the Door of Vanishing, there would be a line of angry customers demanding their money back. Crossing his fingers and praying to the Heavens, Wilkinson had Dominic cleaned up and thrown onto the stage.

Though drunker than he ever recalled being, Dominic managed to work his way through the show, saving the Door for last — partially as a show-stopper, and partially in the hopes that some magic might whisk him away from all of this. But no magic arrived.

Laura wheeled out the Door, and he went through the routine that he had perfected long ago. For the tiniest moment, a sliver in time that froze before his eyes, he had the notion that he might make it through the performance without any trouble. All might be well.

"I remember it clearly," he told Duncan. "I stood there speaking to the audience of far off lands where I had supposedly traveled to learn the secrets of magic, and while I did this, my assistant wheeled the fake Door behind the set piece. And for that moment, it all had been going so smoothly. And then ..."

"Then what?"

He licked his dry lips. "I don't know when it happened. I was so drunk, I don't recall making the signal. Maybe I was reliving the horrible night I sent those men off. Maybe I didn't make the signal at all and my dear Laura made the mistake. I don't know."

"She switched the doors," Duncan said.

Dominic nodded. "I didn't know. I would never have had that boy and his mother on stage if I had known. I swear I thought Laura had kept the fake door. I asked the boy to check out the Door and I watched him — eager and joyful and so in love with his Mama. He hurried to his place and she came to my side. I gave her a little nudge towards the Door and I watched that boy's face, his astonished look when she disappeared. He was so excited. Every gleeful utterance drove me deeper into the floor. I knew right away what had happened. And, Lord help me, I actually considered sending the boy after her — so he wouldn't have to live with the horror that would follow. But I told you that I'm no killer. I couldn't willfully do it. So, I ended the show, and I watched him from the wings.

"He sat in the front row, an empty seat beside him, and he waited. And he waited. And he waited. It didn't matter that I had swallowed more alcohol than many men drink in a lifetime, I was sober and devastated. I kept watching him, praying that he would give up and run away, but after the place had cleared out, he still sat there, waiting. I went to the boy and told him to leave. I figured he had a father somewhere or maybe a brother or sister. He wouldn't budge. I screamed at him, I think. I don't know exactly, but eventually I lied. Told him his Mama was waiting at home. That little tyke got all happy and sprinted out of the theater."

Dominic finished his beer. "After that, I was done. I had to get out of there as fast as I could. I cut the Door in half so nobody could use it and I ran. Shacked up with a gal I met during my travels. Turned out I had a son I didn't know about and she wanted to dump him on me. Didn't even occur to me that the cops would be after me, but when I figured that much out, I did what I had to do to vanish from the world. I love my son, but since I'm admitting the truth here, I'll tell you that I took him on with me out of selfish reasons — figured the cops were looking for a man, not a man and his boy."

"Huh," Duncan said. "That's a bit different than Wilkinson's version."

The corner of Dominic's mouth rose. "I'll bet. That man never liked the truth very much."

"He said you had more than one door you used."

"I had several fake doors, but that was the real one."

"Then you don't have another? Because I came through one, so there has to be more than the one you cut apart. And I need to find it. I have to. It's the only way I'll ever get back. And I have to get back."

Dominic set his beer on the table with a precise motion as his brow furrowed. He clambered to his feet and stepped passed Duncan. "Come with me," he said and headed out the back door.

The dead tone in Dominic's voice chilled Duncan, but he

followed anyway. Getting away from the house, away from Freddie, sounded like a good plan. It would buy them time, at least.

Dominic walked straight toward the barn, and with every step, Duncan saw that barn as something evil. Bits of old horror movies played out in Duncan's mind — movies that had yet to be made.

When they reached the structure, Dominic paused with his hand on the latch. He didn't say anything, never looked back, just halted. Whatever awaited them inside the barn, he seemed to want to warn Duncan but could not find the words. Duncan was about to say something when Dominic yanked open the door and stepped in.

If Freddie had not been waiting back at the car, Duncan might have left at that moment. The side of him that always could read people told him to run. But the rest of him said that he had to go forward, see this thing through. Because if he ran, he would never be able to stop. The answers he sought were here.

To run away meant abandoning any hope of home, and without home, he would just keep running from one bad situation to another, ruining anything good on purpose in order to force him to run again. He knew that life in one form or another. It wore a man down, convincing him that he was an adventurer but taking more of his heart each day until the man woke to find that the years had gone, that he had become old and alone and no longer strong enough for another adventure, another run. He had seen that sad, longing, hopeless look in Pappy's eyes but until this moment, he had never understood it.

That won't be me, he thought and stepped into the barn.

As his eyes adjusted to the dusty light, his jaw dropped open. He stood there, mouth agape, unable to process the sight before him.

Doors.

A hundred at least. Probably more. They hung from the rafters, leaned against the walls, piled up in towers with narrow alleys between. Each one covered in bizarre symbols. No two the same.

"When I left the show, I thought I was done with all this. But about a year later, I read an advertisement for a new magician and his Amazing Door of Disappearance. I had to con the man into a card game and cheat him out of the Door. Others I found long forgotten in basements and attics and elsewhere. I'd read the obituaries, I made inquiries, over the years I became quite good at finding these things. In a way, I think they sought me out."

Finding his voice, Duncan said, "Which one is mine?"

Darkness clouded Dominic's eyes. "I'm afraid you don't understand. I've learned from those who owned these Doors and gladly gave the burden to me. I've learned all about them. Every Door is a unique passageway to a specific time and place. One way only. There might be a door that'll get you close to when and where you came from, but the odds that it's one of these is highly against you. And since the only way to find out if it is what you want is to go through, well ..."

Duncan's legs shook and he fell to his knees. "All for nothing." Breathing became difficult and his chin moved up and down but no words left him. The Doors seemed to close in on him. Endless rows of Doors. Endless places and times to go. But never where he wanted.

"I'm sorry. I truly am. You're not the first person I've met who has gone through a Door and tracked me down. I'll say to you what I've said to the other few. Just because your old life is gone, doesn't mean life itself is gone. I don't know what the world was like where you came from, but this one ain't so bad. And, since you know about the Door, you can help me find them, store them here, make sure others don't suffer the same fate as you."

Duncan lifted his head. One Door after another entered his view, each one taunting him with the false promise of a way back to 2013. He could try. After all, one of them probably did get him home — or close to home. The rest, however, did not. With this many doors, the odds were against him. If he picked wrong, where would he end up? When? At least in 1934, there were cars and phones and a life that was antiquated but recognizable. What if he ended up in 1470 or 1212? What if the only people around were Native Americans who had yet to see white men? Or he might end up even further back. What if he stepped through a Door and found himself facing dinosaurs? The downside went too far down to take the risk.

Dabbing at his eyes, Duncan accepted Dominic's hand and stood. "I don't know what I'm going to do, but thank you for the offer to help."

"I understand. It's a lot to think about."

"Yeah."

The barn door opened and a deep voice said, "Well, well. Looks like I found something special."

Nelson Walter entered the barn. Lucy, Victor, and Dominic's son followed. Brandishing his .38, Freddie brought up the rear. Walter could not hold back a boyish grin, but Duncan saw nothing childlike in the man's excitement. He only saw a demon capable of horrific violence. He only saw the coming death of the woman he loved.

CHAPTER 33

THE SUMMER HEAT STUCK TO EVERY BREATH. Sweat trickled down Duncan's back, but he couldn't be sure if that came from the heat or his nerves. Walter held a handkerchief and constantly patted his balding head.

Despite the Doors hanging around them, Lucy looked straight at Duncan. He wanted to leap across the barn floor and sweep her into his arms. He wanted to beg her forgiveness for all the trouble he had caused and apologize for things he had yet to even consider. Anything to keep her heart beating for him. But she turned away.

Vincent looked at the Doors in disbelief. Different styles of doors from different time periods, each with unique markings, yet all equally dangerous. Even Freddie appeared impressed, though he returned his focus to the three hostages.

"Look at all those Doors," Walter said, stepping around the barn like a conqueror inspecting a newly won city. "Unbelievable. Even though I've always known they existed, to actually stand here in front of them. And so many. I never imagined there were so many."

Dominic scowled. "Just who do you think you are? Give me my boy and get the hell off my land."

Walter stomped over to Dominic and shook his hand. "It's

an honor to meet such an accomplished magician as yourself. Even before the Door of Vanishing trick, I found your work as The Amazing Verido to be impressive. I've read about you in the magazines, and I must say that I think you should have become a much bigger star than you did. The close up work, the big illusions, all of it showed me that you were a master of the art. Houdini himself would have been challenged by you." Duncan saw Dominic wince, and he knew Walter must have clamped down hard on that hand. "As for me, I am nothing more than a man you do not want to cross."

"You've got it all now," Duncan said, stepping forward. "You know it doesn't matter what this farmer says. You'll take all these Doors before the day is out. So why bother with threats? You've won."

Walter turned toward Duncan, wheezing from the stifling barn. "You got a lot of gumption. I'm truly surprised. You worked real hard to stay ahead of me, but in the end, it doesn't matter. I got your friend, I got your girl, I got all the cards."

Duncan paused, then grinned. "Not all of them."

"Oh?"

"If you had it all, you wouldn't be threatening anything. You'd have either let us go or killed us. But we're still here which means one thing to me — you still don't know how this all works."

Walter walked right up to Duncan and patted his cheek with a wet hand. "You've been a smart one this whole time. Hasn't he, Freddie? Been a real smart one." Freddie grunted. "Well, let's see how smart you really are. Tell me, what am I going to do if The Amazing Verido holds out on me?"

Dominic said, "You want to use the Door of Vanishing? It's not a trick to be played with. It's not a trick at all."

"I know," Walter said, snapping his head toward Dominic. "So let's start this off the most painless way I can think of. You tell me how to make the Door work or I'll call in the police and they'll arrest you for several old unsolved murders."

"I can't do that. These Doors are too dangerous."

"Sure. I understand. Let me restate my request so you can

comprehend this situation a bit clearer." From his coat pocket, Walter pulled out a handgun and pointed it at the boy. "Tell me how to use the Door, or I'll kill your son."

"Oh Lord, no." Tears rushed down Dominic's cheeks.

Duncan locked eyes on Freddie. He shook his head as if to say, "See the kind of monster you work for." Freddie squirmed under Duncan's gaze. As if fighting off the accusation, he tightened his hold on Vincent's arm.

"Well, Papa? Are you going to talk or does your barn get painted with your boy's brains?"

Duncan cleared his throat. "I'll tell you. Let them all go. I know how this works. That's what we were discussing in the house. He told me everything."

"That so?" Walter moved away from the boy.

"Yes. I'll tell you what you want to know."

"Then I guess I don't need Verido anymore." He pulled the trigger.

The little gun made a loud noise and Dominic fell to the ground, clutching his side. Blood oozed between his fingers. Lucy cried out and covered her mouth while Vincent stared in shock. Dominic's son leapt to his side.

"Still not talking?" Walter said.

Duncan looked at him like he was a madman. "I told you I would if you just let them go."

Walter shrugged. "You can waste time negotiating but The Amazing Verido's going to die soon if he don't get any help. I'm pretty sure he doesn't have a trick for patching up a bullet wound."

Duncan strained to find the right avenue out of this. There had to be an angle to work, some way to protect everyone. But Walter wouldn't give him the time to think.

The big man strolled around the barn, looking upon the Doors as if viewing an art gallery. "Freddie, put your gun to Ms. Lucy's head. Maybe that'll get some answers for me."

Freddie did as instructed. Lucy looked to Duncan, tears streaming down her face, every muscle in her body tense. Duncan tried to calm her with his eyes but he knew it wouldn't work. A gun to the head trumped kind eyes every time.

But Freddie held that gun, and that was the only angle left.

Though he spoke to Walter, Duncan turned his focus on Freddie. "I see now why your bosses stuck you out in the middle of Nowhere, Pennsylvania. You have no honor."

"Excuse me," Walter growled.

"Come on, Mr. Walter. First you threaten the life of a boy and now an innocent woman. Where's the honor in that? The real Chicago men are tough, no doubt, but they would never stoop so low as to use kids and women."

"Don't you talk to me like that."

"Or what? You going to go kill a few grandmas, too?"

Walter wagged a finger at Duncan. "You think you're clever. Rattle me a bit and I'll make a mistake? Something like that? No, sir. I've been waiting a long time to stand here, and I won't have it screwed up by hotheadedness. Why should I care what you think about honor? You've got far less honor than me. You've been lying to these fine people from the start. Come on, Ms. Lucy. What did he tell you was his reason for all this? I'm sure he came up with a great lie."

Lucy shivered and a new wash of tears streamed down her face.

"I did lie to them," Duncan said. "I did it to protect them from all of this. From you."

"Great job you did there. Ain't that right, Ms. Lucy? He sure is protecting you from that gun resting on your skull."

"I was wrong. Lucy knew that. She tried to get through to me. I should have told the truth from the start but I was afraid." He faced Lucy. "I fell in love and I was afraid the truth would send her running fast from me. I was a fool for that. I'm sorry."

"Aw, isn't that sweet? I might even shed a tear for you. Or I'll just kill the girl and you can shed all the tears. You want that to happen, keep flapping your jaw. Or, you can tell me what I want to know and then you won't have to watch the pretty girl die."

Duncan glanced at Freddie one final time. The man's eyes

darted between Lucy and Walter. His finger touched the trigger, then pulled away and rested on the side of the gun, then back to the trigger. It wasn't enough, though. Whatever incentive Freddie needed, Duncan had not done the job well enough. It was over. There were no more cards to play. Duncan refused to let them harm Lucy, and if things did not resolve soon, Dominic would bleed to death. If Dominic was indeed a relative, Duncan didn't want to know what that would do to his own existence.

"Okay," Duncan said. "You win. I'll tell you how to use the Door."

Chapter 34

Nelson Walter crossed his huge arms. He knew he had won but he wouldn't give Duncan any room to rest. Duncan expected no less. Walter was that kind of man — he didn't take joy in the winning but rather found pleasure in grinding his opponent into the ground.

"I won't wait for long," Walter said.

Duncan glanced around the barn at all the Doors. Without a clear plan, he decided to stall as long as he could. At least that would buy time, and in some cases, that's all one needed. A little time, a little hope, and an open eye, looking for an advantage he could use.

"All of these doors are Doors of Vanishing. Every last one. And each Door is a gateway to another time, another place. You told me recently that you knew there was real magic in the world. Well, here it is. The most powerful real magic in existence. No two Doors go to the same location or the same time. Each one is unique. These markings are part of the ancient spell that makes them work. We don't know where this magic came from, but history is filled with tales of powerful people with hands deep in the dark arts."

Walter spit to the side. "I don't need a damn show. Freddie, put a hole in the girl's pretty leg."

"Okay, okay, wait!" Duncan said, and Walter put a hand out to halt Freddie. But Duncan noticed that Freddie hadn't moved to begin with. Maybe he had some room to work with the thug, after all. Walter's word *show* flashed in his mind and he had an idea. "I'll dispense with the formal part, but in order to grasp the complexities of this apparatus, allow me to demonstrate the full trick. It'll make things far clearer than my mere words."

Even if Walter's criminal senses warned him away from this, Duncan knew the magician in him would never decline. Walter's face lightened as his excitement grew. "Yes, sure. Show me the trick." Walter jutted his chin toward Dominic's crumpled body. "Better be quick, though. He won't last long."

Duncan rubbed his sweating hands on his pants. "I'll need an assistant and some other help."

He stepped towards Lucy, but Walter put out a cautioning hand. "Not her."

Before Duncan could respond, a voice called out from behind. "Ladies and gentleman," the voice said. Duncan turned around to find Dominic's son standing next to a Door set into a platform. "Prepare to be astounded by this final trick, the most dangerous trick ever attempted by any magician anywhere in the world. In just moments, The Amazing Verido will give you the Door of Vanishing."

Duncan stared at the boy, unsure if he could believe what he was seeing. The only reason he could think that the boy wanted to perform the trick was because he knew the end result. If they did it right, Nelson Walter would walk through a door and that would end their problems. Could this boy really be suggesting that? That would require an amazing amount of bravery and cunning from a child. Then again, this child seemed to love his father. What wouldn't he do for that kind of love? And even if the boy wasn't making the suggestion, the thought now existed in Duncan's mind. It froze him despite the hot day.

"I guess I'll be Verido for this," Vincent said and stepped forward. He patted Duncan on the shoulder. "I know the performance. I've read plenty of accounts. I just don't know how the trick actually works. What do I need to do?"

Duncan shook his head. "Just do the show. I'll take care of the rest."

Vincent winked and spread his arms wide. "My dear guests, it is a pleasure to perform for you this singularly incredible trick. You'll please take note here that this is an ordinary door in an ordinary frame that's been set up on this platform for ease of use."

Vincent knocked on the door, the frame, and the platform to indicate solid wood. Vincent's charisma could not be denied, and both Walter and Freddie watched carefully — cautious but somewhat enthralled by the show.

"To further prove this is nothing but an ordinary door, I shall walk through it," Vincent said. While he spoke, Dominic's son rotated the platform until the door stood in profile. Vincent then opened the door and stepped through it with ease. Once on the other side, he closed the door, gestured to the audience as if to say, "See, nothing odd here," and then opened the door again, and went back through. "Just a door like one you no doubt have in your very homes."

The boy rotated the door so it now faced the audience. "And now," Vincent said, his voice rich and mysterious, "I will send this boy to another realm." The boy walked up to the door, glanced back at Walter with an unsure look — all excellent acting on the boy's part — and stepped through.

From where he stood, Duncan watched the boy close the door and immediately slip through a trap door in the platform, curling under and closing the trap above him. Even watching it happen, it looked impossible that he should be able to fit, but he appeared to have no trouble. On the other side of the door, the side facing the audience, Vincent continued the routine with a barrage of faux-magic words and hand gestures.

"And now," Vincent said, placing his hand on the doorknob, "the boy is gone." He opened the door to reveal the empty platform. He closed the door again, and talked about how difficult it was to bring somebody back. As he spoke, the boy slid the trap door open and uncurled from the platform.

When Vincent finished his performance, he opened the door and there was the boy.

Despite the situation, Freddie actually clapped his hands until a sharp look from Walter stopped him.

Vincent walked to the left, far from the door frame as if in deep thought. "Now, here is where things get interesting." In Verido's performance, this marked the point where he would talk of faraway lands, witch doctors, and whatever else he came up with. Vincent tailored his talk to the moment at hand. It was a subtle, brilliant move that demanded the attention of his audience. "You've seen the Door in action and you obviously want to harness its power for yourself. Since we are dealing with authentic magic and not the clever sleights-of-hand that are the mainstay of many a magician, you must learn the proper words, the incantation, if you will, that allows these Doors to function."

As Vincent continued to talk, bringing Nelson Walter closer in as he imparted the "secret," Dominic's boy rolled the door over to Duncan. He looked at Duncan with pragmatic eyes. He knew what he suggested they do, and he had no moral qualms about it. His steady stare shined on Duncan like an interrogator's harsh lamp, demanding answers, not letting him shift into the shadows to escape. Though he felt less sure than the boy, he nodded.

Together, they removed the fake door from the platform, grabbed the closest Door and inserted it into the platform. Then the boy wheeled it back as Vincent continued his remarkably gripping tale.

"One last time. Repeat the words while you lay your hands upon the door. Just as I had done."

Walter mimicked Vincent's wide hand gestures and said, "*El eto ich zarus zanuc cantilo.*"

Listening to Walter struggle with the made-up words made Duncan want to laugh, but he contained the urge. Vincent had almost finished, and Duncan decided to take one final risk. He inched towards Lucy. Freddie saw him and frowned. Duncan shook his head and raised his hands. Then with a pleading look, he lifted one finger — *One second, please.* Freddie glanced at Walter, saw his boss mesmerized by Vincent, then nodded.

Duncan moved close to Lucy and whispered, "I'm sorry about everything. I wish I could make it right. But whatever happens, no matter what, do not go through any of the Doors in this barn. Don't doubt me on this. Please. Do not go through the Doors."

She nodded, her fear clipping the motion.

Looking right at Freddie, Duncan added, "And don't worry. This guy doesn't kill woman or children. You'll be fine."

"And now Mr. Walter," Vincent said, and Duncan hurried back to the platform, "will you kindly step up to the Door of Vanishing."

Walter strode to the Door, leering at Lucy as he did so. When he reached the Door, he put his hands on the wood as Vincent had prescribed, and he said, "*El eto ich zarus zanuc cantilo.*"

"Good, Mr. Walter. Excellent. Now, step through and this great power will be yours."

Walter straightened his back, readjusted his pants, and opened the Door. Nothing could be seen — only pitch black inside. He leaned closer, squinting, but not even a sliver of light escaped.

"Go on, sir. Nothing to be scared of," Vincent said.

Walter closed the Door and laughed. "I'm not stupid. I know what happened to the people who went through this Door before. They went through and were gone forever." He leveled his dark eyes upon Dominic's son. The boy coward back, but Walter yanked him to the Door with one mighty hand.

The boy struggled, but he was no match for Walter's bulk. Walter slapped the boy in the face and that knocked out all of the fight. Walter went on, "Tell me, boy, before your Papa bleeds out. Is Vincent here telling me the truth? Do these magic words really control this thing, or do I have to say something else? Tell me right now or I'll throw you through this Door." He pulled out his gun and pointed it at the boy's head. "Maybe this'll get you talking better. How 'bout I shoot you in the gut and then throw you through the Door? You can die something like your old man."

"Stop it," Duncan said. "He's just a boy."

Walter's eyes narrowed to a half-lidded scowl. "There are no boys anymore. Life is too hard to waste time playing ball and pulling pigtails."

"What does that mean? You'll kill any child that gets in your way?"

"It's like I told you — I'm willing to make the tough calls. You think the New York families, the Chicago families, will roll over so easy because I've got a magic door? It'll be bloody. It'll require tough calls every single day. But I can make those decisions. I'll kill every man, woman, and child that I have to in order to take over. It's ugly but nobody ever done anything great without hurting a few people. And I'm going to start right here with this kid."

"Enough!" Freddie said and turned his gun on Walter.

A flash of confusion crossed Walter's face. "What the hell are you doing?"

"We got your door and Duncan or Vincent will tell us how to use it. They can put up a fight but we'll get it out of them. There's no need to hurt this kid or the woman."

Walter raised an eyebrow. "Never knew you had a soft spot for anybody."

"Now you know. Let the boy go."

"I saved your life. I raised you as my own. You'd be scavenging trash off the streets if it wasn't for me, and you turn a gun on me?"

"I appreciate everything you've done. But killing a kid is going too far."

"The problem here," Walter said, wrenching the boy's arm high enough that the boy yelped, "is that you've forgotten who I am."

"Please, Mr. Walter. Don't do this." Freddie took two long strides forward.

"Freddie, I'm proud of you. It's hard to stand up to your

father. It takes guts and conviction. Most men spend their entire lives never taking that risk, forever living in the shadow of a man they love and fear. But once you've stood up to your father, once you've crossed him, he can be proud of you knowing you'll do just fine in life, standing up for yourself. Unfortunately, I'm not your father, and I don't like being crossed."

Walter wheeled his arm around to shoot, but Freddie reacted faster. He shot Walter in the arm and pulled the trigger two more times. Both shots missed — one went wild but one pierced the Door.

A high-pitched whine like wind whipping around a house filled the barn. All eyes turned toward the Door. The wood around the bullet hole cracked. Like a dark lightning bolt, it made its jagged way up the middle of the Door. Another crack formed below the bullet hole, stretching down toward the platform.

To be heard over the storming wind, Duncan cupped his mouth. "Get away from the Door!"

The boy had enough time to look at Duncan with startled, innocent eyes. Then the Door shattered inward, the pieces falling off into the dark nothingness beyond. It was as if a door on a passenger jet had blown open. The high-pitched whine became a thundering storm, howling and roaring around them. The air from the barn rushed into the Door, sucking in everything it could take hold of — including the boy and Nelson Walter.

Duncan whirled back and tackled Lucy to the ground, pulling her behind a stack of Doors. From his vantage, he saw that Vincent had also secured a safe hold, wrapping his arms and legs around the hayloft ladder. The boy and Walter both clung to the edges of the Door frame, their legs dangling straight back as the winds blasted by them.

"We've got to help him," Lucy said.

Duncan had no doubt she meant the boy. He nodded, thought for a moment, and undid his belt. Even as he looped it around the latch of the middle Door in the stack near them, even as he wrapped it around Lucy's hand, he thought he had devised one of the stupidest plans ever. But nothing else came to mind, and he could never live with himself if he let that boy fall through the Door to be trapped in another time and place. He would spend the rest of his life seeing that boy's face, hearing that howl, knowing he had done nothing.

"Ready?" he shouted.

She nodded, and though the wind swirled her hair around her face, Duncan could see the terror poking her beneath the surface.

He took her other hand and edged toward the Door. Once free from the protection of the stack, the rush of air yanked them straight for the open Door. The belt snapped taut, Lucy's arms extended their fullest, and Duncan stretched toward the boy.

"Come on," he yelled. "Get my hand."

The boy tried to pull himself through the Door but to no avail. Walter attempted to pull himself out too, but his massive size kept him from any real progress. The boy tried swinging his legs to hook them on the frame, but again nothing. Even if he had succeeded, he wouldn't have been able to reach Duncan's hand.

"Stretch!" Duncan said and he felt Lucy find another inch but it still wasn't enough.

Walter lost the grip on one hand. He screamed, and his body flapped like a flag in a heavy storm. Uttering a war cry, he reached over and latched onto the boy.

"No!" Freddie yelled and rushed across the barn. He linked onto Duncan's hand and reached out for the boy. "Take my hand, kid. You can do it."

With Freddie added to the chain, they were close enough to the door frame. But the boy struggled worse with Walter holding onto him.

"Let go of me," the boy cried.

"Tell me how to use the Door, and I'll help you live," Walter shouted.

The boy kicked back at Walter but the big man could take

the weak strikes without trouble.

Duncan's heart dropped as he saw the frame cracking. To Freddie, he yelled, "We've got to get him now. Look."

And Duncan watched the most beautiful, most horrifying thing he had ever seen. He saw Freddie eye the cracking frame, then gaze back at Lucy, her face taut as she strained to hold on. He looked to Duncan, then the boy, then back to Duncan, and a cold decision relaxed the man's face.

"I'm not a killer," he said, sounding exactly like Dominic. "I'm sorry."

Before Duncan could do anything, Freddie let go of his hand and hurled himself upon Nelson Walter. Walter's screams blended with the wind as both men tumbled into the darkness.

"Vincent!" Lucy called out. "Help us!"

Vincent hurried over and took Freddie's former position. With longer arms, Vincent could barely touch the boy's fingers. Now free from Walter, the boy tried again to pull himself out. One, two, three, four attempts but he still could not beat the thrust of the wind soaring into the Door.

"I need something to reach him with," Vincent said.

Duncan thought of Vincent's belt, his jacket, anything to give the boy something to hold on to. But all of those things required them to pull back in order to free up their hands to get the object. The crack on the top of the door frame would make it through any moment. They lacked the time.

"The Door," Duncan said. "Lucy, pull hard. Get that Door loose. All of us. Pull!"

As if they were in a tug-o-war with the stack of Doors, they pulled hard on each other's arms, leading back to Duncan's belt. The Door in the middle of the stack did not budge.

"Again. Pull!"

Two more times they yanked on the Door. Duncan glanced back at the cracking frame. They were too late. The crack had made it through. Any moment, the whole thing would fall apart, sending the boy into the darkness. Who knew what else might happen? The Door might continue eating up their world. All of them might die.

Duncan's right arm went slack. He shot his attention to Lucy who was smiling. "It's loose," she cheered. "Get the boy! Get the boy!"

They all stretched out again. Vincent grabbed the boy's wrist. "Got him! Pull us back. Hurry."

Duncan dug his feet into the dirt floor and used every muscle to bring that boy back to the barn. He pulled until his arms burned with the struggle. The top of the frame splintered, and bright lights flashed from the cracks along the rest of the frame. With one final surge of strength, Duncan growled and yanked and he felt Lucy pulling and Vincent digging in and as if a great warrior had finally given up, the Door let the boy free. Lucy, Vincent, Duncan, and the boy toppled over each other as the frame ripped into pieces, the wood crackling like bones breaking, the pieces falling in on themselves.

And then it was gone.

The wind, the noise, the Door — nothing remained but an empty platform.

Vincent sat up first, his body shaking as he stared at the space where the Door had been. He looked back at Duncan, his lips pale white. Duncan scooted to his feet, worried that Vincent might vomit on him. But Vincent didn't move. He watched that space as if waiting for the Door to return.

Duncan put his hands out to Lucy and was rewarded with a smile as she allowed him to help her up. "You okay?" he asked.

Her smile widened. "I guess you weren't kidding. This was quite a secret." She surveyed all the doors leaning and hanging and stacked. "If I had known, I would never have—"

"I don't know if I would've believed me either."

"Any more secrets?"

"Don't worry. I'll tell you everything."

"You better. I'm not one to give second chances, but considering all this." Lucy glanced around the barn, a shiver taking over.

Duncan put a finger under her chin and gently prodded her head back up. He gazed into her eyes and hoped she could see the depth of his passion for her. Arching back her head a bit more, she opened her mouth — hesitant yet willing. Duncan leaned down, but as his lips neared hers, he heard the muffled tears of a boy.

Across the barn toward the entrance, Dominic's boy huddled over the body of his father, weeping as the pool of blood muddied the dirt floor.

Chapter 35

It's all over.

The thought repeated in Duncan's head with a dampened cadence. Nelson Walter no longer could touch any of them. They had learned all about the Door of Vanishing and the Amazing Verido — and there would be no going back to 2013.

While Lucy rushed to the boy's side, wrapping her arms around him in a motherly way he appeared to appreciate, Duncan could only wonder what would become of Duncan. Selfish thoughts, he fully admitted, but how else could he react? He would never see his old life again, never see the world he understood, never have a chance to fix things with his family, never indulge in an afternoon learning card tricks from Pappy. Only the quaint but antique world of the 1930s remained.

He watched Lucy mothering the boy. Sweet, beautiful, lovely, smart and funny Lucy — could they ever be together again? Or had too much passed to make that work? Had the secrets he kept to protect her caused too much damage to repair? He never put real effort into the life surrounding him because he knew deep in his heart he would be leaving. He would find the Door and return to where he belonged. Except that he would never be leaving now.

Vincent finally found the strength to stand, and he slid up

next to Duncan. "What are we going to do with that boy? And all these Doors?"

Something in Vincent's voice, perhaps the questions themselves, snapped Duncan from his self-pity. "First things first," he said. "What happened to you? Where have you been? I was worried about you."

"All these Doors," Vincent said, his usual state of mirth lost to an unsteady whisper.

"Are you okay?"

He pushed back his hair and plunked his hat back on his head. "Walter's men got me. Beat me up a bit and locked me away. In the evening, Walter came and pressed me to tell him where the Door was and how to use it. I didn't tell him anything or even let on whether I knew anything or not. But the funny thing is now I think I didn't have much to tell."

"Good thing Walter didn't know that or you'd be dead right now."

"Perhaps. But he did kill this boy's father. What do you think we should do?"

The strangest thought popped into Duncan's head yet the more he considered it, the more it made sense. "I could take over the job."

He meant far more than acting the role of parent to this boy — a difficult job in itself. He also meant taking over the farm and the house and the responsibility of the Doors. Because what other life did he have set out for himself? He had no real identity in this era, no credentials, no way to earn his keep other than playing cards and fooling people with magic tricks. He could have succeeded in that realm, of course, but that would be too easy, almost like cheating. And while he had never been above the idea of cheating men at cards, he also didn't believe in sullying his own backyard. It felt like all of 1934 was his backyard.

Because if he took over for Dominic Rose it would explain why he never heard family stories of some relative that had died young or simply disappeared. He could raise the boy as his own. "No, not could. I already did," he whispered. That boy was Frank Rose, his grandfather. A quiet man who never spoke of his past.

Now I know why.

Growing up, Duncan always heard that Pappy had raised his son on an old farm. All of this had already happened. Pappy knew all along. Duncan had spent some time worrying about the effects his actions would have on the future when all along, he had already done all of this. He'd been through this cycle before. All of those using the Doors had a first time through and then it was like this — a cycle. That's why the Timeline was safe.

For Duncan, taking over Frank's parenting meant taking Dominic's role in the family line, too. "Oh, crap. I'm Pappy. I'm my own great-grandfather."

PART V
1934 - 2013

Even though you have purchased this book
long after we wrote it, and even though
there is no way we could know
which card you'd pick
or
what your secret number would be,
we made this prediction:

The face down card is the furthest one to your left.

Not only is it the only face down card on the table,
but it is also your selected card.

Chapter 36

Life was hard at first. Duncan and Frank didn't get along. Though the boy understood that Duncan would stay, would take care of him, Duncan did little to encourage confidence. He knew nothing about running a farm, raising a boy, or maintaining a family.

They had to keep the farm to house all the Doors, and the chickens produced eggs but beyond that, Duncan had no interest or aptitude in an agricultural life. He recalled Pappy's stories of performing magic whenever possible to make some money and even more so, Pappy's tales of card-cheating. After all, that's where Duncan learned it all — from Pappy.

Nope. I learned it from myself.

So, when times got too rough, Pappy — for that's how Duncan decided he should be known from then on — headed into town for a poker game, or took the weekend in Philly and cheated his way to enough money for a few months. Lucy and Vincent moved to Lancaster and set up a magic shop of their own. Lucy struggled to keep it running, but she refused to give up.

Vincent didn't seem to care much about where they were. He had lost his vigor for life, and many of the nights that Lucy spent with Pappy, they discussed their fears for Vincent. Seeing that Door disappear, seeing real magic, shook the young man to his core.

One afternoon in late-autumn, Pappy called his son into the kitchen. The boy rarely spoke, but he was respectful enough. Pappy knew Frank couldn't wait to be old enough to head out on his own, and in fact, in six years, he would join the army and head off to Germany to fight the Nazis, but for now, they had to live together. Pappy thought it only fair to give the boy a say in their future.

"I got something to show you," Pappy said.

The boy listened politely enough, his narrow mouth never more than a flat slit on his face.

Pappy pulled out the small box in his pocket and opened it to reveal a diamond ring. Nothing fancy, but perfect for a straight-forward, honest gal. "I'd like to ask Lucy to marry me, and that would mean she would be part of our family. She'd be living here. I know we don't have a typical family, so I figured you might have some feelings about all this. Now's the time to speak up if you got any thoughts."

The boy offered only a stoic shrug that reminded Pappy of his grandfather. It was hard to remember that the boy was his grandfather, too, but whenever it struck Pappy, an uneasiness wriggled along his skin as if a ghost had crossed his shadow.

"Okay, then." Pappy closed the small box with a sharp snap. He placed it in one of the kitchen drawers. A car engine grumbled in the distance, and he pulled back the curtain on the kitchen door window. "I invited her over for the afternoon. She'll be here in just a moment. You go feed the chickens. Give us some time alone."

Another shrug and the boy left. Pappy paced the kitchen, futzing with the tablecloth as if such little touches mattered to him. He had placed a single rose in a glass on the table thinking it looked sweet and romantic. But as he listened to Lucy's footsteps approach, the rose now looked all wrong — sad and ridiculous.

She knocked on the door. As he rushed to answer, he snatched the rose out, made to throw it in the garbage, then tossed it back in the glass instead. He inhaled a deep breath and opened the door. One look at the tear stains on her cheeks stopped him from saying anything stupid.

"What happened?" he asked, escorting her to a chair.

"Oh, Duncan, what am I going to do?"

He was about to correct her — he wanted everybody calling him Pappy — but thought better of it this time. Instead, he said, "Did someone hurt you?"

She shook her head. "It's Vincent. He's gone."

"Somebody took Vincent?"

"No, he's just gone. He left."

"What? Why would he do that?"

"He hasn't been the same since the barn. He sits around our shop and scowls at everything. The few customers we get, he berates them. 'There's bigger stuff out there,' he would say. 'Card tricks are nothing.' I wanted to tell you before but he made me swear to keep it secret. I'm so sorry. It's terrible of me to have kept a secret after all I've said about such things but Vincent said you wouldn't understand, and he got so crazy when I broached the idea of telling you."

"Slow down. What exactly did he do?"

"Here." She pulled a wrinkled piece of paper from her purse. "Read it."

Pappy took the paper and leaned toward the sunlight coming through the window. He read:

> *My Dearest Lucy,*
>
> *You know the struggles I've had of late. Everything I thought I understood about the world was turned on end by what we saw. Frankly, I don't see how you or Duncan can slip back into your lives but perhaps it's easier when you're in love. Before you start to argue, I know you love him. I can see it clear even if you can't. But I don't have a love. I don't have somebody to hold onto, to pat my head, to tell me the world can still make sense. That door was real in a way that it*

shouldn't have been. How do we come to terms with that? I'm not fool enough to believe a door like that was just a one-time thing. That would be crazier than the idea that magic is real. So, I've decided to find some answers. I've heard about a man who can deal middles from a deck of cards as smooth as I can deal seconds or from the bottom. Middles? Can you imagine? I have to find this man and figure out if he is amazingly skilled, or as I suspect, he is using some real magic to accomplish this feat. From there, I'll see where the trail leads me. I'm going to find out all I can about real magic, and someday I'll come back to you and show you all that I've learned. Maybe even show the whole world. Don't be sad. You've got Duncan. My love has always been magic but now it's real instead of tricks. I suppose we should both be happy for me. In all honesty, though, I'm a little worried. I'll miss you terribly.

Love, Vincent

Pappy rested the letter on the table. He stood behind Lucy and embraced her. "I'm sorry, dear. I know how much Vincent means to you."

"He's gone. He left me. He said we'd always be there for each other, but he left me. How could he do that? And now I'm all alone."

"Never." Pappy stepped around and knelt before her. "You've always got me in your life. I won't go anywhere. I promise."

Lucy sniffled and pressed a handkerchief upon her eyes. "That's sweet. I'd love to believe you, too."

"Then believe me."

"But you've been trying to leave here from the start."

"You know I can't."

"But if you could. What if Vincent finds a Door to help you? The one you need."

"You're not alone. And I know now that no door exists for me."

Squaring her shoulders, Lucy tried to smile. "I should have known this was going to happen. I did know. Vincent's been itching to go for a while. When we finished that day at the barn, I knew he would be leaving me, but ..."

"You convinced yourself it wouldn't happen."

"What else was I going to do? Vincent and I have stuck by each other for so long. I couldn't, I can't, believe he'd go." With a cleansing breath, she said, "This all just happened. That's why I'm a little late. I'm sorry. But I am here and you said you had something important to discuss."

"Oh. That. Um ... now isn't a good time for that. You're upset and you need to figure out what you're going to do."

"Nonsense. If Vincent wants to cavort around the globe without me, I can't spend all my days crying for him. He's gone. That's the way Life is. One day you have something; next day it's gone. Enjoy it while you can. Right?"

"I guess. But this thing I wanted to talk about — maybe it was a mistake to bring it up."

She looked to her lap sadder than before. "I see."

Frank walked in with a filled egg basket. Looking from Pappy to Lucy, he frowned. He set the basket on the kitchen counter and then slid open the kitchen drawer. He pulled out the ring box and rested it on the counter.

Pappy looked at him. "You're sure?"

The boy nodded.

Lucy looked from one to the other. "What's going on?"

Smiling, Pappy reached out and the boy handed him the box. Looking in the soft eyes of the only woman to ever capture him, he said, "Lucy, I have a question for you."

Chapter 37

The years rolled by quite strangely for Pappy. After marrying Lucy, he set about having a steady life, but that was never easy. Gambling and farming only went so far with more than one mouth to feed.

On numerous occasions, Pappy was tempted to invest in the stock market. He didn't know the day-to-day outcomes, he had never followed Wall Street much in his old life, but he did know the big companies that would succeed. He had the ultimate line on long-term, insider trading. But he didn't want to call attention to himself, and he didn't want to screw up the future by out-performing everybody else. Besides, he remembered his youth well enough and his Pappy never had a huge bundle of money. So, he invested a little here and there, enough to keep his family comfortable but never so much as to draw unwanted focus from the government.

He also started destroying the Doors. Dominic had done it — he and Lucy had seen the cut Door in Wilkinson's basement — and they had all seen it happen in the barn. Based on the differences between these two Doors, he thought that if he could cut a Door in half without it opening, straight through the frame, he would be okay. The bullet hole that pierced the activated Door had caused all the trouble. Or so he hoped.

Cutting a Door, however, proved more difficult that he had expected.

When he took a saw to the Door, the teeth ground to a nub and only the slightest indent showed in the wood. He tried an ax, too, but it failed. He imagined Dominic must have worked steadily for years to break that one Door. He knew a bullet had the force required but small holes would never do the trick. Pappy knew the technology would exist years later to make the job possible. Until that time, he had to be content with housing the Doors in the barn, and collecting any others that might turn up.

Two years later, he read of an up-and-coming magician's astounding trick called The Door of Destiny. He checked out the show, and as he had done many times before, he pulled out the sketch of his door that he had made those first nights at The Walter Hotel. Unlike the other times, however, this time the Door matched.

He tried to buy the Door, gamble for the Door, even steal the Door. The magician refused to give it up. He finally brought the poor fellow to the barn and explained it all. The magician scoffed, and to prove he would never be so gullible, he walked through a Door. It wasn't how Pappy wanted things to go, but he had his Door.

And so the years went on. Frank grew older and started dating. Watching him meet the young woman who Pappy knew as Grans was odd, to say the least. He had only known her as a wrinkled, hunched woman who smelled bad but baked wonderful treats. Frank, on the other hand, dated a sleek woman with gorgeous lips and a sultry voice. Most importantly, she made Frank happy. Their wedding came about quick, and Pappy found it to be more than a joyous occasion. It felt like a prophecy coming true.

Vincent never returned, and that hurt Lucy deeply. She suffered through great bouts of depression and there were no prescriptions Pappy could acquire to help her. Decades would have to pass before anybody thought of depression as an illness.

During one of her downturns, she drank so much alcohol, Pappy had to rush her to a hospital and have her stomach pumped. Though he could never prove otherwise, when he tried to cheer her with a vacation to the Jersey Shore and she drowned from an undertow that took her far out to sea, he suspected her death had not been an accident. But suicide or not, his Lucy was gone.

He spiraled into his own depression, slipping through his days, seeing her in every room, every mirror, every breath of the house. He even thought of joining her, he wanted that more than anything, but knew he had to stay alive for the future. If he died now, he would never get Duncan to go through the Door. He would change the loop, never go back to 1934 and meet Lucy. No matter how deep his pain or dark his thoughts, he would never want to undo the love they had shared.

He knew he would never find another love, too. He remembered well growing up and wondering why his Pappy always seemed so alone, looking at old photos of a strange woman. Sometimes even crying.

Pappy spent a day at the hospital when his own father was born. He watched his father/grandson grow up, but he kept his distance. He knew this would be part of what shaped Sean into such a bitter man, but he refused to take any chances with his own life. If he altered the type of man Sean was, then he might inadvertently alter the various outcomes of his own youth as Duncan. That could not be allowed to happen. He wanted to make sure that he always went back in time to live a life with Lucy.

Weirder still was watching his own birth. Watching a young version of himself grow. It was then that he took on the true role of Pappy — introducing Duncan to magic, guiding him on all the key principles, testing his abilities, showing him how to cheat at cards and then admonishing him for doing it, letting him see the Door and then repeatedly warning him away from it, insuring in every way he could control that the boy was prepared to make all the crucial decisions that sent him through that very Door.

As for the other Doors, they all went away. Circular saws with diamond blades did the job. It was still difficult work, but he found that if he took care of a Door or two each day, he could manage. After he cut them in half, he learned that if he opened the Door soon enough, it would implode like the one in the barn minus the hurricane winds. Just a pop and it disappeared. If he was too slow, he ended up with hunks of wood that burned well.

And that was his life. Destroying the Doors and recreating his youth for little Duncan. Nudging and teaching and working hard to make sure Duncan lived the life he was supposed to live. He even encouraged Duncan to befriend Pancake, led him deeper into the life of a card cheat, pretended to suffer dementia so that Duncan would not feel as guilty trying to steal from him, and then denying the boy money when he needed it most. All for the purpose of getting that boy ready to act on that final night — the night Duncan would go through the Door.

CHAPTER 38

PAPPY CHECKED THE TIME on his cellphone yet again. He remembered it all as if it had only happened the day before. He could never forget it, of course — it had changed his entire life — but waiting for it to happen again, knowing he would soon relive it from the outside, filled him with a queasy sensation he had not anticipated. After all he had seen and done, yet his stomach still turned on him.

Any moment and Duncan would sneak into the apartment, intent on stealing anything valuable, and Pappy's nausea might send him running for the toilet. Well, not really running anymore. His body had held out incredibly well for a man over one hundred years old. He required a cane throughout the day and adult diapers at night, but the rest of him worked. He often speculated that passing through the Door had benefited his physiology in a unique way, but he never pursued an answer to that question — some things are better left unknown and enjoyed as a mystery.

The front door to the building opened and Pappy's heart jumped. He hid in his bedroom, listening as Duncan slipped down the hallway toward the apartment. He recalled how each step weighed so much back then, trying to screw up the courage to steal from his Pappy, messing up the opening of the stubborn door, and that sickening feeling that he did not belong in the apartment, that he was an intruder.

"Pappy?" Duncan called out. Pappy covered his mouth, his heart hammering harder than it had done in decades. The living room light flicked on, and he heard Duncan gasp as the young man learned what ol' Pappy had been up to all day. The living room had been cleaned out.

All the books, all the papers, all the magazines. The jewelry, the glasses, the little porcelain figurines. Every bit of junk Pappy had hoarded over the years was gone. Way back when he was Duncan staring at that room which suddenly looked like a display model, he had imagined how hard his Pappy would have had to work to clean out this place. He even thought Pappy had called Mary just to mess with him.

But standing behind the bedroom door, listening to a young man's shock, Pappy reveled in the truth. At his age, he could never have done the work and he didn't trust Mary — after all, he was still Duncan, too. No, Pappy had simply arranged for a maid service to come. Paid the two ladies an extra hundred dollars under the table to work double-time — why not? He didn't need money anymore. And those ladies did a great job.

A loud sigh was followed by the hiss of air squishing out of the couch cushions — Duncan flopping on the couch, fighting back tears, not sure what to do, fearing he and Pancake were dead men. It was all going exactly as it had before. Pappy's hands trembled. Sweat dampened his shirt. Duncan teetered clueless on the verge of the most amazing experience in his life.

Pappy pressed his ear against the door. He knew what Duncan was thinking, what he himself had thought, in that long silence — suicide. It would be so simple to stomp into the kitchen, grabbing a sharp knife, and end all the worry. It would be on his terms and would probably be less painful than whatever psychotic torture scenario the Boss would think up.

Oddly, Pappy had been thinking about suicide for much of the last year. Every day that had brought him closer to this moment, he felt the world closing in on him. He even started collecting some of his meds, hoarding them for a simple, painless, maybe even pleasurable way out. For the first time, he caught a hint of what his dear Lucy had experienced — a desire to end it all on his terms, to not let age or malady destroy what he had left.

But Duncan would not do it. He couldn't. And neither could Pappy. At least, for the moment.

Pappy licked his lips. He knew he should simply wait, let young Duncan go on his journey into the past, but how could he not take a peek? In moments, Duncan would be hurtling back in time — would be meeting Lucy for the first time. He turned the knob on his door and pulled it slightly ajar. Swallowing against the thick lump of nerves in his throat, he edged his eye to the crack in the doorway.

Though long ago he had overcome the shock of seeing himself, nothing had prepared him for the horror of seeing his condition this night. Duncan sat on the couch, his eyes wet, his hair disheveled, his appearance lost and crazed. He stared at the Door of Vanishing, not knowing what it was, only sure of one thing — Pappy had spent a lifetime keeping him from opening that Door.

He approached the Door. Pappy watched like some bizarre television show based on his own memories played out for his amusement. He saw Duncan jump back as the young man felt waves of energy pulse off the Door, but then he realized it was his own heart beating. Duncan licked his lips and took a deep breath. His hand hovered over the doorknob, his fingers tapping out a fast rhythm.

Come on, Pappy thought. *Do it.*

Duncan glanced back to the clean room. He turned away from the Door and stepped toward the exit.

No, you idiot. Go through the Door. If Duncan failed to go through the Door, then he might start a paradox. Or if Time did not work that way, then he might destroy Pappy's history.

Pappy's mind started working furiously to come up with contingency plans. At his advanced age, he had limited options. He was too slow to attempt rushing Duncan and tossing the fool through the Door. He still had skill as a cheat — he could lie to Duncan, tell him that a fortune waited on the other side of the Door, entice him to willfully go through. But if he managed any of those actions, what would be the outcome in 1934? Would that Duncan behave the same way? Would he be too angry at Pappy to care about the same things? Would he be filled with a sense of betrayal so great that it blocked him from seeing Lucy the way Pappy had seen her? From falling in love?

"Damn," Duncan said as Pappy whispered the same word. Duncan turned back, hurried to the Door, grabbed the knob, and yanked it open.

Pappy's wrinkled mouth opened as he widened the gap in his bedroom door. He knew what Duncan saw. A pitch black emptiness as if all the light from the living room stopped at the door frame and refused to go any further. Duncan inhaled one last time and stepped through.

Pappy waited.

He listened to the world around him, wondering if everything would change. But it all remained. His younger self had gone to 1934 and had lived out a wild adventure that brought him successfully to this moment.

"Yes!" Pappy cried out. He raised his arms high and took a triumphant lap around the living room. "Yes, yes, yes! Duncan, you sweet wonderful boy, yes!"

Dancing a jig into the kitchen, Pappy hummed "Chattanooga Choo Choo," his favorite tune from 1942. From the refrigerator, he pulled out a bottle of vodka and a shot glass. Two full shots and a satisfied exhalation broadened his smile. He felt lighter in his chest and shoulders. The last year had been one of great increasing tension culminating in these past minutes.

And he had succeeded.

The toughest part was over. Only a few details remained, but for the first time since going through that Door, Pappy could sleep without worrying about his every single action. The future was unwritten now.

He flipped open his cell phone and tapped a number he had not used in a lifetime.

"H-Hello?" a meek, high-pitched voice answered.

"Pancake, this is Pappy."

"Pappy?"

"I'm Duncan's great-grandfather."

"I know who you are. I ain't an idiot. I just don't got time for you right now. I got problems and ... Oh, crap. What happened to Duncan? Why are you calling and not him?"

"Shut up and listen. I know all about your problems. I've seen to it that Duncan's disappeared and you won't ever see him again. But you won't be able to get away so easily."

"He bailed?"

"No. He provided for you. I got your money here. All of it. Everything you need to get those bastards who cut off your hand to back away. You come to my apartment, door'll be open, three envelopes with all the cash is in my bedside table. Got it? Anything else you see that you want, take it. My gift to you."

Before Pancake could blubber his thanks or ask a single question, Pappy cut the call.

He then went back to the Door. For a second, he considered stepping through it. To go back and see Lucy again. He even reached out for the knob. To hold her, kiss her lips, feel her warmth and hear her voice. But he was too old for such foolishness. Duncan was back there now, falling in love, and she fell for him. After all Pappy had done to orchestrate this moment, why risk destroying it?

"No," he said to the Door. "You've got to go."

From his bedroom closet, he pulled out his circular saw. It weighed a ton in his weakened arms, but he didn't care. The Door had to be destroyed.

In a few minutes, it was over. Perhaps he still rode the adrenaline or perhaps he had done this to so many Doors that he no longer had to struggle through. Whatever the case, he cut through the Door and frame with ease, severing the last tie to Duncan and 1934.

He unlocked the front door for Pancake and shuffled back to the kitchen where he poured a water glass full of vodka.

From the back of the counter drawer, he pulled out a small container — his hoarded pills. He sat at the table, placed the glass of vodka before him and lined up the pills.

With a sigh, he gazed at the far wall of the kitchen where he had placed a Door — the very last he had discovered. Nobody ever used it because Pappy had piled boxes in front of it. Nobody had known it was there. But when the cleaning ladies had come, he asked them to clear away the boxes.

He stared at the Door with its strange markings and wondered where it would lead. And when. He knew he should destroy the Door, but how could he? At his age, with nothing to look forward to, nothing to preserve, nothing but his own darkness. Those he loved had died long ago, and now that Duncan had gone back to 1934, there was simply nothing left.

That was the point of the pills. But if he went through the Door, even if it meant ending up in the middle of the ocean or a volcano or being hunted by angry Neanderthals, he would have a few thrilling moments. That would be a better death than suicide.

"Why not finish with a little excitement?"

He walked over to the Door. He opened it and stared at the endless darkness. Like looking into tomorrow.

Tomorrow — he had no idea what would happen. How strange. Tomorrow was an unknown quantity. Not a second, minute, or hour. Nothing about tomorrow could be predicted.

How beautiful, he thought and stepped through.

AFTERWORD

I suspect I will be crossed off a few Christmas card lists because of this.

One of the major axioms among magicians is "Don't reveal the secret, especially to a layman." And yet here I have helped to write a book in which I explain how to do several strong card tricks. A book geared toward mass consumption, no less. Kind of a no-no in the magic world. Some of my magic friends won't be pleased. Dai Vernon must be rolling over in his grave.

However, I don't believe I have exposed anything to laypeople. My theory is this; in order for a trick to be exposed, the exposee must comprehend what was just explained. In the case of this book, you have to actually read the tricks and go through them, cards in hand, in order to understand the secrets. That takes work. And if you are doing that, then most likely you have an interest in magic. And if you are actively pursuing an interest in magic, then you're not a layperson anymore. In fact, you're probably an aspiring magician. And I have no problem at all explaining certain tricks to aspiring magicians.

If you read the book and didn't following along with the effects, then you probably find magic amusing but aren't really interested in learning it. That's cool, too. No hard feelings. But if you did pull out a deck of cards and messed around with even some of the tricks, then at the end of this afterward, I'll share a few magic books with you to help further your magic education.

First, a warning and short rant. Do not learn magic from free YouTube tutorials. Let me say that again but this time a little louder: DO NOT LEARN MAGIC FROM FREE YOUTUBE TUTORIALS. Most tricks given away for free on YouTube are performed badly and explained worse. Overall, the magic tutorials on YouTube are dire. Yes, you can learn the "secret" to many, many tricks on YouTube, but magic is a lot more than just the secrets. Secrets are usually boring. As you know from reading this book, most of the time, the most powerful effects in magic have the simplest of secrets. Magic is about presentation. It's about you, your personality, and how you perform and sell the effect to your audience.

That's not to say there isn't some good free magic on the Internet. There is. But you have to be kind of "in the know" in order to find it. And in order get "in the know", you have to earn the respect of some good magicians, people who can guide you in the right direction. The best way to garner the respect of more experienced magicians is to study the classics. Know your stuff.

If you are reading this, then you are a reader; someone who actually enjoys reading (quite the observation, eh?). Therefore, I suggest starting your magical journey with books. Learn the fundamentals and then advance from there to instructional DVDs.

Although I am a creator of magic tricks, because the story of *Real Magic* is set in 1934, I knew that the effects performed by most of the magicians in the book would need to be appropriate to the time period. Being from the future, Duncan could get away with performing things that were a little more modern. At the same time, he wanted to fit into the period so he couldn't do anything too outlandish. With all of this in mind, when it came time to collecting material for the book, I went back to the classics. Tricks that have stood the test of time. Below is a list of some of the books from which I culled and adapted the tricks you read in this novel. These collections are excellent magic resources and are available very cheaply in either PDF or hard copy format. Trust me when I say that while they are all very old books, the material is top notch and will still fool most anyone who witnesses them. Even a lot of magicians!

You may have noticed that all of the tricks explained in this book are "self-working." In other words, they do not require any sleight of hand. This was a conscious choice Stuart and I made so that anyone would be able to perform the tricks included in the book regardless of skill level. Well, regardless of manual dexterity. Because, like I said before, the real trick of magic isn't the method, it's the performance. Now, I told you before to stay away from free YouTube tutorials on magic, but that doesn't mean you shouldn't watch magic performances on YouTube. Look up performances of some famous magicians you might know: David Blaine, David Copperfield, Criss Angel, Cyril, Derren Brown, Dynamo, Penn & Teller and analyze them. Study what makes them so engaging.

I do believe magic is a great art form. Yes, many bad performers have cheapened it and many in the general public think of magic as child's play and completely frivolous. However, when it is performed well, magic can be transcendent. Although some are too cynical to admit it, we all want to be astonished. We all crave to be amazed. No one wishes for mundane experiences. In our heart of hearts, we all want to believe that magic is possible. And even though most rational people realize that when a magician pulls out a deck of cards, he will be doing a "magic trick," they cannot help but to be emotionally overwhelmed when something completely inexplicable happens. Just remember that *you* have to make it magical for them.

As promised here is a list of some great card magic books. This list is by no means comprehensive. There are literally thousands of books published on just card tricks, let alone other types of magic. These five books, though, are some of the best, especially when starting your magical studies. Just pop the titles into your search engine and you'll find many retailers who carry them.

Close Up Card Magic by Harry Lorayne, 1962
Encyclopedia of Card Tricks edited by Jean Hugard, 1937
Expert at the Card Table by S. W. Erdnase, 1902
Royal Road To Card Magic, The by Jean Hugard & Fredrick Braue
Scarne On Card Tricks by John Scarne, 1950

If you are a more experienced magician looking for some powerful, practical magic to add to your repertoire, feel free to visit my website, *www.cameronfrancismagic.com*, and check out some of my DVDs and downloads.

Enjoy the journey.

Cameron Francis
May, 2013

ABOUT STUART JAFFE

Stuart Jaffe is the author of The Max Porter Paranormal-Mysteries, The Malja Chronicles, the Gillian Boone novels, The Bluesman series, and much more. His short stories have appeared in numerous magazines and anthologies. He is the co-host of The Eclectic Review - a weekly podcast about science, art, and well, everything. For those who keep count, the latest animal listing is as follows: one dog, four cats, one albino corn snake, one Brazilian black tarantula, three aquatic turtles, one lop-eared rabbit, four chickens, and a horse. Thankfully, the chickens and the horse do not live inside the house.

For more information, please visit *www.stuartjaffe.com*

ABOUT CAMERON FRANCIS

Cameron Francis is a professional actor, writer and magician currently living in Orlando, Florida. As an actor Cameron has appeared on stage in New York, Baltimore, Philadelphia, Washington, DC, and Gainesville, Florida, and has also be seen in numerous commercials, television shows and films, including Never Back Down, starring Oscar nominee Djimon Hounsou.

As a magician, Cameron has created many original effects and has lectured on his magic in seven countries including the U.S., England, Germany and Austria.

If you are interested in learning more of Cameron's magic effects, please visit *www.cameronfrancismagic.com*

Printed in Great Britain
by Amazon